ACCIDENTAL MURDER

A Novel

JP Davis

Machete Books. Chapel Hill. North Carolina

Library of Congress Control Number: 2019903646

FIRST EDITION 2019

ISBN 978-1-7338473-0-8

To Penny,

a hard-charging Aries with a literary eye like DiMaggio

ACCIDENTAL MURDER

To Karl,
with best wishes,

06/19

CHAPTER ONE

A bus stops in the morning twilight picking up passengers.

Two begin to argue.

The bus driver looks into the mirror to see what the commotion is.

"I have my headphones in my ears," says one rider to the other.

"I don't care. It's too loud. I can hear it all over the bus."

"I can listen to my music with my headphones. No one else is saying anything. Why don't you just move?"

"Ladies sit down while the bus is moving," the driver says.

"I don't have to sit down."

"I'm driving this bus, and if I say you must sit down, you must sit down."

Avinash begins his morning jog stepping out into the street.

"Stop!" Two people on the bus scream and the driver looks down just in time to hit the brakes, stopping within feet of Avinash. He looks up, his mind so preoccupied a normal day-to-day occurrence could have killed him. In a life of preparation, a lapse.

He steps back, motioning for the bus to pass. The annoyed driver waves Avinash across in front of his bus, refusing to go first. Avinash scowls at the driver and moves across the street, shaking off the near-death experience, and resumes his morning jog.

Avi, the name his friends would call him, if he had any friends, has a less formal, more approachable feel that allows him to exhibit the human qualities often required to do his work; patience, compassion, and peacefulness are all tools of his trade, tools that make it much easier to commit murder.

After his jog, part of his morning routine at the Hotel Royal Riviera in St. Jean Cap Ferrat is to practice yoga in preparation for meditating.

Once finished, Avi reaches for his iPad and checks his email:

From: VKR@mg.serb.com

Domestic.

He reads the email and responds, accepting the job. He views the online Wall Street Journal. Not very interesting—continued unrest in the Middle East, Washington says blah, blah, blah… He feels some satisfaction as he notes the market was up 270 points yesterday. He has a substantial portfolio, much in contrast to his dismal prospects growing up as an untouchable child in Calcutta.

Avi picks up the phone in his room.

"Yes, monsieur."

"Please send up my latté."

"Of course, sir, right away."

Soon, the doorbell rings. Avi opens the door.

"Bonjour, Monsieur. May I come into the suite?" the waiter asks in French.

Avi does not respond but points out onto the balcony. The waiter places the tray on a large table surrounded by six chairs.

"Shall I pour for you, sir?"

Once again nothing is said. Avi simply sits down at the table in front of the tray. The waiter pours hot milk and coffee into a large cup in the usual amounts with a slight tremor in his hands.

"You have a fabulous view from this suite," the waiter says as he does almost every day when he brings the hot latté to Avi in his villa.

"Yes, it is the best," Avi finally says to the waiter. "That will be all."

"Very well, sir," the waiter says and sees himself out of the villa.

In the walkway outside, the waiter stops, leans against the wall and breathes a sigh of relief. A beautiful young hotel maid asks, "How was he today?"

"Just like every other day: scary. He does not speak to me very much."

"He is so mysterious but dashingly handsome," she says to the waiter.

"I would suggest you be careful and make sure you keep your uniform on around him, my love."

She winks at the waiter, disregarding his comments with her dust brush and continues walking.

Avi will neither shower nor shave today; nondescript French tourist wear is the appropriate attire. A brief pause in the lobby to make sure all is clear, then he takes off on his Vespa, this time looking carefully for buses.

The drop is late. Strange. He makes his way to the local bakery, orders a coffee and a fresh pastry, picks up a newspaper and waits. Just as the coffee arrives, it happens: the drop is made. He hates not being able to take the time to enjoy the leisurely French coffee experience. In perfect idiomatic French, he tells the lovely waitress he will be right back. He hands her a 20 euro note, "Please make me another when I return. I'm terribly sorry." She smiles as only French women can and pockets the 20 euro note while taking the coffee back to the kitchen.

He reaches the park, sits down on a bench next to a folded newspaper. He picks it up carefully, gripping the package within; no one notices, and no one is watching. This park is the perfect place to blend in and not be noticed.

Avi returns to the bakery to finish his coffee and then another as the waitress playfully flirts with this handsome Latin-appearing man. He decides flirting back will have to wait for another day; the business Avi is involved in is especially dangerous when one gets distracted. The waitress turns to wait on another customer.

He peeks inside the envelope finding a dossier plus $50,000 in cash. He pulls the dossier from the envelope and silently reads.

Donna McCally, Caucasian female. 5 feet 6 inches, 143 pounds, brown hair, brown eyes, aged 37. Occupation: Homemaker. Mother of two—Josh 10, Mary 13. Lives at 105 Stemphill Lane, Tucson, Arizona. Husband, George McCally, procurement service associate for Lockheed. Travels extensively. Gone 3-4 nights a week.

Avi closes the dossier and strides to the sidewalk outside. It is time to go to his local "office," one of many he has stationed in various parts of the world. He rides his Vespa to a taxi stand at a nearby hotel where he has a cab take him to a commercial freight district about 30 minutes away. He gets out at the dock and waits. A short while later, he walks down the road about a half-mile, then turns back and makes two lefts and a right to make sure no one is following. Once he is convinced, he walks through the storage area to the shipping containers. He slips familiarly through the maze of containers and stops at an orange one. The cargo manager is walking across the yard smoking a cigarette. He nods but does not stop as he passes.

Avi unlocks the container door and walks over to a cabinet containing an elaborate filing system and collects some documents. For this job, a British passport for Mr. Harry Hareem is needed. Avi uses the names of lost boys for his identities, boys he grew up with who died as children and no one cared enough about to even bury. He has kept their names all these years. The boys live on, working for Avi now. It's easy to assume the identity of someone who had a record of being born, but no record of dying.

Avi goes online to book a first-class ticket for Mr.

Hareem. He adds in details required to complete this assignment using a network of contacts he acquired over the years as the guy people call when they have no one left to call. He puts the documents into a backpack and returns to his villa. There he orders dinner and gets ready for his departure tomorrow.

The following day, Avi arrives at the Nice airport, boards his first-class flight and settles into his window cubicle.

A lovely French flight attendant appears beside Mr. Hareem and asks in French, "How may I serve you, sir?"

Avi smiles at the attendant and says, "Perhaps I will have a Bloody Mary now, and leave the invitation open for additional requests later." He then opens a novel, and his journey to close the Donna McCally transaction begins.

CHAPTER TWO

When Avi arrives in Mexico City as Mr. Harry Hareem, he boards an Aero México flight to Nogales International Airport. Landing in Nogales, Mr. Hareem clears customs and walks into the airport bar near the exit. He sits down and the bartender walks over.

"A Blue agave, please," says Avi.

A man sitting just down a few seats moves next to Avi. "I'll have one of those as well," he says.

The two men drink their drinks silently and leave together.

"My car is just outside. Are you ready to go now?" he asks Avi.

Avi nods and they walk to a nearby car.

For Avinash, crossing the border poses none of the usual challenges. His contact is a Mexican federal policeman on the payroll who drives Avi across the border in full sight of local border patrol personnel. No ID, no worries. It's a pretty busy crossing and nobody is looking for Harry Hareem.

In Green Valley, Arizona, Avi buys a car. The purchase is settled like many transactions along the border, for cash and with a title to be issued someday. The thirty-day license tag should suffice for Avi's purposes.

He dials another Arizona contact.

"Yep, it's Lloyd. Leave a message."

Avi hangs up; he will not leave a message.

He waits. Two minutes later his burner cell rings back. Clearly, it is Lloyd as Avi did not block any callbacks for this phone. He connects but says nothing into the phone.

"Hey, man," says Lloyd. "I'm sorry about missing your call. I have your van and it's ready to go." Lloyd has a somewhat fearful strain in his voice. He is your basic low-level criminal with a few busts for drugs, car theft, and a scam or two. He is Avi's local contact from the CIA's master list. While Lloyd is on the list, he is still a YOYO (you're on your own) contact, which means he is not sanctioned or approved, but reasonably reliable.

Avi picks up the van at the designated location and drives it to a cheap, not very secure storage facility with no cameras about 10 miles out of town. He drives the van into the unit he rented online, turns off the engine, closes and locks the door, and pockets the key. He then walks out to the gate where Lloyd waits to drive him back to his car.

"How was your flight, man?" asks Lloyd nervously.

"The rules go like this—I speak to you and you answer me; nothing else," Avi replies.

"Sorry, man."

Lloyd drives Avi back to his car. Avi then drives to his

room at the no-tell motel and gets ready for his first day on the job tailing Donna. He settles into this dive of a motel, a world away from Cap Ferrat, and again reads over the assignment information. 'George is often away traveling for work.' Avi reads on. 'Donna is a homemaker.'

Beginning the next morning, Avi uses his Ford Taurus to watch Donna daily. He is patient with this part of the job. Watching is the most important part of getting it right.

Donna drives her kids to school every morning at around 7:30. On Monday, she shops for groceries, driving all the way to Costco. Avi follows her from a distance; in this part of the world, a tail can stay a long way back since no trees interfere with the line of sight. He goes into Costco and observes her filling a cart, checking it against a list in her hand. With an earpiece, he can hear everything going on with her from his cell tap. Once he captured her digital signature, he turned her phone into a full-time bug.

Donna runs into a friend: "Hi, Doris."

"Oh, hi Donna. How's it going?" says Doris.

"It's going fine, just still getting used to the traveling again—George is on the road. He's in Vegas working a convention or something. I'm not really sure what he does when he's out."

"At least your kids are older now," says Doris.

"That's true. How about you?"

"Just home and working some part-time. I'm doing an internet teaching job. It's really cool."

"I'm glad. It's really good to see you, Doris."

Donna finishes up her shopping and goes home for

lunch. On Tuesday, she returns home from dropping the kids off by 8:15 and then only leaves the house twice: once to go to the mall and once to the post office. Donna's phone rings on Tuesday at 8:45 pm.

"Hi Honey, how is it going?"

"Oh okay, I'm just so tired. The kids just went to bed, and so am I."

"Okay, I'll see you Thursday night. I love…you." She hangs up before he finishes his sentence.

With George returning Thursday, Avi now knows Wednesday will be the best day to complete the McCally assignment.

On Wednesday morning, Avi retrieves the van from the storage unit and drives to Donna's neighborhood, arriving at 7:30 as school buses and commuter traffic fill the streets. He parks two houses away from the McCallys', pulls on his Cablevision uniform, and places an orange cone behind the van. A few minutes later, Donna drives past taking her kids to school. Avi sees her leave, and he waits until 8:00 when the traffic has died down. He walks to the McCallys' front door, removes his lock tools, and finds the door unlocked. He enters the house and checks for an alarm system but finds none. He walks the house looking for pets and makes an assessment of his plan. He goes up to the master bathroom, sees the tub is a nice cast iron which will work well. He begins to fill the tub with water and replaces his Cablevision uniform with doctor's scrubs and plastic gloves. He turns the water off and listens for Donna to return. He waits.

Eventually, he hears sounds downstairs. The door from

the garage to the kitchen opens, and some keys hit the counter. He turns the water in the tub back on as Donna walks up the stairs toward her bedroom. Her last thought is, "Why is the water running?" Avi steps out of the water closet behind her as she reaches down to turn the water off. As she straightens up, he delivers a massive blow to her head with a wrench, killing her instantly. He undresses her and lifts her into the tub to get her body wet. He pulls her from the tub, turns her around and drops her head against the side of the tub to give the proper effect of a blow to her head, and lets her body slide to the floor. He checks the water on the floor to make sure it gives the impression Donna slipped getting out of the tub. He reaches into his bag for the blood-viewing blue light to make sure the scene is convincing. He finds blood residue in most of the right places, just enough splatter to give it randomness. He removes his scrubs and places them and Donna's clothes into his bag. He selects an outfit for Donna and lays it out on the bed in the master bedroom. Then he puts his Cablevision uniform back on. He goes out the way he came in, leaving the front door unlocked just as he found it, not leaving a trace.

CHAPTER THREE

Detective Rachael Lopez reaches across her current bed partner, Deputy Police Chief Ed Hillman, to answer her phone.

"Yes?"

It's Detective Al Johnson calling. "Rachael, where the hell are you? It's 2:00 pm."

"Hey, I haven't had lunch so I'm just getting some." She looks over at Ed and grins.

"Bull shit," says Johnson.

"Okay, if you have to know, it's that time of the month and I had blood running down my leg, so I came home to change."

"Oh, shit, don't tell me any more," says Johnson.

Rachael lights a cigarette as she gets out of her bed and pulls on her jeans. "What's up?" she says to Johnson.

"We have a body. Woman fell getting out of her tub. Looks like an accident. Not sure. Get over there and check it out. Call me when you get to the scene. Paramedics are there with a hysterical cleaning lady. I'm texting you the address now."

"I'm on it," says Rachael.

As she hangs up, Ed looks at her from the bed.

"We have a body," Rachael says. "Looks like a woman fell getting out of her tub. I'm off to investigate."

"How about tomorrow for lunch again?" Hillman says.

"Jesus, don't you think you ought to save some of that thing for your poor wife?"

"Damn Rachael, I don't get you." He jumps up from the bed and begins to dress.

"What's to get about me? It's just sex. Let's not complicate it any more than it already is, Boss."

"Oh, real nice. Thanks for the added barb. What are you doing to me?" asks Ed.

"Hey, you're the one that's married, not me. We have sex, you're my boss. Big deal. I'm off to make you look good." She puts on a tight shirt, her cowboy boots, grabs a pack of smokes and her 38 revolver and goes to her car as Ed watches from the door. "Lock up, big guy. And don't steal anything."

"Funny, very funny," Ed says as she drives off in her car.

Al and Rachael arrive at the scene at the same time. "I thought you said to call you when I got here."

"I got tired of waiting, so I came on."

They enter the house and move upstairs. Rachael enters the room and every man in the house turns to stare at her. She is used to this. She's about 5 ft 8 inches tall and around 120 pounds with beautiful caramel skin, thanks to her father, the Latino in the bunch.

"What's the situation?" Al asks the paramedic.

"Looks like she fell getting out of the tub."

"That was a hell of a fall," says Rachael.

Al looks at her with obvious contempt. "Come up with a motive yet, Detective Lopez?" he asks condescendingly. "How about suicide?" says the paramedic as Al and he chuckle.

"Nice, you two," says Rachael. "Where's all the blood?" The paramedic looks at her. "If she hit her head, there should be more blood. I don't see as much on her back as I would have thought from this head wound."

"Rachael, the coroner will be here soon. He can explain the physics to you," says the paramedic. "Plus, it's probably mostly internal, since the tub hit her head. It's not like she got stabbed to death," he says sarcastically.

"I find it hard to believe she could simply slip and fall, hitting her head in exactly the right place to kill her, bam, just like that."

"Don't waste a lot of time on this one, Rachael," says Al.

"Al, cool your jets, you'll be back asleep at your desk in no time. Let's see what we actually have here, okay?"

Al walks away muttering under his breath.

Downstairs Rachael meets the maid who found Mrs. McCally, a Hispanic woman from Mexico. She seems very nervous.

"Ms. Dominguez, it's all right. I just have a few questions," says Rachael. "What time did you come in today?"

"Around 12:30."

"Was the water running in the tub?"

"No."

"Did you touch anything upstairs when you came in?"

The maid looks nervous. Rachael tries to sound reassuring, "It's okay, just tell me what happened."

Rachael listens to the trembling maid.

"I came into the house and cleaned the downstairs first. Then I went upstairs, and she was on the floor. I saw blood there, so I ran downstairs and called 911."

"You ran downstairs?"

"Yes, my phone was inside my purse on the kitchen counter."

"The call came in around 1:08 pm," says Al, walking up. "Her story seems right."

"Did you clean another house this morning before you came here?"

"Yes, Mrs. Lang's house. I finished there and came here."

"Okay, that's all. You may go," Al says. The maid leaves quickly.

Rachael looks at Al shaking her head. "Hey, I was speaking with her."

"Rachael, what the hell else can she tell you? She doesn't know anything. The woman slipped and fell. Why do you have such a bee in your bonnet about this?"

Rachael thinks about Al's question. While not showing it to these guys on the force, she's upset about Donna McCally's death. Not because she knew Donna but because this incident reminds her of her mother's death, an accidental fall which led Rachel to find out about her mom's cancer. She never said a word about her cancer.

The forensic investigator walks up with a puzzled expression. "Irregular accidental death, I believe," he says.

"I want it treated like a homicide," says Rachael, and all the eyes at the scene roll when they hear her.

"Rachael, we have enough open homicides without you creating new ones from thin air," says Al.

"The husband has been notified. He's in Vegas," says one of the detectives.

"Nice," says Rachael.

"According to the report, he works at Lockheed. He's there for a conference." Al says, scanning the report on his phone.

"I want him at the station tomorrow morning," says Rachael.

"Why?" Al questions. "You think he raced home this morning, beat his wife in the tub, and drove back to Vegas so we could get him out of a meeting that has been going since 8:30 this morning?"

"I still want his story."

CHAPTER FOUR

Rachael's phone rings. It's Sheila, her best friend.

"Girl," Rachael says. "What's up?"

"Can you pick up Joe from school for me today? I'm tied up at work, in the middle of a crisis with a patient and can't leave and Mike is out of town."

"Sure," says Rachael.

"Hey Rach, he has a friend coming home with him."

"Bring the friend to your house?" asks Rachael.

"Yes, and Rachael, it's a girl so try not to, you know…"

"Embarrass him in front of his date? I got it."

"Why don't you stay for dinner tonight? Like I said Mike's out of town. I miss you girl."

"Okay, I'll be there especially since that rat bastard is gone. I still want to shoot him."

"I know. Mike has always had one eye open thinking you were coming to kill him."

"I don't like the way he treats you or Joe."

"Let's not get into that today, ok?"

"Fine, I'll see you tonight." They hang up.

Rachael thinks about the days when she lived with Sheila, Mike, and young Joe after her mom died. It was a tough time in her life. Rachael's father had worn out his welcome at all the army bases almost everywhere around the globe due to beating up privates under his command who would not do what he told them to do. His superiors were sympathetic to the sergeant but had to move him around often because of his anger issues. They finally wound up in Yuma as part of an army support unit at a marine facility.

When her mother died, Rachael moved in with Sheila to finish high school. At 17, Rachael decided there would be no more moving around the world with her father, a Great Santini knockoff. That was where she got to know Mike, Sheila's alcoholic husband who sometimes beat Sheila and Joe. Rachael knew how to take care of herself and had been in this scene before with her father. She managed to put fear into Mike while she lived there, and for a few months, it was mostly quiet at Sheila's house.

Rachael leaves her gun in the car and walks into the school to pick up Joe. When the bell rings, she is sitting outside the main door when he comes walking toward her with a girl in tow. "Mom said you were going to drive us."

"Hi, hot stuff. Man, when did you get so good looking?" asks Rachael.

"Rachael, this is Sherry."

"Ah Sherry, hello."

"Are you really a cop?" asks Sherry.

"Why? Don't I look like one?"

"Well, not really. I mean, you're really pretty."

"You can be pretty and still be a cop. Want to see my badge?" Rachael holds out her badge for Sherry to see. "I also have a squad car today, so I'm taking you both for a ride. Want me to cuff you in the back seat?"

"She's just kidding, Sherry," Joe says.

"Let's go."

They get into the squad car and school traffic is everywhere. Rachael hits the siren and the cars begin to move over as she drives through the school zone and takes Joe and Sherry on a joy ride at a high speed.

"Anyone up for ice cream?" Rachael asks.

"Yeah!" they both scream between laughs.

After ice cream, they get to Sheila's.

"We're going to do our homework," says Joe.

"Cool, I'll be here if you need me."

Rachael goes into the kitchen, opens a bottle of wine and sits down with her laptop to begin to work on Donna McCally, specifically on her husband, George. Affairs: nothing she can find easily from phone records. Insurance: nothing noteworthy. How about his job at Lockheed? High-security clearance.

"George, if you didn't do it, what are you working on that would get your wife killed?" Rachael says out loud in the kitchen.

She finishes her first glass and pours the rest of the bottle into the big wine glass.

In about an hour, Sheila comes in the door.

"Any problems picking up Joe?"

"And Sherry, too," says Rachael.

"Is she still here?"

"Yes, they're back in his bedroom doing homework, I guess."

"Rachael, you haven't checked on them?"

"Hey, I'm working here and I didn't want to bother the little guy if he might be getting some."

"He's only 12, Rachael. They're probably playing video games," says Sheila. She walks back to check on them and they are playing video games.

"Sherry, can you stay for dinner?" asks Sheila.

"No ma'am, my dad is on the way to pick me up," says Sherry looking down at her phone.

"Okay."

Sheila goes back into the kitchen, gets out a glass and picks up the open bottle of wine to pour herself a glass and notices it is empty. She looks at Rachael.

"What?" asks Rachael.

Sheila opens another bottle. She picks up her glass and the bottle, comes over and sits next to Rachael who is typing on her laptop.

"What are you working on that requires a whole bottle of wine?"

"This case I have. Young mom was killed at her home today."

"Killed, why isn't it on the news?"

"Because it looks like an accident."

"What do you mean?" asks Sheila.

"I mean all the hard dicks at my office are convinced it

was an accident, but I'm not. This woman has two young children, a husband who was in Vegas while she was being killed. That bastard was in on it somehow, and I intend to prove it."

"Whoa, girl, you seem to be moving pretty fast here. Have you talked to him?"

"No. I just got the case this afternoon. He's coming in tomorrow and I plan to get to the bottom of it then. All I've done is pick up the kids and come here."

"Don't shoot him or beat him up, promise me, please."

"What? Jesus, what is wrong with everyone around here? First Al, now you, what the fuck?"

Sheila looks at Rachael.

Rachael knows why Sheila is concerned. A few years back, Rachael beat a suspect half to death who might have killed his wife, and she has threatened Mike often.

"You're a protector," says Sheila. "This woman is dead. Maybe it was an accident. Please be careful and stay by the book on this one. I don't want you to have to move away again."

Rachael pours herself more wine but Sheila stops her from pouring the rest of the new bottle into her glass.

"This hits too close to home for you, honey. Be careful." Sheila hugs Rachael but does not get hugged back.

CHAPTER FIVE

George McCally comes into the police station the next day at 10:00 am and meets with Al and Rachael. George looks like the perfect fit for Donna: 5 foot 9, about 200 pounds, carrying most of the extra pounds around his waist, sporting a deeply receding hairline which will certainly make him bald by 50. He is completely distraught. "We can't stay at the house. My kids and I are staying at one of our friends... I don't understand. How could this happen? . . . I need to be with my kids. Why am I here? I have to plan a funeral! Oh, God!" He tears up.

"Mr. McCally, we are sorry for your loss. I just need to ask you a few questions," says Rachael.

With tears in his eyes, George says, "Okay."

"Is anything going on at work that would alarm you or make you more cautious?" Rachael asks.

"No, I mean, what do you mean? You think someone killed Donna? How? Why?"

"Calm down, Mr. McCally. These are just standard questions we ask when we're investigating an accidental death," says Al, as he scowls at Rachael.

"I don't know. Some of my work is classified because of who I work for and what I do, but no one has ever approached me." He seems irritated and impatient.

"Mr. McCally, you seem angry. Is there anything you want to tell us?" asks Rachael.

"What do you mean? Look, I need to be with my kids. I don't know why you dragged me down here! And yes, I am mad—I'm very angry about all of this! I don't know what happened. I'm sad, I'm angry, but mostly I'm confused. What in the hell is going on?" George breaks down again. "I don't understand," he says. "Why was she taking a bath?"

"Why wasn't there a rug beside the tub?" asks Rachael.

"A rug? I don't know. I don't remember a rug there."

"You walked into that bathroom every day, what, twice a day or more for how many years and you don't remember if there was a rug there?" asks Rachael.

"There are rugs at the toilet, sinks, and shower, just no rug at the tub?" Rachael asks again.

"I don't know. I don't remember about the rugs. Maybe there was one there. We hardly ever used the tub. I don't remember. I don't think I ever used that tub. We have a shower right next to it." George continues to tear up as he tries to talk.

"Mr. McCally, we're sorry to have added to your troubles. You may go," Al says.

George stops crying, looks angrily at Rachael, and walks out of the room.

"Well, Rachael, I guess you've got your man," Al says

sarcastically. "He sure seems guilty to me. Maybe he smothered her with the missing rug."

"Maybe," says Rachael.

"Jesus, Rachael, what's wrong with you? Don't you have enough to do? McCally's life looks harder with his wife gone. He's no Brad Pitt, and I don't see anything to draw a sugar baby to steal the McCally fortune away from Donna."

"You don't need a fortune to have someone want to beat you to death, Al."

"Oh, I get it now: it's a woman thing. You think he hated her so much he wanted her dead?"

Now Rachael is really pissed at Al. She stays quiet a moment remembering what Sheila said.

"Answer me this one question," says Al. "What is the motive, Detective Lopez?"

Rachael paces around the room for a moment and finally answers Al.

"George's story seems to make sense, but something is missing, and I just can't put my finger on it. She was killed. I believe that. I just don't know why."

CHAPTER SIX

As Rachael walks down the stairs to check on Donna McCally's autopsy she remembers. Oh shit, Vince is down here today.

Vince Craft, in appearance, is a forgettable 5'8", 227 pounds, with a receding hairline. He looks like, and is, a government employee-for-life. His father was a mortician and, for lack of imagination or ambition, Vince went to mortuary school. When his father died, Vince was too lazy to keep the family mortuary going, so his aunt, a city councilwoman, got him a job in the Tucson coroner's office. People don't care about Vince one way or another—he's a non-entity, like the furniture. He wants to work his 20 years and then retire and do nothing.

Tucson is not the murder capital of the world, so having Vince as one of the coroners is not a major deal. But Rachael really dislikes him, even more than the average man in her life. He's slow and lazy and not very bright whereas Rachael is quick and energetic and very, very bright.

Rachel knocks on the glass door to the autopsy room.

Vince gets up from reading the newspaper in a chair near the basement window and pushes the button to let her in.

"Hey, Vince, where are you on McCally?"

"I was just about to start. Want to assist?"

"No, not really. But I need you to get it done."

"Okay. Shall I crack her open?"

"Probably not since it appears the only issue is a head laceration. We can let the family have her mostly intact."

"Geez, Rachael, I thought since you were here, we'd do the full works."

"Not this time, okay?"

Vince shrugs and turns on a tape recorder. "Severe head lacerations. It appears the victim was nude. No evidence of additional trauma to the body. The lacerations appear consistent with a severe pipe trauma directly to the head."

Vince examines her scalp closely, looking for anything unusual, and then opens her skull to view the underlying brain. "No flakes of metal or other material in the wound. The underlying cortex has an indentation caused by a long hard object, possibly a metal pipe or a tub," Vince dictates.

"What do you mean 'a long metal pipe'? She hit the side of the tub."

"Yeah, I guess that makes more sense. The gash looks longer, but I can see where the tub edge could have done this," says Vince.

Rachael rolls her eyes. "Vince, if you think a metal pipe did it, I need to know that."

Vince looks at Rachael seeming a little intimidated. "No, let's go with the tub. It's hard and would leave the same impression." Vince rewinds the recorder and speaks into the device: "Skull damage appears to have been inflicted by severe blunt trauma force, most likely from the side of the tub." He stops the tape. "The tub is cast iron, Rachael. That's why I'm thinking about how metal would react to her skull, that's all."

Sternly, Rachael asks, "In your expert opinion, Vince, what happened to Mrs. McCally?" She's irritated, and it shows.

"It looks like she was taking a bath, somehow the floor got wet, she slipped on the water and hit her head on the side of the tub judging by the indentation in her skull and, bam, that was it."

"Bam, that was it?" says Rachael.

"Bam, that was it," repeats Vince.

At the end of the day, Rachael goes home, checks her emails, and opens a bottle of wine. It's only Wednesday, and this is bottle number three so far, this week. So what? She gets a frozen meal ready for the microwave: baked chicken, rice, green beans. Wine first.

Rachael cannot get Donna McCally out of her head. She is really pissed off this thing has happened to this innocent woman. She can't let go of thinking it was a murder. Instinct maybe. Al and his bunch of cronies just want to clear cases as quickly as possible. They do not care, in her opinion, one bit about this woman. Make it go away is their motto.

It is just too close to how she feels about her own Mom's death. Was there neglect from George the way there was for her mother? She is mad at men, mostly because of the way her father treated her Mom and her. He was angry most of the time and when Rachael and her Dad got into a fight, she gave as good as he could give her. She remembers a stare-down with him at 12 years old after he had hit her Mom. She stepped in and he left for a few hours. She has a love-hate relationship with men thanks to him.

While finishing her third glass of wine and waiting for her dinner to cool, Rachael accesses the federal database online to continue to dig into George but finds she needs a deeper clearance; some of his information is classified. She flips through the names on her phone. Charlie, Dale, David, Don, Dwight, Earl, Ed. She stops on Ed. She's lonely. She wants to scratch this itch of being alone but thinks he's probably home with his wife. Three glasses of wine sometimes make the itch stronger. Instead, she calls Charlie, a guy from work who she knows is sweet on her.

"Charlie, hi. It's Rachael."

"Rachael! Hi, it's nice to hear from you."

"You're so sweet, Charlie. Listen, I kind of need your help."

"Okay, what do you need?"

"I'm digging for information on a guy who has very high-security clearance, and I can't figure out if his wife was killed because of him or if he had a role in her murder. Can you access whatever he was working on at Lockheed?

"Maybe, but not likely."

"Ah, Charlie, I have more faith in you than that."

"That's probably federal stuff, Rachael. We're just Tucson PD. They'll never let us near anything like that."

"I was just speculating. Maybe he sold some classified material or was being blackmailed or something."

"I don't think I can help, but I'll try."

"Charlie, I would be so appreciative if you could pull this off for me," Rachael says, sounding a little tipsy.

"What's his name?"

"George McCally. Lockheed Corp. His wife's name was Donna. See what you can find out about both of them, will you dear? Thanks, Charlie."

"Sure, I'll work on it right now. Hey, Rachael?"

"I've got to go now, Charlie. Let's talk tomorrow."

"Oh, okay then. See you tomorrow."

The following day Rachael gets a call from Charlie.

"Rachael."

"Hi, Charlie, what have you got for me?"

"George has been working on a very secret project through Lockheed for the Defense Department. While he's only a procurement officer, at times he needs to be brought into the loop on some sophisticated purchases and stuff. Records show he has been traveling all over the world meeting with various technology firms to bring in the software, weapons, and munitions required to pull off some very up-to-date fighting gear."

"Damn, Charlie, that's some good intel. How did you come up with it? Never mind, I don't want to know. What did you learn about Donna?" asks Rachael.

"Donna's parents, the Cartmans, are well-off but not rich. They own a nice-sized farm in Iowa. Been there their whole lives. Donna and George have 'I love you' wills: you get my stuff, I get your stuff."

"Thank you so much for this. I mean, wow, this is so much more than I thought you could come up with," says Rachael.

"So, Rachael, can we get a coffee sometime or maybe a drink after work?"

"Maybe. I'm kind of seeing someone right now, but I'll keep you in mind, okay?"

"Oh, okay. I just thought after your call last night…"

Rachael interrupts. "Thanks again, Charlie, I've got to run. You're the best. Bye."

CHAPTER SEVEN

Avi is back at home #2 at the Hotel du Cap-Ferrat, sipping a glass of Veuve Clicquot while relaxing by the pool, enjoying the stunning French Riviera and one of his favorite relaxations, savoring the view of beautiful young girls sunning by the pool. One waiter rushes over to refill his glass from the bottle sitting in the ice bucket by his chair, while another one follows to refill the bucket with ice to keep the rest of the bottle cool in the warm French air.

Avi takes a nice long breath, sips a little more champagne, and begins to read a new dossier.

Adam Sodkoff, the CEO of Quantum Corp. According to Yahoo Finance, he makes $2,000,000 a year salary plus bonuses and options that bring the total to $5,000,000. An insider: Andover, Columbia, Harvard MBA. He was born a rich kid and grew into a richer adult. Lives in Manhattan in an Upper East Side co-op, a building his grandfather built. It has a security guard and a required sign-in. Sodkoff's office is at 612 Fifth Avenue.

The next day, as William Patel, MD, Avi arrives at the

Air France first class check-in in Nice after quickly going through security. The lovely French gate attendant seems happy Dr. Patel is flying with her airline. Dr. Patel boards, settles into his roomy first-class seat, and departs for New York City, sipping a very nice Veuve Clicquot champagne once again.

After arriving in New York, Avi checks into the W. He makes a call from his room, and a voice answers by saying only "Yes."

"I need to be able to come and go as I wish at 612 Fifth Avenue."

"That's easy, you need Carlyle. They run maintenance for most of the 600 block, and most of the city for that matter. I'll take care of it."

Three days later, Avi gets his badge—Supervisor, Carlyle Maintenance—with a universal key to access all Carlyle properties worldwide. For the next few weeks, he enters the property at 612 Fifth Avenue at all hours of the day and night carrying a clipboard as if checking to make sure the cleaning has been done to his satisfaction.

He finds it impossible to gain access to Sodkoff. Sodkoff is not a late-night worker bee. He works about a 35-hour week in the office and from home using email and phone. He is virtually never alone. He has people on him all the time: at work, at home with his family, and during his time at the gym every day. He has a full-time chauffeur to drive him back and forth. For a day or so Avi was hopeful a meeting of the Bronx Zoo Board of Directors would give him a chance to get to Sodkoff; but even there his target was surrounded by other members of the Board.

After another week of following Sodkoff, searching for the slightest wrinkle in the security around him, Avi determines this assignment is too risky. Working from another of his cargo container offices, this one located at the Red Hook Terminal in Brooklyn, Avi sends an email with the subject: "contract canceled."

His phone rings immediately.

"You are already in place," an Eastern European voice says, "and no other assets are available. I am on a very short schedule. I need this to happen soon."

"I'm out. Too risky," says Avi.

"I will pay you an additional $50,000. Does that adjust for the risk?"

Avi prides himself on only doing work he can accomplish on schedule and with perfection. He thinks about the new offer.

"Okay, the risk has been adjusted. Done in two weeks."

"Excellent," the voice on the other end says.

They hang up.

Avi looks around his container office, one of a series in strategic locations all over the world. Each container has a complete office with multiple passports and files, anything he needs, even a Lily cappuccino machine. He can work safely in any freight yard in the world, as most comings and goings-on there involve people who know how not to pay too much attention. He can have a container shipped out of anywhere anytime he wants. It's very hard to trap him in one location given the intricate network of paperwork he has on hand.

He steps out of the container to take a break and looks up into the sunlight shining on his face. He is concerned he has made a mistake taking on the Sodkoff job after his research and instincts have told him to walk. Is he slipping? Is the work from Viktor weighing on him? He doesn't really like working for Viktor, but the money is good. His usual job is to kill really bad people for one side or the other, and he is having a hard time finding a good reason to kill some of these people for Viktor. He prefers to kill people who he believes need killing or at least people his employer has a moral justification for wanting dead, misguided as it may be. He takes a moment to reflect on the light. It gives him pause. Then the light fades behind a cloud.

Avi sits at his desk doing more research, looking for a way to get close to Adam Sodkoff. The wife, Constance Sodkoff, is the perfect wife for a rich guy. An attractive socialite, well dressed and well connected. He uncovers some photos of her in Gotham magazine from a Boys and Girls Club fundraiser with her teenage daughter.

The following day, Avi buys a pedal assist bike to use as a follow vehicle in Manhattan. Who would have thought New York City was bike friendly? With the electric motor, he can pedal everywhere, and there are no parking problems.

He spends several days following Constance. When she's not in front of the camera, she drinks her way around Manhattan's social circles. Three lunches with friends in three days, each accompanied by quite a few martinis.

After the third day's lunch, her next stop is Divinity Country Day High School, where she picks up her teenage daughter and drives to a nearby Starbucks. Avi finds a good spot to watch. The girl is raising cane.

"Jesus, you're sloshed drunk, and it's only 4:00! This is embarrassing. It's my senior year! I don't want you around me anymore. Why are you driving anyway? Where is the driver?"

Having heard enough, Avi slips out of Starbucks and returns to his office. He makes a Chai latte to compare against Starbucks and fires up his Mac to do further research on Constance and her daughter. It turns out the girl is Jackie Sodkoff, age 18, pictured in Gotham with her mother in the Boys and Girls Club fundraiser photos. Avi peruses the Divinity Country Day yearbook online, learns about Jackie's classmates, and checks for a Facebook account. Bingo. He cross-references "friends in high school." One of Jackie's classmates, Jane Hyland, has no Facebook account. He creates one for her. It's a bit of a risk; she and Jackie may be close and could compare notes. But he goes ahead as this seems to be the only chink in Adam Sodkoff's armor.

Jane "friend requests" Jackie, Jackie accepts, and Avi is in. After a few days of lurking on Facebook, he learns the Sodkoff family is going to the Hamptons for the weekend, except for Jackie's older brother who lives in the Village. Avi accesses Google Earth and his government access software to find the address of the Sodkoff beach house.

This ability to be both tech-savvy and a cold-blooded killer makes Avi one of the best assets in the post-Cold War era. During the Cold War, there were many targets and many hits. It was a busy time, and there were lots of hired assassins. Once the Berlin Wall came down, many of those assets suffered the same fate as their victims. With no enemy, they became targets in some border negotiation. The new spy says, "Give me the guy who killed Ambassador Vikkts, and I'll give you Boardwalk and Park Place."

CHAPTER EIGHT

Avinash is a leader in the industry of warfare, an industry most don't even know exists. There really is a boogeyman, but he's not under the bed. He's in Starbucks. He wears Italian clothes, gives money to green charities, drives a Vespa, works out at the gym, and has an apartment nearby. He gets looks of desire from your sister when she sees him walk by. He looks and acts just like you and me except when he's working.

Through his work as a contractor for the Company (the code name for any of his intelligence network partners), Avi has access to a network of contractors, people who can get him any item he needs in any part of the world so long as he has a code and a trail no one can follow. Once he takes delivery of any good or service, the trail dies. Even the contractor who provides the service is not really sure what is happening. That's why it works so well.

Avi is the CIA's asset #57. He uses this and other networks to initiate a plan similar to the McCally job using a van.

On Wednesday, he collects the van and drives to East Hampton to tap the beach house phone. He uses a tracker to set up an attachment to Constance's phone which will activate once she accesses the Wi-Fi.

Back in Manhattan on Thursday, Avi rents a Sea Ray cruiser for the weekend and sails out away from the city. He pulls into the Harbor Marina. an easy sail for a guy who has every kind of training from various stints in the navy and other military services all over the world.

Now he waits. He waits well. He knows how to wait better than anyone. His time in the Mossad prepared him for a career as an assassin-for-hire. Thirteen-year-old Avinash, who witnessed his first murder in Calcutta, saw a pathway out and followed it. He had one goal when he left Calcutta: to own a Mercedes and some nice clothes like the first hitman Avi ever saw practice his craft.

Each year in India, 1.7 million children die. By the time Avi was 17, he had seen hundreds of children die for various reasons. Many died from smallpox, typhoid, and roundworm simply from drinking dirty water, many from much more heinous causes. He kept a list of every child he knew who died and made up names for the ones he didn't know. These names became Avi's paper army. Today when a new identity is required, he simply goes to this list and creates it.

He found his way in with a group of men who employed children to beg on the streets. Most of these men lived very well but most of the kids, like Avi, were born untouchables with little prospect of ever moving out of a life of constant hunger and poverty. Avi was different. He was a smart kid, working his way into the management of these begging organizations by recruiting additional kids to beg.

One time, Avi was sent to the docks to retrieve a group of kids who would be arriving by ship. He could drive by then and they sent him in a truck. He waited, leaning on the truck smoking a cigarette as he had seen the assassin do years earlier. Eight kids were brought to him to deliver to the slave master. Strangely each kid was missing either a leg, an arm, or an eye. Avi delivered the kids to the slave boss and asked him what had happened to them. The older man laughed at him and took the kids away.

Avi went directly to the camp where the crippled children were staying. "How did this happen to you?" he asked each one. Only one or two could respond.

One said, "I was running by the train one day begging for people to throw food or money. When I went back with the money, the boss called me over and gave me something to drink. It tasted bad but I was thirsty. When I woke up, my arm was missing."

Another boy said, "The same for me but my leg was missing."

When Avi approached the boss the following day he said, "Those kids, we had their arms and legs cut off?"

The slave master responded, "You have to make the most of these kids. People will pay us more if they are maimed. I'm surprised you didn't know that."

This incensed Avi. He went to the man who stored his money, who had always been trustworthy, and said, "I need my money; can you get it all for me? I'm moving." Any time Avi wanted part of his money, the man would get it for him.

"Sure, meet me here tomorrow at 4:00 pm."

The next day Avi returned at 3:50 pm. At 4:00, no man. 4:30, no man. He waited until the next morning, but the man did not show up. Avi went back to the slave camp. When the maimed children left to begin to beg, Avi accompanied them. At the end of the day, he gave the children a large percentage of the money and kept the rest. He drove them to the police station and dropped them off. Avi took the money and went into town where he knew a factory existed that produced guns for the military.

Avi hung around the entrance to the factory as the workers came off their shift. He was sitting in his car when a man he had met before came out. He offered the man a cigarette and they smoked together leaning on the car.

"I need a gun," he told the factory man.

"It's 3,000 rupees."

Avi handed him 1,500. "The rest tomorrow with the gun and ammo," he said.

The following day when they made the exchange, the man asked Avi, "You don't know how to use that gun, do you? You need instruction. Bring more money tomorrow and I will introduce you to a man who will teach you how to use it."

Avi went back to the slave camp where his employer was waiting on him.

"Where have you been? Where are the kids?" He beat Avi.

"Wait! A man came and took all of them. I've been in jail. I just got out."

"What man?" the boss asked.

"He was a man in a uniform, not a cop."

The boss had no reason not to believe Avi as he had been steadfast during his time with him.

Once he had convinced the boss, Avi went to the prostitutes.

"I need money," he told the group of women. "I have to escape. I will come for you tomorrow and help you escape if you give me the money I need."

None of the girls would listen to him except one, Zeba. She was a beautiful woman and was making lots of money for the men in the camp.

"I will give you money, and I beg of you to return," Zeba said to Avi.

"I will."

Avi went back to the factory and met with his contact and another man, Nuvvuru, an assassin who worked in India, who would teach Avi to use a gun.

Avi paid his contact and gave Nuvvuru the rest of his cash. Nuvvuru laughed at the amount of money, but said, "OK, kid, follow me." Avi followed Nuvvuru, who was driving a black Mercedes.

"I will teach you how to kill. Is that what you want?"

"Yes."

In the course of 24 hours, Avi learned how to use the gun. He next went back into town and bought more ammunition. At 4:00 am he returned to the slave camp which was quiet everywhere except at the prostitutes' tent. Avi entered his boss's house where he found the boss asleep with two girls in his bed. Avi walked over to him and shot him in the face at point-blank range. He shot him again in the stomach and blood spattered onto Avi and the two girls.

Screaming, the girls ran out of the room.

Avi took all the money the boss had in the side drawer by his bed and stuffed it into his pockets. It was a substantial amount. Hearing men running up the stairs, Avi slipped into the closet. The two men stopped and looked around the corner, finding their dead boss in the room.

"What happened here?" one of the men asked. "Do you think one of the girls shot Rohan?"

The other man looked at him and said, "Go down and get the girls."

Avi heard one man retreat down the stairs and then heard the flip of a lighter and smelled a cigarette. He stepped out of the closet and the man, who could not see the blood on Avi in the darkness, asked, "What the hell are you doing here?"

Avi stepped right up to the man, pulled the gun from behind his back and shot him in the chest once and in the face once, double tap style as he was taught. More blood spattered on him as his victim fell to the floor.

Avi went back into the closet, kicked a hole in its back wall and climbed through grabbing a shirt hanging in the closet to wipe his face from the blood splatter. The other man came running back up the stairs and found his friend dead on the floor along with their boss. No one else was in the room. He walked over to the window. Nothing. He walked over to the closet. He pulled his gun and opened the door. Nothing. It was dark in the closet, but he noticed a hole in the back. He moved into the closet and crawled through the hole. As he came out the other side, Avi shot him in the back of the head, then moved in closer and shot him again in the head. He reloaded the gun with six bullets and climbed out the window and down the stairs to the ground. He ran to the prostitutes' tent and walked into Zeba's room. She was with a man. Avi shot the man double tap to the head.

He turned to Zeba. "Get dressed," he said. "We need to go."

They walked to a small hotel in town. It looked as if Avi had hired a prostitute, so no one noticed them much at all. They showered and changed clothes. Avi gave Zeba his car and some of the money from the boss's drawer, and they parted.

Avi returned to Nuvvuru for further instruction. He had found the mentor he was looking for. He continued to hone his skills over the following months and years by joining various forces around the world, mostly in the Middle East. Each army was glad to sign Avi as he already had skills when he came to their camps. He was taught more and more and became more and more valuable, allowing him to sign on with almost any organization he wanted. His build and skin color allowed him to fit into most Middle Eastern and northern Asian cultures. Through all of his assignments and training, he was able to learn the customs, accents, and languages of many countries.

At the end of their military service, most snipers go back to a life of peace and quiet with a family or some semblance of one. Most have something to go back to. Avi does not. This is all he has, and he is good at it.

CHAPTER NINE

On Friday evening, Avi leaves the shelter of the Harbor Marina for a 10-minute walk to the Sodkoff house. He is familiar with beach advancements, having made many during his service in various military and mercenary roles over the years. Almost all are different, and they are the most difficult type of assault. Usually, the only cover is darkness, and most coastlines are being watched by a team anticipating an attack. A beach insertion, Navy SEAL style, usually involves a force of 6 to 12 people in two teams in full dark and an electric engine pushing small rubber boats. This assault is entirely different.

Avi appears to be a tourist walking down the beach on a nice evening stroll. There is no security from the beachside. He sits down on the beach near Adam's house and slips on a pair of thin gloves. He is as relaxed as he can be in combat mode. He waits, listening to his monitoring device through his earpiece. There's a big argument going on in the house. Nothing new, from what Avi has experienced so far. Adam has perhaps had one too many scotches, and Constance

45

sounds plastered. Jackie is clearly annoyed and begins to shriek, just like at the coffee shop in the city a few days earlier.

"Great!" she says, "I'm going to my room. There's nothing to do on this island, and you wouldn't let me bring a friend. I just have to sit here and watch you two fight all night. Thanks for nothing!"

Jackie slams the door to her room and retreats to the Internet to hang out with her friends in cyberspace.

"I've had enough of you today as well. I'm going to bed," says Constance as she staggers to the stairway. Adam pours himself another scotch, neat, lights a Cuban cigar, and walks out onto the deck.

As Adam settles into the rocking chair, Avi hears its creaking. He can now see as well as smell the lighted cigar. Adam is staring out to sea from his porch, slightly drunk from three scotches. He doesn't notice the dark figure moving to the porch's side steps. Avi steps onto the porch and in one motion is behind Adam before he even notices him there. Avi pulls the rocker back and as Adam leans back in the chair Avi reaches his left arm around Adam's head and places his right hand on the right side of Adam's head. Instinct almost takes over as he turns Adam's head to snap his neck. Avi stops himself, remembering he needs to leave his victim in an accidental state. With one motion, he pulls the vial of Rohypnol from his fanny pack and shoots it into Adam's carotid artery, killing him as the drug courses through his system, leaving no sign of the assault. It's easy to murder when someone is so drunk they cannot put up much of a struggle. Avi knows the Rohypnol will burn off leaving no significant levels in Adam's bloodstream for his autopsy. He used this method before on dictators.

Avi allows Adam's body to slip down into the chair and places the cigar in the ashtray on the table. It is still lit. "Cuban," Avi says to himself, hating to leave the fine cigar behind.

Avi then disappears down the beach into the night. No dark boat. No team. No black make-up. A tourist taking a walk.

Constance wakes slowly in the morning and notices no Adam sleeping in the bed next to her. With earplugs, eyeshades, sleeping pills, and a lot of alcohol on board, she wouldn't have noticed if he had flown out of the room in a 747. Slightly hungover and groggy from Lunesta, she slowly works her way downstairs to the kitchen to make coffee. She waits for the pot to finish, anxious to taste that first hot cup. Where the hell is he? Probably gone out on a 30-mile ride with some biking buddies, she decides. She takes her coffee out onto the deck where she finds Adam slumped over in a rocker. She takes a seat on a chaise and sips her coffee.

He must have been really drunk last night. I can't believe he can sleep in that rocker. What a joke! "Don't say anything about me," she says. She moves to the rocker beside Adam, drinks her coffee, and waits for her husband to wake up. Jesus, you really look like shit in that chair, white as a ghost. "Adam," she says, "wake up and go upstairs to bed. Adam, get up!" She leans over and shakes him. "Adam, Adam!"

CHAPTER TEN

Arthur Cannon, Long Island coroner, takes a good, long look at Adam Sodkoff's body. Long Island, especially this part of it, while not the murder capital of the world, is highly competitive for heart attacks. This guy, while in pretty good shape for his age, looks like just another high-powered executive who pushed too far too fast. Cannon decides Adam Sodkoff died of a heart attack. No foul play. Another stressed-out executive works himself to death.

Two days later, Detective Frank Holland, NYPD, reads of Adam's death in the Times. He and Sodkoff actually rode bikes in the New York City Bike Club together, and while he didn't particularly like Adam, he finds it strange the guy would die of a heart attack. He decides to check it out. He calls out to the LIPD to ask for a copy of the autopsy report. The operator connects him with Arthur Cannon.

"Dr. Cannon? Frank Holland, NYPD. I wonder if I can get a copy of the autopsy report on Adam Sodkoff. I think you did the autopsy."

"Yeah, I did it, for the Long Island Police Department,

Detective … Hollins, was it?"

"Holland. Would you be good enough to send over a copy of your report to me at NYPD?"

"Now why would NYPD want another death report to look at? Don't you have enough of your own?"

"No, it's nothing like that, Doctor. I'd just like to see this one. I knew the guy."

"Well, I tell you what, Detective—you get your boss to send an official request for the autopsy report and I'll send it to him."

"Okay, if you're going to be that way, I'll do that," Frank says, hanging up. He goes down the hall to get a cup of coffee and before he can get back to his desk, he hears his name.

"Frank!" the police captain yells, giving him the look that says, "get into my office." Frank walks into the captain's office and has a seat across from his boss.

"Detective," the captain begins.

"Yes, sir."

"Why am I getting a call from Long Island to sign off for you to get an autopsy on some heart attack out there while I've got legitimate homicides here the people of New York City are paying your salary to solve?"

"Boss, this guy was sort of a friend of mine. We rode bikes together, and I just thought I would take a look and see what killed the guy. He seemed in pretty good shape to me."

"You just thought you would take a look? You have time on your hands to look at closed case autopsies for a hobby, do you?"

"Boss, I don't know. I just was curious about it. Like I said, the guy was in pretty good shape, 30–40-mile rider at a 12–15-mile pace. Not a fat guy on a bike. I just think, man, what could happen to me if this guy goes out with a heart attack?"

The captain walks around his desk and leans on it. He looks down at Frank.

"Frank, I know you. You're a good cop. Probably too good since this job has kind of ruled your life as priority one. I'm going to sign off on your autopsy request, but if you plan on investigating this thing, I need to know. This belongs to the Long Island PD, and they will not be happy for some NYPD cop to be opening closed cases for them to deal with. I'm not happy you're looking at closed cases either."

"Boss, I get it. I'll keep this on the QT unless it turns into something, and I'll come to you first with anything."

"This better not turn into anything. I mean it. Go close something that's still open."

"I will."

"Oh, and Frank," says the captain as Frank walks out his door. "I've got a real homicide for you down in Chinatown. Get on it."

"Right, boss."

Frank reflects on the captain's comments about the force being number one in his life and feels a certain sadness. He's sure his ex-wife could see this every day she lived with him. He really misses her. She was a great wife. He was married to the job, and she knew it and just couldn't take it anymore.

Frank gets his team opening a murder book on the

downtown homicide. A Chinese guy whacked in Chinatown, likely drug-related. Part of a new boss moving in to take over the territory. The team goes down to work the scene, but Frank is thinking about Sodkoff.

CHAPTER ELEVEN

At the end of the day, Frank drives home. He makes himself a Bacardi Gold Rum and Diet Coke, cuts in a lime, and sits down in his two-room apartment by the train tracks in Brooklyn. He misses his old life. His wife would come home from work and go right to work at home, making their life. She never complained about their home life. His work life was another story. Frank was out day and night, fixing a city that, in reality, he could not afford to live in. But his job was who he was.

Frank is a second-generation cop. He never even thought about another profession. His dad had been his world, and he had been larger than life. His dad would tell stories about saving the city from bad guys, and in his dad's day, there were plenty. Big name gangsters, Mafia. Every night, it was on TV. Being an NYPD cop was all Frank ever dreamed of doing, but he never knew how difficult it was on Camille. He thought every woman could handle it like his mom. Her dad had been NYPD as well.

Frank never understood what Camille was going

through. Every day when Frank left for work, she held her breath. She was never sure if he would be alive that evening. If he was on a case he might not even call for days, and he would not come home if he was hot on a perpetrator's trail. He wouldn't want it to go cold for something like family or a phone call to reassure her he was okay. Looking back, it was just plain unforgivable. Some nights, when he got home really late in the early stages of their marriage, Camille would say from a sleepy slumber, "Honey, I'm glad you're home. I hope it all went okay."

Frank wakes up from his reflection.

"This drink must have fallen over," he says to himself, noticing his rum and Coke glass is already empty except for slightly melted cubes. Frank stares at the ice cubes. His life has melted away and what does he have to show for it? He goes to the kitchen and makes another drink. He returns and starts to tinker with his bike, which he keeps on a trainer stand when he can't ride outside.

CHAPTER TWELVE

These envelopes are getting too big. Avi calls Viktor. "I want my assets deposited directly into my Cayman account from now on."

"As you wish," says Viktor. "Why don't you invest some of your cash in my fund? It generated a 75% return last year."

"No thanks," Avi says. They hang up as he counts the $200k for the Sodkoff assignment. $150,000 bonus on top of $50,000 up front.

He loads the cash into a gym bag and takes it down to the Hotel du Cap Ferrat concierge's desk. "Allo, may I have access to my safe box?" he says in French.

"Of course, monsieur."

The concierge gladly goes with him to the drawer. It is on the bottom row in the vault as it is one of the biggest boxes they have in the hotel. They both place their keys into the keyholes and turn them. The manager takes his key from the open door and waits. Avi takes out his box and follows the concierge to a private vestibule.

Avi opens the box and finds it is completely full. The box is about 2 feet wide and 3 feet long and 7 inches tall and it is full of money. Avi does the math and figures there is $10 million in hundreds in there, and there is no room for more.

He sits at the table in the vestibule for a few minutes. Then he returns to the safe area and slides his large box back into the drawer and closes and locks it with his key as the concierge comes over to lock the manager's lock with his key.

Unlike in a bank, Avi has 24-hour access to this box, and with the tips he showers on the staff as well as his reputation at this hotel, he gets whatever he wants. Avi is in the deluxe sea view terrace suite, one of the few in the entire hotel. He keeps a room in this hotel for months at a time, and when he is not in the hotel, he rents a regular room just to be able to come and go as he pleases and maintain his safe box. The hotel has many eccentric guests who want a room here so badly they keep a small room rented so they can at least have a room on the premises until the manager can vacate their regular room for them if they show up unannounced. The regular hotel guests are treated like royalty, which many of them are. Avi is a mystery to the staff, and they have no reason to pry. Many think he is a black sheep heir, cast away from the family as he rarely has any guests except an occasional beautiful woman. Some think he is an arms dealer, but most of those are Russian. He seems to be of Middle Eastern descent, but no one dares to think any further. They just know he is very good to the staff. He wants absolute privacy and to be left alone unless he needs something.

Avi reads a new dossier.

Reverend James Shook. 5'10", 192 pounds, born 05-05-1960. Church Word of the Lord Fellowship Witness, 22 Clover Street, Los Angeles, CA. Home address: 1215 Coldwater Canyon Drive, Beverly Hills, CA.

Shook has a congregation downtown but lives uptown. I wonder how many in his congregation know he lives up in the hills. Well, let's see what we can find out about the good Reverend.

Avi accesses his database to take a look.

Well, it appears our friend, the Right Reverend, spent a little time in upstate New York for possession with intent to sell. Interesting. This guy is not going to shake easy. He has a good gig and he's been to the rodeo. Looks like I'm going to need to go to church.

Avi follows the right reverend for a brief period of time and sees he will be an easy target. The problem will be the setting. Avi will need to get him while he is at the church or nearby.

Avi goes to the Wednesday night service. It's a big church with a crowd of about 200 on a Wednesday night, and the service is being televised. The sermon goes on for 40 minutes, there is some singing, and it rounds out at about one hour. Avi greets the reverend as he leaves the church.

"Enjoyed your sermon, preacher," Avi says in a southern accent.

"Where are you from, son?"

"Alabama sir, I was adopted by a family down there as a baby," Avi adds to explain his appearance of Indian or Latin origin. "I am moving here to work with an orphanage I am trying to open right down here by your church. Perhaps you could walk over with me to see what my plans are sometime."

"Of course, son."

Avi moves on through the line and goes out to his car and waits for the preacher to finish greeting his flock. In about an hour, the preacher walks out alone. Avi gets out of his car and walks up to the preacher. "Sir, can you walk with me over to my site for a second?"

Shook looks around and sees no one watching. "Well son, I really have to be somewhere right now, perhaps another time."

Avi puts a gun in his gut. "I insist, Reverend."

Now Shook looks panicked. They walk around the corner.

"You know, son, this is not any way to raise money for an orphanage. What is it you want?"

"You'll know soon enough."

Avi hands the reverend 2 grams of crack cocaine and pulls the trigger twice. No one hears the puffs of the silenced 9 millimeter as the reverend falls. Blood drips onto one of the bags of crack. Avi grabs the other bag and dusts it on the reverend. He puts the gun in his jacket, removes his gloves, and walks around the corner to his car.

The 9 millimeter is the essential drug dealer gun of choice. A nine-millimeter bullet is designed to fit in many different types of guns, and it can be purchased almost anywhere. The machine gun takes a nine, a tommygun—

like they killed Al Capone with—will hold about 50 rounds. Interestingly, when the police arrive on the scene, they too will likely be carrying nines.

LA Times headline: "Beloved Reverend Shook gunned down five blocks from his parish. Police suspect drugs were involved."

Details are sketchy, but it appears he was shot, and drugs were found nearby. No one is sure how he became involved in this situation, but sources report a James Shook had been incarcerated at Shawshank Prison in New York for drug possession with intent to sell 15 years ago. Police suspect it was a drug deal gone badly.

CHAPTER THIRTEEN

In Tucson, Rachael cannot let the McCally case go. She still thinks Donna McCally's death was no accident. How much of her obsession with this case is coming from a desire to solve her mom's case no one can say. Perhaps she sees this as a way to heal her own life from the wounds of living a life of an army brat, on the move. Every time Rachael got settled into a school, met some people and made a few friends, the nervousness of her own soul would start. It was almost a panic. She knew once she got too comfortable in a setting, her dad would come home and announce they were moving to Timbuktu or somewhere else on the other side of the world. She learned to keep people at enough of a distance that when she had to leave she did not get hurt. At least she thought she was not getting hurt. She just learned to medicate the hurt.

Knowing full well Roger will pitch a fit if she keeps working on this case, Rachael flies to Iowa to check out Donna's parents. To add insult to injury, she uses a police voucher to buy the ticket.

At the airport, she rents a car for the drive to the Cartmans' house which is in the middle of nowhere. She comes to a crossroads—two ways dirt, forward paved. She turns right, down the side road and drives about six more miles to their house. It is a beautiful farm with several windmills and cattle in the fields. She drives up to the front of the house, and before she can get out a woman comes out of the house to greet her.

"You are Detective Lopez?" says Mrs. Cartman.

"Yes, and you are Charlotte Cartman?"

"Yes."

"I am so sorry about your loss, Mrs. Cartman."

Mrs. Cartman seems to assume an American Gothic stare as she fails to react to Rachael's comment, but turns and leads her toward the porch of the white farmhouse. They enter the house where Mr. Cartman is seated in a recliner wearing coveralls and smoking a pipe.

"Mr. and Mrs. Cartman, I am so sorry to bother you in your time of grief."

No one says anything for a moment.

"I guess I'll just come right out with it: I'm not sure Donna's death was an accident, but I have nothing but my instinct to go on. Can you help me?"

"Honey, we feel the same way," Mrs. Cartman says eagerly. "Poor George and the kids. This is a real mess. . . I just don't know what George is going to do. She did so much for those kids and for him to make their place a home." She tears up as she speaks.

"Do you have any reason to believe anyone would want to hurt Donna?"

"No. I can't think of anyone. She was always such a good girl. But it seems so strange to me, her, you know, her…" Mrs. Cartman cannot bring herself to say 'death.' She hands Rachael a glass of lemonade.

"Thank you."

"We just can't seem to figure it all out," continues Mrs. Cartman. "It's not like Donna to be taking a bath in the middle of the day. I don't see it. And then to slip on the floor with as much farm work as she has done that was more difficult and dangerous. I just don't believe it."

Donna's father so far has said nothing. He sits in the rocking recliner, smoking his pipe and listening.

"We've been talking about how we can help them now. We were hoping a life insurance policy we took out on Donna years ago would be there for them in case something awful happened, but after George lost his job at HP and they needed money, I think they cashed it in to tide them over. It seems like that's what Donna said . . . Miss . . . Mrs.?"

"I'm a detective. Please call me Rachael."

"Can you think of any reason why someone would . . . I mean who would . . ." Donna's mom cannot say the word 'murder,' and she tears up again. "You know, as a detective?"

"Police experience shows most homicides are committed by someone who knows the victim."

"You think George was connected to this?"

"No ma'am, I don't have a suspect. I haven't even been able to convince anyone this was anything other than an accident, so far. I'm just trying to figure it out."

"We just can't believe it. It's just not like her. A bath."

"Is there anything else you can tell me about Donna that might help? Did she have any old boyfriends? Did she know much about George's work?"

"Well, she had an old boyfriend, but he is married and farms about 30 miles from here down Highway 122. He is pretty much always on his farm. As farmers, you don't get away much. Cattle don't care if it's Christmas, Detective, they still have to eat."

"I understand."

"As far as George and his job goes, Donna never mentioned to me anything about his work other than the fact he had to travel a lot. We were all just glad he had the job. He went almost two years without work after he got laid off from HP."

"I don't know what I'd do if I had to go two years without a paycheck," says Rachael.

"Well they cashed in that life insurance policy like I said, and I guess they lived off it. We helped them along as best we could at that time as well. It's a shame George won't have the insurance now."

They sit a few more minutes and no one says anything.

"Thank you both for your time. I guess I will head on back."

"Please let us know, dear, if we can help any more. I believe you will find out what happened."

"Thank you, Mrs. Cartman. I will."

CHAPTER FOURTEEN

Avi has finished his business with the Reverend and is working out of his latest office, this one located at Guardian Cargo Logistics in Los Angeles. He is readying himself for his return flight to Cap Ferrat when his email pings.

From: Viktor.

Subject: Employment Required – Domestic.

Avi opens the email and is introduced to a new, thoroughly unpleasant target.

Harrison Chester DelGotto: March 28th, 1956. Lives in Los Angeles, California. Known address: 13 S Mapleton Drive. Occupation: Real Estate Developer, 162 Sepulveda Blvd., Los Angeles, California, and Las Vegas, Nevada. Thrice divorced.

Avi does a bit of research and feels pretty good about this hit. His kind of hit. Typical bad man. Shoddy real estate developer. Bad houses and bad deals. Hookers. Drugs. Older guy who is in bad shape and will move slowly. The perfect mark. He may die before I get to him.

Avi stakes out the Sepulveda office address. Around

10:35 am, he believes he spots his mark getting out of a Rolls across the street from the office. The guy has his own designated parking space with his name on a sign. Right car. Right tag number. Fat guy moving slowly. That's him. Avi curses himself for not checking the parking lot for the parking space. He just can't get his head around how lax most people are around security. A sign on a parking space with the guy's name. It can't get much easier.

Chester heads toward the building with Avi close behind, but not too close. Chester's office is on the first floor. No private entrance.

Avi walks down the hall to the men's room. No one is in there. He walks back out, takes a turn around the small lobby. Not a high-end property by LA standards. He walks back out of the building, down the street four blocks, and then four blocks left and makes a few more turns checking for a tail until he doubles back over to Starbucks just across the street. He has a latte while he sits outside watching Chester's building. Nothing noteworthy is going on. No signs of surveillance. He watches and he waits. Although it may not seem important to the inexperienced, it can truly trip you up if you wait an insufficient amount of time. If you do wait, either things happen or things don't happen, and it gives you a sense of when to attack. After a while, Avi feels all is clear at Chester's office and reenters the building.

It is a fairly typical office building, but it has no door security, which is a little unusual for California. Avi double checks for cameras: none. Avi expected there to be cameras. The egos in LA require everyone to take notice. Even the nobodies usually have doormen, even if it doubles the rent. The unimportant have to become important somehow. It's their first step on the way to the top. The harder they can make it for you to get in, the better they like it.

Avi is frankly surprised to see the men's room does not at least require a code to enter. Chester really is a bad guy if he has a building in LA in which there is no way to stroke his ego coming or going. Avi goes into a stall and waits. He waits some more. Avi has been waiting on something or someone, it seems, for his entire life.

CHAPTER FIFTEEN

The things one thinks of while waiting.

He was a poor, young boy growing up in Calcutta. His mother was an untouchable, his father a Brahmin, or so he was told anyway, as he never met him. His father never showed up at the hovel they called home. It was basically a box surrounded by and stacked up with other boxes and sheets of stolen tin.

Avi and his friends would run around all day trying to figure out where to steal food or get into pranks, making nuisances of themselves. It was the only way most people knew these kids were alive. They would get in the way of civilized life in the city.

The lost boys are a source for identities for Avi's operation. In modern civilization, it is not so easy to make up a name or go to a cemetery and assume the identity of a "resident." Computers keep up with births and deaths. Try going through an airport with a dead guy's passport, and you will find yourself in a little room being questioned for a very long time.

Ideally, you have a source of births with no reported deaths. They must be people society doesn't care about alive or dead, or at least no recorded death. That's where the lost boys come in. Almost daily during Avi's childhood, one of his young friends died of something. Disease, trauma, dysentery. Avi never forgot their names, although most of society did. Avi attended the services as the children's bodies were burned, if the family could pull together the money for the wood pile, although most of the time they were just dumped into a hole with other bodies and lime was sprinkled over the potter's grave, just like Mozart. Avi would find something belonging to each friend who died, a stone they picked up or a branch or a piece of string, and he would keep it, not knowing these memories and mementos would one day come in handy in his chosen profession.

Avi has a list of names with birth certificates and no death certificates, so he can easily develop a new identity on the internet almost anytime he needs one without any questions. He also sees this as a way for these boys to pay back the world that cheated them out of life.

Avi remembers the first murder he ever witnessed.

Deep in Box Town one day, he noticed a guy talking to a man in a big, shiny black car. Avi had never seen a car like it. It was bigger than his house. The man in the car was smoking a cigarette as the other guy pleaded with him in a language Avi did not understand. The man did not look at the pleader but looked straight out the windshield and smoked his cigarette. When he finished the cigarette, he tossed the butt at the pleading man, pulled out a gun, and shot him in the head. The man fell backward and Avi saw blood pouring from the back of his head like it was coming from a hose.

For a moment the street became quiet, but soon all the noise returned. The man who did the shooting eased out of his car, pulled out another cigarette, then leaned back against the car and smoked it, taking his time, as if nothing had happened. He was dressed in a nice suit with beautiful shoes and dark sunglasses. Once he finished the cigarette, he got back in the big car and left, in no particular hurry.

Avi stood still for a few moments as his friends ran toward the body. Then he snapped to and ran over to take the dead man's wallet, shoes, and belt. He ran away fast, outpacing his friends easily. When he saw he was alone, he looked in the wallet. It had a huge stack of rupees, which Avi counted: 7837—about a year's pay for a Box Towner. That was it for him. He took the money and left Box Town for Calcutta proper. He never went back. He was 13.

If a man in a car could leave a dead man's wallet behind with all that money in it, and with no apparent care in the world, he must be richer than all the maharajas. Avi would learn to kill people as well.

CHAPTER SIXTEEN

Avi hears the door to the men's room open. Chester comes in for his morning constitutional.

From a stall in the men's room, Avi dials Chester's cell phone number, given to him during a brief phone call yesterday. Chester answers from the next stall saying "hello, hello." Avi's number is blocked on Chester's phone, showing up as "unknown caller" while Avi sets the triangulation. When Avi hangs up he has the location of DelGotto's phone locked in. No more need to follow Chester.

Once the men's room clears, Avi drives to his office at Guardian Cargo to get to work. He uses Chester's phone to get into his computer where he finds his credit card numbers, flight preferences, hell, even his favorite hooker's phone number.

Once he has cleared things at the office, Avi heads to the Beverly Hills Hotel, where he has already checked in as Mr. Royce, from Boston, another name from his lost boys' list.

It appears Chester is headed to Vegas on Delta Flight 984 LAX to LAS at 8:31pm, last thing Monday. Avi decides to drive over. Less hassle. He stays checked in at the Beverly Hills Hotel, telling the front desk he'll be in and out for the next few days, and he may have to spend a night or two in San Francisco, but to keep the room for him. He leaves a "do not disturb" sign on the door.

Avi is there to meet Chester's plane as a limousine driver, holding a sign for Mr. DelGotto, supposedly providing complimentary service from TSI distributors. Chester has no idea who TSI is, but a free limo is a free limo. Avi drives Chester to the Strip where he has a suite at the MGM Grand. Avi himself is checked in down the street at the Bellagio as Dr. Rove from New York City.

"Mr. DelGotto, you qualify for complimentary return service to the airport also. When are you returning?"

Chester fishes out his itinerary. "Flight 4598, leaves at 4:20 pm on Thursday."

"Good, sir. Shall we say 3:00 pm?"

"Sure."

"Very well, sir."

Avi keeps tabs on Chester periodically over the next few days. He also has a little vacation in Vegas. The Bellagio is a nice hotel, but not the top-of-the-line hotel she was years ago. Still, it's nice enough for Avi to go unnoticed. Ever cautious, he changes his hair style three times over the next four days just to keep the Bellagio cameras from noticing the same man over and over again in the hotel. Avi has a penthouse suite overlooking the famous fountain. It is a penthouse in name only, as it is on the 38th floor and not the top. It seems the Bellagio has floors and floors of penthouse suites.

Avi calls the concierge, and they send up a bar cart to his room, with a fifth of Grey Goose, St Germaine, Baker's, cranberry juice, limes, club soda, and various other liquors and mixers all on a rolling table to leave in his suite for his stay. Las Vegas. Ask for anything, pay some money, and they can make it happen. Avi does a quick 40-minute workout in his room while he listens to Italian opera. He has a drink sitting in his luxurious robe and then goes into one of his two bathrooms to take a shower. He emerges dressed to impress—a rich, dark, Latin-looking executive, handsome and lean.

Avi walks down the strip to the Metropolitan. He goes to the bar upstairs and has a light meal alone. He then goes down to the large bar. After a couple of drinks, he is feeling pretty loose for a hit man. He sees a group of girls sitting on a couch with a coffee table in front of them. One girl in particular catches his eye.

"Excuse me," Avi says to the bartender, and the bartender breezes over while he is making a drink for another patron. "Please bring a bottle of Crystal and five glasses over to this table with me."

The bartender stops making the drink. "I am sorry sir but the most expensive champagne we have is the Moet Chandon Brut."

"Ok. Then, let's have two bottles on a bar cart with a fifth of Grey Goose, a fifth of St. Germaine, two sliced limes, a bottle of cranberry juice, an ice carafe, five highball glasses, and someone to make drinks personally for me at the table with those four ladies." He hands the bartender five one hundred-dollar bills.

"Johnny," the bartender says to his co-worker, "take over the bar. I'm taking a break."

The bartender pulls together a rolling bar and rolls it to the table where the four girls are sitting. They look up surprised as the handsome bartender opens the champagne, pours four glasses, and begins making each a cosmopolitan martini, Avi style.

"Whoa, we didn't order this," says a pretty auburn-haired girl sitting in a chair at the end of the coffee table.

"No, but he did," the bartender said, pointing at Avi. "I'm here for the duration of your stay to make you free drinks from this cart."

Avi makes his way over to the table as the girls high five each other over the free bar for the evening. They now see Avi in his finery, an Armani suit—lean, tall, and Latin-looking. Avi uses a Latin accent as he speaks to the girls.

"Ladies, I hope it was not too presumptive of me to send over a bar."

"Why, no," the auburn-haired ringleader says, mostly in unison with the other three girls.

The bartender places a chair beside the auburn-haired girl, and Avi sits down. The evening advances and Avi learns she has a child at home from a mistake she made as a young girl. She works as a dancer, but not a showgirl dancer yet. That is what she aspires to be. A Vegas story. They dance and drink more. The night begins to weigh into the scene. It is the time of night for things to happen or not. It is sensed in a place like this. Avi stands and hugs the girl, gives the other three kisses on the hand and begins his departure.

"That's it?" the auburn-haired girl, who has been happily consuming the free bar, stands and asks of Avi.

"Sorry, my dear, but that's it."

"Have I done something wrong?"

"My dear, you have done something too right, and I am not in a position to advance forward with you."

"Oh, so you're married. Married men never talk about themselves . . . So, that's it? You're married?"

The easy thing to do here would be to tell her he is married.

"No, I'm not married and I'm not gay. I am just not in a position to have a relationship at this time. You are a nice girl, and you need a nice man. A man who can be a father and a husband. I am not one of those. Goodbye, my dear."

"Wait, maybe I'm not looking for a husband tonight."

"Sorry, I don't believe you even if you believe yourself."

Avi walks away feeling regret with his decision, but many decisions trigger sadness. This young woman could have been someone to build a life with, a life with kids and a white picket fence and a dog. It's a recurring dream that dies with every new murder. A new murder moves this life further and further away from reality. Avi cannot allow any strings in his life. Strings get pulled, and people can follow strings. When the night ends, he arrives at his suite alone and goes to bed.

The next day, more time, more waiting. A major part of this occupation is waiting. It would drive an ordinary person crazy to have this much alone time. Luckily, Avi doesn't have that problem.

When he was a child in the Box Town world of Calcutta,

there was never silence—always noise, noise, noise. The silence was welcomed; Avi found it to be his friend. In spite of his profession, he enjoys silence.

Avi thinks about Viktor and how his life led him to this place with this guy.

CHAPTER SEVENTEEN

YUGOSLAVIA 1989

The CIA assigns Avi to eliminate a political target in Belgrade.

The CIA is the best group to work for. First class. Easy in, easy out. They arrange everything but the kill.

When Avi does a job for the CIA, transportation is provided. This time he is met at the airport by a young driver. Avi notices the driver keeps looking at him in the mirror, which is a no-no. He is only supposed to drive—no interaction with the asset.

The driver, whose name is Viktor, works for the Company in Belgrade. Viktor is a runner, one of the people who make the pick-ups and drop-offs when assets arrive in or depart from a city. Never is the same runner used for the drop-off and pick-up. There should be no connections between anyone in any scenario, so if someone sees something, it would be difficult to tie any one person to the scene except the asset.

"Can I get you anything, sir?" this kid asks Avi.

Avi says nothing; he simply looks at him as if to say, "Shall I kill you as well?"

The kid kind of stands out. First, he has a mouth on him, which is a liability in this environment. Over the 122 jobs Avi has done for the Company, no runner has said a single word to him. He likes it that way, and that is the way of the Company. No communication leaves no room for runner error.

"Sir, we are having great weather here right now, and the hotels are excellent."

Does he think I am a tourist? "Hey kid," Avi finally says, "shut up."

"Sure thing, I should know better. I just figured you might need to know a few things once you got here, that's all."

Avi never snitches on the kid for talking. They both have something to lose if he does. Avi can use this error to his advantage later if needed. He finds himself reluctantly liking the kid. Avi's life is mostly a lonely existence. There's something odd but comforting about the way the kid interacts with him—like Avi is a human, not a killing machine. The kid can't say anything to anyone about this; he knows the rules: there would be consequences if he did.

Avi is curious about this kid. He is somewhere between 20 and 27. Avi is in his 30s. Not much difference, but at the same time considerable difference.

YUGOSLAVIA 1991

Avi is back in Yugoslavia for a big job, the Belgrade mayor. When he arrives, the same kid picks him up.

"Hi, sir," says Viktor.

"Kid, you just don't get this thing, do you? Shut up and drive."

Viktor drives Avi to a building in downtown Belgrade where the target is to be eliminated. Avi makes his way into the building and up the stairs and sees no one. This is supposed to be a municipal building with activity going on, but the scene is too quiet. He continues up the stairs to the second door on the left as instructed. The mayor is sitting at his desk, not moving. Avi moves in to eliminate him, but the mayor does not react. Avi checks. He is already dead.

Shit, it's a set-up. Avi moves back to the door only to find two armed gunmen lying in wait. Both take shots. Avi kills one and is hit by a bullet from the other before he is able to kill him. He works his way down the stairs and out the front. No car. The getaway driver is nowhere to be found. Avi is wounded and out on the street with no ride.

He moves down the street to a pay phone as inconspicuously as a wounded man in Belgrade can. He makes a call to what is supposed to be the bailout number in case something goes wrong, No answer. Shit, I've really been set-up. A black car is slowly moving down the street, but it's not Avi's ride. It's two more gunmen out to kill him. Avi jumps behind a two-foot wall and drops down flat protected from oncoming gunfire by the wall. He fires two shots at the car. The passenger in the car sprays the wall and the scene with AK47 fire, trapping Avi. Then a second car screams down the road with the driver shooting an AK out the window in every direction except at Avi. The AK fire from the second car sprays the back glass out of the first car, and the car pulls away. The second car slows to a crawl right in front of the wall Avi is concealed behind it, and the passenger door swings open. "Get in!" yells the kid as he shoots the AK out the driver's window. Avi moves from behind the wall shielded by Viktor's car. He jumps in, and the kid drives him out of town.

The kid takes Avi to a farmhouse where two old men come out, one missing a hand. They open the doors to a barn and the kid drives the car inside.

Avi has his pistol pulled, ready to kill everybody on the scene, but the kid says, "Wait, they are here to help us. Please don't shoot."

Avi allows the old men to help him from the car. They take him to a nearby table set up inside a horse stall. The man with two arms pulls Avi's shirt off to see where the bullet entered his side, while the one-armed man gives Avi a bottle of something with no label.

"For pain. Drink, drink," the one-armed man says.

Avi takes a swig of what is clearly some home-grown hooch and almost loses his breath; pure alcohol. The first man takes the bottle and pours some on Avi's side as Avi breathes in and out as he was taught during his time with the Mossad. When it comes to pain, the yoga method works best. Avi begins to calm down as the hooch has the desired effect. The man with one hand gets the bullet out of Avi's side and drops it into a metal pan. Then he sews Avi up with help from the other man. When they finish, the men pull bales of straw to the back of the stall. They move Avi there and place him under a horse blanket, then put straw over the blanket, almost completely covering Avi in the back of the stall.

Viktor sits on a bucket in the stall with the AK in his lap and waits as Avi falls asleep. Two days later, he drives Avi to the airport to catch a commercial flight out of Sarajevo.

CHAPTER EIGHTEEN

Ten years later, Avi's phone rings. He picks it up but says nothing.

Avi hears the voice of Viktor, the kid: "Sir, I don't know if you remember me from Yugoslavia? I'm sorry, but I do not know your name."

"Yes, kid, I remember you. I remember people who cover me, and I remember those who don't."

"Oh . . . ah . . . great," Viktor says nervously. "I just know you are the very best at what you do. I picked up several assets when I worked in Yugoslavia, and no one else performed at your level. You see, even though I was told to drop you and leave, I usually went around the corner to see what you were actually up to. I did this with most of the assets I drove. I saw you work with precision, while I saw other assets get the job done without any concern about collateral damage. You, sir, are a solid professional."

Avi says nothing.

"Sir, are you still there?"

"Yes," Avi says.

"Well, I would like to develop a relationship with you for a project I am working on."

"I'm listening, but only because of Belgrade. I don't need or want any relationships."

"You are the best at what you do. I am in need of your services," says Viktor.

"I am still listening."

"I have certain elements that need to be addressed similar to what you have done for the Company. I am in a position to pay you what I believe would be a significantly higher fee," says Viktor. "You know who I am since I was there for you once. I am a man of my word. I have a business model which requires your expertise to enhance my circumstance. We both know that is all it is ever about with your current employer. We are not naive enough to think there is any patriotic or larger-than-life reason for our work with the Company. It is strictly a commerce model. Just like mine. They just keep the money, but I am willing to provide a larger split with you. That's all. No difference."

"What type of circumstance?" Avi asks.

"Regular people," says Victor. "Not necessarily bad people. Just people who have made bad choices. They will not even know you are coming for them because they have no idea there is any reason for their demise."

'I will do one of these for you as a test. $150,000 in cash delivered to my designated place. No questions from you about methods or time horizons or I will add you to the list."

"Excellent. Thank you. I look forward to a long and profitable relationship," says Viktor.

Avi awakens from his day dream while he waits to do his work in Vegas. He assembles the murder kit he uses for point-blank killing, including a toilet paper roll. He checks out of the Bellagio and drives the rental car to his Vegas office, a public rental storage unit. He puts on his chauffeur's uniform with hat, switches his car for the limo he has stored in one of his two units, and drives to the MGM to pick up Chester. As he pulls up he sees Chester waiting out front with his rolling bag. He steps out to open the back door as the bellman moves to load the bag in the trunk.

Avi motions him away; he stops. Avi closes the door, gets the bag from the bellman, and loads it into the trunk himself. Avi tips the bellman as it appears Chester missed that part. He gets behind the wheel of the limo, and they depart.

"Mr. DelGotto," says Avi with his best Texas twang, "you look like you could use a drink."

"You know, I probably could."

"Well, sir, I have something made up for you right here."

"Damn, how did I qualify for this service?"

"Oh, sir, people are dying to get this service," Avi says.

Chester takes a big sip of the special potion and nods right off. Another easy mark.

They head toward Stoddard Wells Road and Quarry Road in Nipton. Unfortunately, Chester begins to awaken after a little while.

"Hey!" Chester says in a raised voice. "This isn't the way to the airport! Where are you going? I need to make a stop on the way."

Avi swerves the limo to throw Chester, still groggy, against the side of the car. Chester falls over pretty easily and Avi stops the car, gets out, and takes Chester's phone. Chester realizes he may have made a mistake with this limo driver.

"Relax, sir, we will be where we need to be soon," says Avi as he restarts the limo and drives on.

"What is this all about? You can't just take my phone. I'll report you. What is your name?"

Chester puffs up like a bully. Avi swerves the limo again to knock Chester about in the backseat. He stops the car, opens the door, and hits Chester twice—once in the mouth and once in the throat. Chester is in pain, holding his throat, and the reality of the situation finally hits him.

"Who sent you?" Chester asks through the pain of his sore throat. "I can pay you more, I'm sure. Just let me go. We'll act like none of this ever happened. I swear, I can keep a secret," Chester pleads.

"Chester," Avi states, "I would suggest you drink the rest of your drink or things are going to get very ugly for you."

Chester looks out the window at the Las Vegas desert. He sees a vision of all the houses he has built and all the people he has taken advantage of, and he solemnly drinks his drink. Soon after, he passes out.

Knowing he needs Chester to be found, Avi pulls off the road just past Nipton and uncovers the shallow grave he dug last night—time is always a factor when digging a roadside grave. He pulls Chester out of the back seat of the limo, binds his hands and legs with some twist ties he found at a hardware store. He positions Chester on his knees and shoots him in the back of the head through the toilet paper roll so any blood backsplash will hit the roll and not his uniform. He then covers the grave containing Chester's body and drives back to Vegas. He turns in the limo, takes a cab back to his storage unit, picks up his rental car, and drives back to Beverly Hills.

CHAPTER NINETEEN

Rachael is in the office when her boss Captain Roger Emanuel steps in.

"Rachael," he says. "Where have you been for the last two days?"

"I went to Iowa to follow-up on the McCally case."

"The McCally case? There is no McCally case, Rachael. This woman died from a fall in her bathroom. We have plenty of open cases for you to work where no one fell down until after they were shot. You are not being paid to investigate accidental deaths. What is wrong with you?"

"Me? What the hell is wrong with you? This woman was clearly killed, but I seem to be the only one around here who knows about it or actually gives a shit."

"Rachael, I've taken enough grief around here covering your back and definitely too much from you as well. I'm not having another conversation with you about this case. Do you understand?"

Rachael says nothing more. When Emanuel leaves her cubicle, she calls George McCally.

"Mr. McCally, this is Detective Lopez. I'm so sorry to bother you. I know you're in a bad place, but I have just a few more questions. May I come by your house?"

"Have you found out more about . . . about . . ." George cannot say the words.

"Very little, but I want to get some more information from you that may help."

"Ok."

"How about in an hour or so?"

"Fine."

Rachael drives up to the McCally residence and knocks on the door. The daughter answers. Rachael really does not know what to say to kids.

"Hi, I'm Detective Lopez. I'm here to see your father."

"Dad," the child calls out.

George McCally steps through a swinging door wearing an apron.

"Kids, this is Detective Lopez."

"Yeah, Dad, I met her at the door," the daughter says.

"She's here to help us find out something about your Mom."

The kids look puzzled but let it go and go upstairs.

"I'm sorry, Mr. McCally, have I interrupted dinner?" asks Rachael.

"No, I'm working on it. Spaghetti and green beans from a can, I'm afraid." He begins to tear up. He wipes his eyes. "Have a seat, Detective Lopez. What can I do to help?"

"Mr. McCally, I understand there was an insurance policy on Donna for $700,000, and you were the beneficiary."

"Oh, you still think I had something to do with this?" George asks.

"Sir, I'm just asking so we can find our way through this. I'm not accusing you of anything."

"Well, was is the right term."

"What do you mean?"

"When I lost my job at HP, we had to sell the insurance policy and use the cash just to get by. I was out of work for two years before I signed on with Lockheed."

"You cashed it in for the cash value."

"Not exactly. We sold it. It was a way to get more than the cash value. Donna handled it all. It was her policy."

"Can you tell me more about it, Mr. McCally?"

"I remember we called Hartley Life, the company that wrote the policy, to cash it in but were told we could only get $97,000 cash. Then one of my former colleagues at HP told me about a company that would buy life policies from you for more than the cash-in value. So I told Donna, and she found one that paid us $200,000."

"What company?"

"I don't remember the name right off the top of my head, but I think I still have the paperwork here somewhere. Give me a minute."

George and Rachael walk through the den into an office, and George opens a drawer in a desk full of files. He flips through them and locates a manila file folder.

"Here it is . . . Great Plains International Viatical Settlement Group."

CHAPTER TWENTY

Las Vegas PD detectives have joined the first responders at the scene.

"What have we got here?" asks Detective Emerson, who just arrived.

"A big, fat, dead guy. Head shot. A little beat up in the face but not very bad," says Inspector Clark who has been on the scene.

"This looks like a professional hit. I mean, big hole in the back of the head, shallow grave in a place where it will be found easily—all the marks of a mob hit with a warning to anyone else running afoul of them," says Clark. "We've got his identification here. DelGotto. Heard of him?"

"No. Why? Should I?" asks Emerson.

"I guess not but I sure as hell have. I live in one of his shitty houses. It's been a lemon since we bought the damned thing. I've had almost everything in it replaced but the interior walls," says Clark.

"Oh yeah, I've heard of him now. He's trouble. He's kind of a bad guy, I think. Some mob ties. There should be a list of 250 to 350 suspects to choose from."

"Yeah, I could be on the list after what all the complaints I made after going through them with my house," says Clark. "He owed money everywhere from here to Detroit to Chicago. I checked with a lawyer to see if I had any recourse, but he told me DelGotto was broke. I guess we'd better get on it. You think the FBI may try to jurisdict us out of this case?"

"No way. This case is unsolvable. They won't touch it with a ten-foot pole. We'll have to take the lead. Let's make sure we bury it with some guys who can waste time on it. It's a low priority as far as I'm concerned."

Avi powers up his MacBook Air in the comfort of his home, or at least as close to home as he actually has—his suite at the Hotel du Cap Ferrat. Avi keeps rooms—more like villas—in the south of France in multiple hotels as well as a private residence in Nice. He clicks the bookmark for the Las Vegas Review-Journal online. After three days, he is rewarded with a news story about the discovery of DelGotto's body.

"Bankrupt real estate developer with alleged mob ties found dead near Vegas

Chester DelGotto, 54, a son of the late well-known Southern California real estate developer and builder, Richard DelGotto, was found dead yesterday in a shallow grave not far from Las Vegas. DelGotto was reputed to have ties to the mob and was known to have declared bankruptcy at least twice in the past. LVPD spokesman Douglas Merrill says it is too early to give out any additional information."

CHAPTER TWENTY-ONE

Frank checks the Court database and pulls a copy of Adam's will. It's 74 pages long. He sees that Joseph Stein, attorney, is the lawyer who filed the will with the court. Google has made even a cop's job so much easier. Frank finds Stein's number and gives him a call.

"Stein, Holloway Partners," the receptionist says as Frank's call comes in.

"This is Detective Frank Holland. May I speak with Joseph Stein, please? I'm calling about the death of Adam Sodkoff."

"One moment, please," says the receptionist. Frank holds for a minute or so.

"Detective Holland, I'll connect you now."

"Thank you."

"Joe Stein here. How may I help you?"

"Mr. Stein, I'm Detective Holland with the NYPD. I'm conducting an inquiry into Adam Sodkoff's death, and I would like to come by and ask you a few questions."

"Of course, but I am confused as to the nature of your

inquiry. According to my information, Adam died of a heart attack."

"That is the official report, Mr. Stein."

"Are you telling me there is something more to this?"

"I don't know if there is or not at this point, Mr. Stein. I'd just like to come by and discuss this with you to see if there is sufficient reason for me to look into it further."

"I see, Officer Holland."

"It's Detective."

"Detective Holland, I'm not sure how much light I can shed on any investigation. I was Adam's lawyer, but I don't see how my participation in an inquiry will benefit the family."

"It's not an investigation. It's an inquiry. Look, I was a friend of Adam's. We rode bikes together. I just have some reservations about this being a heart attack and I wanted to speak with one of his close friends who might be able to shed some light on anything that could help me. If you would prefer I work on this without your cooperation until I can make it official, I completely understand."

Joe thinks about the tenor of Frank's answer. "No. I would certainly like to cooperate with the NYPD in any way I can without infringing on my client's rights."

"Understood and I very much appreciate your cooperation."

"Detective, will you please hold while my assistant picks up to get you on my schedule?"

"Thank, you, Mr. Stein." Lawyers! Frank says to himself.

Frank gets scheduled to see Stein on Friday afternoon.

On Friday, he takes the subway to the upper east side and walks the two blocks to Stein's office.

"I'm Detective Frank Holland to meet with Joseph Stein," Frank says to the receptionist.

"Please have a seat, Detective. I'll ring his office for you. May I get you water or something?"

"No, thank you."

Frank has a seat in the lobby and waits.

"Detective Holland, I'm Stacey Gurley. Would you please follow me to a conference room? Mr. Stein will be with you shortly."

They move through a hallway to a small conference room across from Stein's office. Frank sees a name placard on the wall next to an office: Joe Stein. Joe is sitting at his desk talking on the phone. Franks sits down at the conference table. Soon, Stein enters the room.

"I'm sorry to have kept you waiting, Officer Holland."

"It's Detective."

"Oh right, sorry, Detective Holland."

"Call me Frank."

"Frank, how can I help you? I don't mind telling you that I'm a little taken aback by your inquiry and your visit. I saw the death certificate. It says he had a heart attack."

"Like I said, Mr. Stein . . ."

"Joe, please," says Stein.

"Joe, I'm having a hard time believing Adam died of a heart attack. We rode bikes together. Our group had a ride last weekend, and most of Adam's and my fellow riders are having a hard time with his death. Anyway, can you tell me about Adam's situation? Is there any reason to suspect foul play you can think of, based on your relationship?"

"I'm not sure. Do you really think someone may have killed him?" asks Joe.

"Like I said, there is no open case on him at this time."

Joe sits quietly for a moment and speaks "Detective, it's highly unusual to be having a conversation with the police about a deceased client, especially when I've been told by the authorities he died of a heart attack."

"Joe, I'm here trying to figure out if Adam was killed or not. I am not trying to create problems for you or his family unless there was foul play involved, so you have nothing to fear from me. I need your help to determine if I'm wasting my time. I mean, he was your friend, wouldn't you like to know if he was murdered?"

"Of course, I would. Look, I'm willing to speak with you about this but it needs to be totally off the record. Can you agree to that?"

"That's going to be difficult for me to answer until I hear what you have to say, I mean I'm an officer of the law. If there is something illegal, I can't promise you."

"There's nothing illegal, Frank. It's just that Adam and I knew each other very well. I know a lot of personal things about Adam and you need to know that attorney-client privilege survives the death of the client so I cannot tell you anything to incriminate Adam."

"Joe, I'm not trying to find out anything about Adam. I don't care what he has done unless it got him killed, okay?

"Okay," says Joe. "What do you want to know?"

"Tell me about Adam. Is there anyone you can think of who would have a reason to kill him? Let's start with insurance. Who got what? Who would have a reason to want him dead for a payoff?"

"Adam was fairly well liked by most people. He didn't really push too hard to make big waves. He was, of course, the CEO, so he had to make tough decisions. Some people liked them, and some people did not. Adam had a single-pay $6 million policy which went to Constance, his wife, and his company had a $10 million COLA—company-owned life insurance policy. It's customary for CEOs to carry large policies as they are hard for a company to replace. That's especially true these days as a CEO job almost requires prison time, the way they are now treated. It's not an easy hire. Then, there was the $3 million policy we originally got to cover the anticipated taxes at his death; that's the one we sold to a viatical settlement company for $1 million."

"Joe, I need a little clarity on that. What do you mean sold it? You cashed it in?"

"No, Detective, we sold the policy."

"You are going to have to walk me through this. I don't know the difference between sold and cashed in."

"If you no longer need a life insurance policy, you basically have three options. First, you can do nothing and keep the coverage until the cash value of the policy runs out."

"Ok, I get it. At some point, the policy will lapse and no more coverage?"

"Option two is to cash in the policy with the insurance company that issued the policy, like Hartford or New Jersey

Life. In Adam's case, he could have received around $700,000 that way. The final option is to sell the policy to a viatical company for more than the insurance company would have paid if cashed in, but less than the face value of the policy. In Adam's case, the viatical company purchased the policy for $1 million. Then, that company keeps the policy in force, making the regular premium payments."

"How much was this policy again?"

"It had a $3 million death benefit."

"So, this company makes the premium payments just like you and I would if we owned it until the person dies, and then they get the payout? So, the company gets the $3 million?"

"That's right."

"So, they had to keep making the payments to keep the policy in force until he died."

"Well, technically, yes, but they could have used the cash value of the policy to make the premium payments."

"When did you sell the policy?" asks Frank.

"About three years ago."

"Let me get this straight: they paid Adam $1 million for his $3 million policy three years ago. He just died, and now they will pocket $2,000,000 in profit?"

"Yes, Detective, and it's tax free because they are the beneficiary."

"They made $2 million on $1 million in three years, tax free?"

"It looks that way. But they would have no way of knowing Adam was going to die."

"You're right, if he actually had a heart attack. This makes me wonder even more, Joe."

"Frank, there is no way this viatical company could have known Adam's policy was in the tranche of policies they may have bought. These viaticals are pooled with other policies when they're sold just to make sure nobody knows who is in which tranche. Buying an entire pool reduces the risk for viatical buyers. Most of these people who are insured will not die for a long time."

"You're taking away my theory here, Joe. How do you know all this?"

"I worked in the insurance industry for a while. I saw this first hand in the 80s. Frank, it's a long shot for any of these viatical firms to be in on this."

CHAPTER TWENTY-TWO

Viatical settlements were a good idea gone bad, like many government ideas. In the late 80s, people were dying of AIDS at an alarming rate. Most of them knew they were going to die. AIDS patients who had enough money could buy a very expensive drug cocktail to keep them alive, maybe until a cure could be found. People with AIDS who lacked money were screwed. Then some clever person remembered that in 1911 the Supreme Court agreed anyone could sell his life insurance policy to an investment or insurance group. With this court case backdrop, the goal now was to give the dying a chance at living longer using the cash from their policies or allow them to leave some funds to a then-unacceptable same-sex partner. In the late 1980s, viatical settlements were a win-win. People with AIDS, unlikely to live a typical lifespan, gained access to funds to allow them to survive a bit longer or more comfortably. The buyer of these life insurance policies knew it wouldn't be long before the person died, and the policy's face value would accrue to him or her.

Today, where global transactions can take place in minutes in a nonregulated environment, anyone can sell their life insurance policy. However, insurance companies are no fools, and they know it is hard to juice the actuarial tables and make premature deaths pay on a consistent basis. As long as viatical settlements remain just a fraction of their insurance business, the insurance companies continue to turn a blind eye. The insurance company still gets monthly premiums until the insured dies, and that is, after all, their life's blood.

CHAPTER TWENTY-THREE

It's Saturday morning. Frank wakes up early to an empty house and feels the pain of it. What's he to do? His life is as it is. He can't go back to Camille. She can't take a life of wondering, although she still worries because she loves the man, just not the life. He knows this like he knows he is breathing. Frank is moving a little slowly because he walked all over the city yesterday tracking down various leads.

Looks like I logged 9.8 miles yesterday according to my wrist device.

He puts on his riding clothes, grabs a banana, and fills two bottles, one with Gatorade and one with water. He loads his bike with the essentials—cell phone, bottles. Then he checks the bike gears for precision, takes the bike off the rack, and walks with it to the elevator.

"Good morning, Frank," says Mrs. Lorenzo as she gets on the elevator pushing her shopping cart.

"Trying to beat the crowd, Mrs. Lorenzo?"

"I'm 80 now, Frank. I have to get moving early and be careful because of, you know, rapists."

Frank snickers and says, "Mrs. Lorenzo, I'm right here on your floor, so if you ever need me to walk you anywhere just let me know. I want you to feel safe in my city."

"Oh, Frank, you're such a dear, and such a looker. If I was 20 years younger, I'd be after you myself."

"Thank you, Mrs. Lorenzo."

Frank leaves the elevator and walks his bike out to the street in front of his building. He mounts his Cannondale road machine, connecting his feet to the pedals, and rides out the six miles to get to where his group ride will begin. The city is now bike-friendly, but the boroughs are still a life-threatening experience some days as cars, trucks, and bikes are taking up the same space trying to get into the city by one of three routes. Frank enjoys the first six miles as he gets loose for the group ride ahead. There's one hill that will give him a good warm-up. Frank sees a few cyclists pedaling up ahead. He is getting close to the start location.

"Hi Frank" . . . "John" . . . "Frank" . . . "Bill."

More riders arrive and greet one another.

"This is a 30-mile B class ride," states the ride leader to the cyclists in attendance.

This means the riders will need to keep a 15 to 18 mile per hour pace for the 30-mile duration. Not an easy thing to do.

"Riders," says the leader, "I'd like us to take a moment of silence to reflect on one of our riders, Adam Sodkoff, who died a few weeks ago." This is Frank's second tribute to Adam before taking a bike ride. This death continues to be on his mind. He can't let it go.

The group stands in silence for a moment. Then the moment is over, and the riders pedal out together.

"Frank," one rider says as they start off side by side, "what happened to him?"

"Heart attack."

"What the hell was he doing to have a heart attack, trying to bench press 400 pounds?"

Frank does not respond as the riders are spreading out now and will likely break into two groups, the 18 mph or better riders and the 14–15 mph riders.

Frank just can't let it go. Adam was in good shape. I don't think anyone on this ride can believe it as well. I know it happens, but this just doesn't add up. He rides on. The nice thing about riding, unlike surfing or some other sports, is you can ride and daydream or think at the same time. Frank continues with his obsessive thinking about Adam throughout the ride. What am I missing about this whole Sodkoff case? Frank asks himself as he pedals up a long hill. Suddenly, it pops into his mind; he hears Joseph Stein's voice saying, "We sold Adam's large life insurance policy since he didn't need it." Frank sees this as his only real lead, and a lead is a lead in police work.

CHAPTER TWENTY-FOUR

LA Times Headline: "DelGotto Insurance Fraud Alleged"

Hartley Life Group has filed a lawsuit against Wisconsin Viatical Settlements claiming they had no insurable interest in the life of Chester DelGotto. DelGotto, who was murdered in Las Vegas two months ago, had sold his life insurance policy to Wisconsin Viatical Settlements, which ultimately sold it into a fund owned by Diversified Financial Services of Grand Cayman Island. Upon DelGotto's death, Diversified Financial collected on the life insurance policy.

Rachael opens the LA Times and reads the article on the first page of the second section. Hartley Life . . . Wisconsin Viatical . . . the viatical settlement . . . Diversified Financial Services.

"Holy shit! This is what happened to Donna McCally!"

Rachael thought she now had enough to go on to take it to Roger Emanuel. She goes into Roger's office to discuss McCally again.

"Boss, I need to talk to you about something."

"What is it now, Rachael? I can't keep running interference for you with the guys out there. Why are you having such a hard time with them?"

"They're a bunch of pricks," says Rachael.

"Look, I know it must be tough being the only woman detective with these guys but, you know, they pick on each other just like they do you—it's not that they think any less of you. I can't understand why you stomp all over them instead of playing along sometimes. You know, be one of the guys a little more," says Roger.

"I don't know if you noticed, but I am not one of the guys."

Roger says nothing to this comment but any fool can take one look at Rachael Lopez and see beyond a shadow of a doubt she is definitely not one of the guys. She is a vision of a woman: 5 feet 9 inches tall, about 135 pounds of perfect athletic beauty with warm latte colored skin even other women desire. It was a complete challenge for her to keep her distance from the boys her age on the military bases and, once she got a little older, from the service men at all the bases where she lived. Preventing sexual assaults in her world was a daily struggle. Sometimes she failed and suffered the consequences in silence, knowing full well her father would simply blame her for being weak. To protect herself, she earned black belts in the martial arts of Ninjitsu, Karate, and jujitsu. Along the way, she also developed her contempt for men with justification.

Rachael continues to speak with Roger. "I want to actually solve cases and make a difference around here."

"Rachael, you've been busted twice already on shootings as well as that thing with the suspect which made the captain relieve you from duty for a year. You know you don't get along well with some of your colleagues, or with me either, for that matter."

Rachael would like to deck Roger, but she remembers what Sheila said about playing nice, and calms down.

"Okay, Roger. You're right about all of that and I know we've had our differences, but I really feel I have enough to follow-up on this McCally thing."

"I knew you were still working on it after I gave you a direct order to drop it."

"Well, I'm sorry, but you're wrong about it, Roger."

"It's Captain, Detective."

"Oh, it's Captain again now? Okay, Captain, a guy named DelGotto got killed in Las Vegas because of his life insurance, and I think this is what happened to McCally. Listen, Roger, I mean Captain, this McCally thing is starting to look like a hit to me."

"A hit! Have you completely lost your mind? Who's going to hit an average mom with no real motive? I've heard about as much out of you as I'm going to take. You are insubordinate. You shoot everything and ask questions later. No one wants to partner with you. I don't even want to get into how your private life spills over into the station from time to time."

"That's my business, Captain."

"It becomes my business when I have men who separate from their wives or get divorced and can't work because of relationships with you. I'm tired of fighting for you and with you. You've discharged your weapon three times in three years! You're trigger happy, Rachael."

"They were all legitimate."

"I've been here 15 years and fired my piece twice."

"Roger, you sit at a desk."

"That comment's out of line, Rachael. Why are you even working here?"

"You know what, Roger? I'm not sure I know anymore."

"Okay, I will allow you to resign effective immediately. That way, you can get your benefits for a few more months and find something you are more suited to, like being a private detective."

"Fine. I want my vacation pay, all six weeks, now. And my pension money."

"You'll have it when the paperwork goes through. Effectively immediately, you're on vacation, and I'll expect your resignation letter on my desk today."

"You'll have it. I don't know why I ever took a job at this dump anyway."

"Don't press it, just get out of here before I change my mind. You know, if you didn't have such a screwed-up life and such a condescending attitude, you could have made it great. You're brilliant and a damn good detective, Rachael, if you were not just so screwed up in the head."

Rachael storms out of his office and slams the door. She gets a box from the office supply room and begins to clean out her desk. The squad room gets quiet. Everyone heard the yelling coming from Roger's office. No one is surprised by this outcome.

As Rachael fills her box from her desk, Bonnie the receptionist comes over.

"Here, let me help you."

"I got it," says Rachael sternly.

Bonnie steps back, and Rachael picks up her box and walks out of the office. She gets into her car and drives to a bar in her neighborhood.

The bartender says, "Hi, Rachael, what will it be?"

"A white Russian and a straight bourbon."

"Okay, anything I should know? Should I put on a bullet proof vest?"

"Cal, just know I'm paying myself and I don't want any of the guys in here to hit on me. And I don't want to talk about it and I promise not to shoot you."

"Ok, I'll try to fend them off for you."

"Thanks."

Rachael has way too many drinks and Cal the bartender drives her home after work. End of story.

At 3:00 am, she wakes up dehydrated from her drunken bender. She gets up and drinks three glasses of water and opens her computer. She realizes she now has all the time she needs to study this whole viatical settlement thing, including looking into Diversified Financial Services, who ultimately ended up with Chester DelGotto's life insurance.

CHAPTER TWENTY-FIVE

A black Gulfstream 550 lands at Owen Roberts International Airport in Grand Cayman. The pilot taxis to a private terminal. Viktor Ludvidz and three beautiful associates, models from Eastern Europe, exit the plane and slide into Viktor's Maybach 62 automobile, the only one on the island.

"We will be in conference, no need to rush," Viktor says to the driver as he closes the privacy panel. They all pour drinks, and two of the girls help Viktor relieve some stress during the drive to the office.

Viktor enters the office where team members are busy in their cubicles.

"Good afternoon, Mr. Ludvidz," the shapely receptionist says as Viktor walks in the door. A chorus of greetings to the man follows. He ignores most, nods at some, and walks straight to his office. Viktor checks the market and then touches the phone on his desk.

"Yes, Mr. Ludvidz?" his assistant speaks into the phone.

"Send David in."

"Yes, sir."

In less than two minutes, one of Viktor's fund managers comes into his office.

"What is your asset return month-to-date?" Viktor asks.

"I'm up just over 1.4% for the month, sir, and year-to-date, 6.1%."

"For six months, and I take it that is a gross number without deducting fees?"

"Yes, sir."

"Why is it so hard for all of you to bring me a net number after fees? We are the only ones who give a shit about the gross number."

"I'm sorry, sir. It's 4.88% net of fees, sir."

"So, for all this effort and all this work, you have managed to basically break even with the index for six months?"

"Sir, this has been a difficult market to beat the index in. Sir, most everyone . . ."

"Most everyone is not living a dream life in the Cayman Islands. They're back in New York City or worse, living paycheck-to-paycheck and getting fired for these kinds of numbers. They damn well better improve. That is all."

David picks up his laptop and backs out of Viktor's office. Viktor touches his phone again.

"Yes, sir?"

"Send in John."

"Yes, sir."

In no more than five minutes, John Menuso walks into Viktor's office.

"Good afternoon, John," Viktor cordially addresses him.

"Good afternoon, sir."

Viktor walks over to the window and opens a cabinet and pulls out a bottle of Baker's #7 bourbon. He pours two glasses.

"How are the employees doing?"

"Sir, it's difficult on them with the markets going up so easily. It's really hard for them to show better performance."

"Unlike your group."

"Well, yes sir. But it's mostly you. You have an incredible knack for picking the right viatical pools. It really amazes me."

"Your software gives us the edge on the actuarial tables, John. I don't know how we would do it without you. You're a great employee and a dear friend."

"Thank you, sir. I'm happy here and very happy you offered me your villa to stay at."

CHAPTER TWENTY-SIX

Rachael goes to work finding out everything she can about viaticals and about Diversified Financial Services. Google gives her several hits. She checks the news. The most current news is the DelGotto mess and it is only mentioned once. It seems they bought the viatical pool, which is a group of insurance policies, from the insurance company that put it together. Rachael finds an article authored by Simeon Ross, an insurance investment analyst with Maybaum and Smith in London. He seems like an authority on viaticals and investment benefits. Rachael tracks down his London office number and dials it.

A British lady answers on the first ring, "Maybaum and Smith."

"Yes, this is Detective Rachael Lopez calling to speak with Mr. Simeon Ross, please."

"One moment and I will connect you, Detective."

"Ross here."

"Mr. Ross, I am Detective Rachael Lopez of the Arizona State police. May I speak with you about viaticals for a moment?"

"Yes, of course. What an intriguing call—the police asking about viaticals."

"What makes it so intriguing, Mr. Ross?"

"Well, I am quite certain that of all the interviews I have given about viaticals and the investment business, I have never had a conversation with a detective about it. How can I be of service to you?"

"I do not know very much about this business, so if you don't mind, I will just ask a few questions to try to understand it. First, why would someone sell their insurance, and why would a pool be created for people to buy it from them? Also, why wouldn't someone kill all the policyholders once they bought all the insurance?"

"If you will permit me, I will take them one at the time. Why sell your policy? Because you may get more than the cash value from an investor, depending on your age and your health. Most policies are sold and bought by investors on older or terminally ill policyholders, so they have some definite period in which the policy will likely be paid. Now, why would a healthy person sell a policy, and who would buy it? Well, a healthy person would sell if they could get more than the cash value, and an investor would likely be another insurance company who would just assume the actuarial risk of the policy. It's not a very good investment to buy a policy on a healthy person unless you are in the insurance business."

"What if they have an accident?"

"Well, of course, this makes the numbers or returns move up exponentially, but the pools are designed to balance the risks to the insurance companies from paying off."

"Do you know of any firm that buys healthy pools of viaticals?"

"There are some, but, as I said, it's very difficult to beat the actuarial tables. Diversified Financial Services is one, but I think it is part of a much larger insurance and investment business. I don't see how a group could make their returns advance."

"Can you tell me about their operation?"

"My dear, I have written a report about the entire company. I will gladly send it to you."

"Thank you, Mr. Ross. That would be great."

"My pleasure."

CHAPTER TWENTY-SEVEN

Rachael checks her email and finds the report from Mr. Ross. She discovers Diversified is a hedge fund with offices in Guernsey on the Channel Islands in Europe and in the Cayman Islands in the Caribbean. She sees where the viatical business is really not a large part of its total business, according to the report dated the end of the year two years ago. The report is very vague on details around the investments and certainly does not shed any light on who the investors are. Rachael cannot really tell much from the report since it is written for sophisticated investors—and having a 401K does not qualify her as one. It looks like the only way to find out anything about this company is to go to their offices and see what she can dig up. According to the report, the company has an operation and business headquarters in Guernsey. That seems like a good place to start.

Rachael has never even heard of Guernsey, so she does some research about how to get there, where it is, and the significance of having a business there. Flying into Guernsey the first thing she notices is all the cows. "Oh right, the Guernsey cows," she says to herself on the plane as it taxis down the runway. In her due diligence, she finds Guernsey has very attractive privacy laws around corporations and is some type of tax haven.

Arriving here, however, she finds it to be a dead end, similar to all her phone attempts. No one will tell her anything; it's a very tight-lipped community. Talk about privacy. She stops at the Victor Hugo House and browses his museum. She finds out he was exiled to the island and wrote many of his works here including "Les Miserables." The only things Rachael found of any interest are the amazing tomatoes and Victor Hugo's house and, thankfully a one-stop flight to the Caymans via Miami. A vacation is much deserved so long as her credit card holds out. Her vacation pay will be arriving soon, so she decides to run down the only lead she has left and take this flight to the Caymans.

After 30 hours of travel, she arrives. She stops at the tourist information desk at the airport.

"I'm looking for a hotel near the business district."

"Price range?" a man behind the desk asks.

"As cheap as you have."

"I think you would like the Comfort Inn. It's fairly cheap but clean and nice enough. It's also by the beach, so it's a good vacation."

"Can you book me?"

"No, but you can with their phone right over there." The man points out a Comfort Inn phone on the wall.

Rachael walks over and picks up the phone.

"Cayman Comfort Suites," someone says as he answers the phone.

"Do you have anything available for tonight?"

"Let me see. . . We have one ocean view room available for $188 per night."

"Do you have anything cheaper?"

"That is all I have open for now. How many nights do you need?"

"I'm not sure."

"Oh, I love those kinds of vacations," the reservationist says. "Well, if you take it for 5 days, I can give it to you for $168."

"Ok, I'll take it. Do you have a shuttle from the airport?"

"Yes, it will be along very soon. Just go to the curb, and you will see where the shuttles arrive."

Rachael gets her bag and goes out to meet the shuttle. She now has a week to wrap this thing up and go home.

She arrives at the Comfort Suites, checks in, and decides she is going straight to Diversified to try to come up with some answers. She looks at the report for the address and finds it's a relatively easy walk from her hotel. She puts on a nice dress and heels and walks down to Diversified to have a look around.

The first thing she sees is a gorgeous female receptionist sitting at a glass desk revealing her long legs and high heels as you come in. Rachael approaches the desk.

"He will be with you shortly," says the receptionist.

"He will? I mean . . . of course." Rachael takes a seat.

Another beautiful woman comes out to meet her. "You're early."

"I'm sorry," Rachael says.

"Most of you are late. Come with me."

The lady escorts Rachael to Viktor Ludvidz's office where Rachael waits — for what she does not know — but she continues to play along. Eventually, Viktor walks into the office.

He asks, "When did you get here?"

"Today," Rachael states.

"You are not from Croatia."

"No, I'm from LA," she lies.

"Who are you?"

"I think there must be some mistake. I'm just here to pick up a job application."

"Oh." Viktor squirms some as he had other intentions. Viktor speaks into the phone rather harshly in a language Rachael does not recognize. The beautiful lady who escorted Rachael in reappears.

"Sorry for the confusion," she says and sees Rachael out providing her with an application for employment.

Rachael is escorted quickly out the door. She stops by the Ritz Carlton bar on her way back to her hotel. She walks in and is virtually attacked by three guys in the bar who want to buy her a drink.

"Hold on big fellas, all three of you. Tell me who you are."

Rachael makes small talk with all three. It seems the Caymans has an abundance of lawyers and a shortage of newbies, people who have just moved here or are single and on vacation. She is not only attractive in her own right, but she is a scarce commodity in the Caymans—a single woman who is not there with a bunch of wedding friends or on her honeymoon. The three lawyers continue to hang around and Rachael sees this cannot go anywhere with all three of them at once. She sees one fairly attractive man sitting alone at a table over by the water. She looks over at him intentionally and he looks back.

"Guys, I will be back in a few."

She walks by his table and out to the beach with her drink. He gets up and follows her.

"I notice you have met the welcoming committee," he says.

"Is that what they are?"

"Lucky for you, you're way out of their league. They were trying to show you some courtesy in hopes it would improve their odds."

"And you?" asks Rachael.

"I'm quite certain I do not have a chance with you unless I am rescuing a damsel in distress."

"I don't need rescuing; I'm pretty good at taking care of myself, but I would like to have a little quiet time away from the welcoming committee."

"Would you like to join me at my table? No welcoming required."

Rachael waves goodbye to the committee and has a seat at the table.

"I'm Rick Stokes."

"Rachael Lopez."

"Nice to meet you. "Do you come here often?" jokes Rick. "Actually, by the reception from the welcoming committee and the fact this rock is pretty small—you would make it about three minutes without being noticed here—I already know the answer is no."

"Let me guess," says Rachael, "you are a lawyer as well?" Rick smiles. Rachael continues: "Is everyone who lives here some type of lawyer?"

"This is a strange place, Rachael. People come here to bury their treasure, vacation or get married and someone has to push all the paperwork for these transactions."

"So that means you are a lawyer?"

"No, I'm a minister, I do weddings."

Rachael looks at Rick and smiles.

"Yes, you're right, just the opposite—I'm a lawyer. I push papers."

"What type of legal work do you do?"

As a result of her research into Diversified Financial Services, Rachael now knows quite a bit about the offshore investment work done in Grand Cayman, but she sees no reason to let Rick know she is anything more than an incredible-looking woman. They have two more drinks.

"Will you join me for dinner?" asks Rick.

"Sure."

"Let's go down the street to one of my favorite places."

"How far is it?" asks Rachael.

"About two miles. You can cab back or even walk if you don't like the company."

"Let's go." Rachael pulls a cigarette and a lighter from her purse and hands the lighter to Rick. He smiles and lights her cigarette.

They walk out to the parking lot, and Rick walks up to a VW bug convertible with the top down.

"This is your car?"

"No. It's the Cayman's; we just get in any car with the keys in it."

They get into Rick's VW. Rachael enjoys the ride in the convertible and smiles with her hair blowing in the breeze for the two-mile journey. The fact Rick drives a VW surprises her, as she figured him for a Mercedes man. The drive gives her a chance to get a better look at him: very handsome and fit; in fact, really well toned.

They arrive at Bacchus, and Rick gets them a nice table in the back off a small alcove.

"Grand Cayman is different. It's nice, but not New York City nice," says Rachael.

"Is that where you're from, Rachael, New York City?"

"No. Not really," she replies but does not elaborate. Rick does not press her. He asks, "How about a bottle of wine? Red or white?"

"Red—Pinot. I don't like it too heavy."

The wine list is most extensive. They select a $168.00 Morgan Pinot 2004.

"Very nice selection," states the waiter. The waiter brings the bottle over, Rick samples it, and two glasses are poured.

"Wow, this is a nice wine, Rick."

"I don't get to take new guests out too often, so I splurged a little. So, do you think you will stay or are you just visiting?"

"Do you mean at your table, in the Caymans, or at your house?" Rachael says.

"I was shooting for maybe in the Caymans, but I'll take whatever answer you want to give."

Rachael does not answer as she looks at the menu.

"Shall we order?" Rick asks.

"Yes."

Rachael tells the waiter: "I'll have the vine-ripened tomatoes, mozzarella, and basil flatbread to begin."

When their appetizers arrive, Rachael checks her flatbread against the Guernsey tomatoes of just a few days ago. No comparison—Guernsey wins.

Rick turns to his amuse-bouche select a la Bacchus.

"So, Rachael, are you independently wealthy? Looking for a place to stash all your money?"

"Hardly, I just needed a change. So far, I like the pace here."

Rachael watches as Viktor and four "girls" come into the restaurant. She could not call them women. They are shown to a table in a private section of the restaurant.

"I see you noticed Viktor," says Rick.

"Well, you could say I met him today, but we didn't actually meet."

"How did that happen?"

"I went to Diversified Financial Services to get a job application, and I think he mistook me for another type of applicant."

"I see. Well, beware of him, Rachael. I know you just met me and can believe me or not, but Viktor is into some next level stuff up at Diversified Financial Services. He does not suffer fools gladly. Watch your step."

"What kind of stuff, Rick?"

"I only know what I hear. I haven't done any business with him directly as he has his own team of lawyers up in the palace—that's what we call his building. It's the tallest thing on the island. Anyway, he runs a hedge fund as almost everybody here does. It's really what keeps the island afloat, more so than the tourists. But I've heard he doesn't mind cutting corners if the returns warrant it. Just be careful, that's all."

"Okay, thanks. I will."

Rachael decides this guy, while maybe not one of the good guys, is at least not one of the bad guys, so she thinks she will dig a little further in with him.

The waiter comes over to refill their glasses.

After serving Rachael, he says, "Madame?"

"I'll have the Thai Red Curry dish."

"Monsieur?"

"The Pork Café de Paris."

"Very good."

Over dinner and a second bottle of wine, the two engage in a little small talk.

"Rick, how long have you been down here?"

"I don't really know . . . Let's see . . . forever. Yale Law in 1982, Wall Street 1984–87. Then, after the crash of 87, the firm I worked for closed and in 1988, I came here."

"What brought you down here from Wall Street?"

"That's a story for, hopefully, another time. I would like another time," says Rick. "Our time together isn't ending, is it?"

"No, I don't think so, not yet," Rachael says playfully.

"Rachael, may I ask you a rather personal question? It relates to your answer to my first question which you haven't answered yet."

"Oh, about my Cayman intentions?" Rachael says playfully. "Fine, what is the question?"

"Shall we have espressos?" Rick asks, implying they will have more time together.

"Why not?" says Rachael. She holds up her wine glass to toast Rick's glass. They toast and order espressos.

They drive to Rick's home on Seven-Mile Beach, not far from the Ritz or the Comfort Suites. Rick holds the door for Rachael to enter. It's a beautiful home right on Seven-Mile Beach with sliding glass doors across the back leading to a pool elevated just slightly with an infinity edge to look over while sitting in the pool. He walks straight through the house and out to the pool and Rachael follows. He walks over to an outside fridge and gets a bottle of white wine. He opens it and pours two glasses.

After they each take a sip, Rick moves closer to Rachael, reaching to put her glass down on a table. She is truly an amazing-looking woman, tanned in all the right places. She reaches out to Rick as he moves closer and they share a warm passionate kiss. Rachael is not the kind of girl who would stop Rick's advances, especially if she thinks it could help her later.

CHAPTER TWENTY-EIGHT

Avi continues to follow the routine one would expect of the best killer in the business, but Lloyd, one of his contacts, screws up and is caught by Tucson PD. He's a small-time low-life with a friend who works for Cable Central in the fleet group. Avi used Lloyd for a van on the McCally hit.

Two Tucson PD officers interrogate Lloyd.

"Lloyd, it looks like you are going to do some serious time on this one, my man. This was not your usual routine of a speedball, Lloyd; you had some serious shit on you this time. You're probably looking at 5 to 10 with an intent-to-sell rap."

"Guys, I can't do any time. You've had me telling you stuff, and you've made some busts based on that stuff. Those guys will get me if I go to prison, man. You've got to help me out here."

"Unless you have a lot bigger fish to snitch on, Lloyd, there is really no reason for us to leave you on the streets anymore. I mean, come on, Lloyd!"

"Lloyd, are you getting ambitious on us, man? We like

you being a small-time thug snitch and nothing bigger."

"Look, guys," pleads Lloyd, "I have something that may be pretty big, but you got to let me back out there. I can bring you some dealers and I promise to keep it small."

"I don't know, Lloyd, you've probably gone too far this time for us to help you out."

Lloyd continues to plead, "I got a guy who's into some major shit, man. I'm not sure what it is, but I get a call from this guy who tells me he needs a van, and, bam, I get $5,000."

"Where do you get the van?"

"I have a guy at Cable Central who hooks me up for two grand so long as I bring the van back. It's not a thief deal, man. He always brings the van back. This guy who wants the van, he's some Arab."

Lloyd plays the Arab card hoping to get a rise out of them. The fact is Lloyd does not know what nationality Avi is.

"The guy meets me, pays me, takes the van for about a week, and then tells me where I can pick it up. There is never anything wrong with it, and I take it back. Easy money."

Lloyd is right, the Arab card gets the attention of the detective who is thinking he may be able to get a promotion out of this if it's Homeland worthy.

"OK, Lloyd, sit tight. We'll see what we can do."

The two cops walk outside. "Lloyd is kind of a stoner, but I think he's on the up-and-up about this van. How do we play it?"

"We play it so we can get a big chip in the game, that's

how. Let's go to the boss and see if he wants to set up a sting. Maybe we'll get to nab a global terrorist."

"Let's put Lloyd back out there as bait and see what he comes up with."

They step back inside and continue the conversation with Lloyd.

"Lloyd, how often does this guy rent a van from you?"

"Oh, all the time," Lloyd lies, "probably is trying to get me now."

"This guy got a name?"

"No man, no name."

"Look, we can't help you without a name, man."

"Let me think . . . I don't know, man! I can try to get it when he calls again. Wait, he has a name tag . . . Hartman, on the uniform!"

"The dude has a uniform?"

"Yeah, a cable uniform!"

"Wait, Lloyd, the guy has a cable uniform on when he picks up the van from you?"

"Sometimes, man."

They step back outside.

"This may be something real, I mean, the guy has a uniform. He must be planning something big—setting a trap or a bomb or something."

The detectives go down to Roger Emanuel's office.

"Gentlemen, what's up?"

"We have a drug low-life we busted for possession with intent. He's been a pretty good snitch for us on small-time dealers, but he may have stumbled onto something bigger."

"Continue," Roger says as he sits down at his desk.

"He has some Arab guy who rents a van from him, according to Lloyd, all the time. The guy has a fake cable uniform and gives him the van back in great shape—keeps it for a week at a time. We think it's enough to set up a tap and try to catch the guy and see what he's up to."

"On one hand," says Roger, "this guy may be some pervert with a voyeur fetish or a stone-cold bomber guy setting something up."

"That's what we thought."

"But why? What target do we have in Tucson with any terrorist value? Why would some jihad organization waste resources on us?"

"Roger, how about we run a phone tap and see where it goes?"

"How about no and let me tell you why: we're going to call it in for the Feds to decide if it warrants any resources. I don't see any reason for us to pursue this. If it's a good lead, we're in over our head. If it's a bad lead, the Feds can make the call and we won't have wasted any time on it."

CHAPTER TWENTY-NINE

Avi's burner phone for Ralph Hartman rings. Avi answers but says nothing.

"Hey man, this is Lloyd."

"Lloyd? I don't know a Lloyd," Avi says in his best Arab accent. "You have the wrong number." He hangs up. Damn! Avi curses himself for not destroying this phone. From this call, Avi knows Lloyd's been caught, and Ralph Hartman is now on the grid.

The FBI is listening in.

"That's him," says Lloyd.

Special agent Jason Cavuto says, "Run the voice through the database."

"I'm not sure there was enough to run," says Agent McGhee. "It sounded faint like there was a device on the phone."

"Look, we probably need to bring in Homeland; they will have the best Arab voice recognition database," says Cavuto.

"Maybe, but whoever that was, he wanted off the phone

pretty fast, like he knew the rules about voice recognition."

"The guy has a cable uniform, and this must be a burner phone. I'm sure if we try it again, it will be disconnected."

"This guy Hartman has a very small history. No arrest, but strangely I don't see a driver's license or a social security number on the guy," says McGhee. "If this is a fake identity it tells me we are dealing with a professional, especially someone who can create a person and not just steal someone else's ID. Maybe Hartman is not a US citizen. Any entries into the country for Hartman for the last 12 months?"

"Let me take a look." Agent McGhee looks on his computer to access the entry manifest across the US. "Nothing."

Lloyd is sitting in a chair across the table from the two agents.

"Lloyd, you're telling me you got this guy a van less than a month ago?"

"Yes man, it hasn't been very long. A month, maybe a little longer, but not six months."

Special Agent Cavuto says, "I think we should spend a little more time on Mr. Hartman. Lloyd, you've convinced us you may have something here. We're going to let you back out there in case he reaches out to you again. And Lloyd, we will be listening 24/7, so don't try to double cross us."

"I won't man, I promise."

In his room in Cap Ferrat, Avi opens his MacBook and looks at Ralph Hartman's profile. A few rental charges here and there but nothing suspicious. Flushing the fake

Hartman ID from the grid would probably cause more suspicion. Avi looks up Lloyd on his secure federal network. He sees Lloyd has been busted for possession of a quantity showing intent to sell. Avi knows a low-life like Lloyd will certainly squeal to try to lighten his sentence. He steps out onto his hotel suite balcony. It's night time; he enjoys the French Riviera view with the lights shining on the water making it peacefully difficult to see where the shore begins and the water ends. He takes a deep breath and goes back inside.

Avi is disgusted to be inconvenienced by Lloyd's weakness. He dresses and rides the Vespa to the office at the freight terminal to design a plan to deal with Lloyd. He decides Ralph Hartman may be of use after all in designing a trap. He decides to keep the old burner phone to call Lloyd back when the opportunity presents itself.

He can use another one of his mules—the people he uses to get him items required to do his job—or perhaps he'll accept the challenge and take out a few bad guys for the freedom fighters, even though he really doesn't give a shit for either side of the cause. He is an unaffiliated killer. He kills for cash, not for king or country. He likes the idea of killing these first world guys who would not even feed him or his lost boys in Box Town. So many of his friends starved to death. He decides, for now, to drop it, even though he owes Lloyd a visit for his stupidity.

CHAPTER THIRTY

Frank Holland is a good New York City cop and a good father to his teenage daughter. She lives with her mom in West Babylon, just off Chelsea, on a street where many of the people who keep the city moving live—police officers, firemen, trash men, and women. They live and die, sometimes the hard way, as in the World Trade Center bombing. They collect a paycheck and live in small houses with few rooms and small yards about an hour away from the billionaires and millionaires they protect and serve.

Frank's ex, Camille, couldn't take the toll it places on a family to wonder night after night and day after day if a loved one is going to come home. It must be like the life of a military spouse except it is ongoing, not off and on. A police or fire spouse has to feel the anxiety and fear every morning. The saving grace is the closeness of the community, with families living near each other, but that also makes Camille feel lonely. She feels the pain with Frank or without him. It's a difficult thing to live with someone who loves his work more than anything else in his life.

Everything plays a close second, family, friends, obligations. It makes it especially hard when you ask them to choose. Frank's dad and his wife of 43 years lived nearby, and many of their retired cop and fireman friends live nearby as well. This place has history, duty, and honor on every street corner. It's more than a community, it's a family.

Frank goes over the coroner's report and autopsy results on Adam Sodkoff with a fine-toothed comb. He can only find one tiny note of interest—trace evidence of Rohypnol in the victim's bloodstream. A very small level, not a lethal one, possibly taken days or even weeks before the heart attack.

Strange. Who would give Adam roofies? His girlfriend already had what she wanted out of him. I wonder if she had a policy on him? No, Joe Stein said Sodkoff had already set her up with a variable annuity worth $300,000. No motive. But roofies? Trace amounts?

Frank heads back into the city to visit with Jean Conwell in the NYPD Coroner's office.

"Jean, can I come down to see you?"

"You know I have them backed up down here, Frank. What's on your mind?"

"I'm just following a hunch, Jean. Can you kill someone with roofies?"

"Sure, someone can OD on them, but it's a tough way to go. It would light up a corpse like a Christmas tree. I could pick it out at the scene. Why, Frank? What's up?"

"Well, I got a guy who died of a heart attack, but he had a trace amount of Rohypnol in his blood, and I'm not convinced it was a heart attack."

"Damn it, Frank! Don't bring another body down here with that weak ass shit. If you hang this on my door, I'm doing your autopsy next!"

"No, no, I got nothing really to go on, just a hunch."

"Okay, for you, only because you're so good looking. If someone were to stick it straight into the bloodstream with a high enough dose, then, bam, the heart stops and they're gone."

"Oh, okay. Thanks, Jean. It would take a high dose? I guess that means he really had a heart attack," says Frank.

"Maybe the guy just pushed it too hard. Don't look for shit to stir up man! There are enough real criminals getting away without you creating ghosts for us to chase. Just focus on catching the ones you can! My plate is full down here, gorgeous."

"Jean, you're a scary lady."

"I guess I am. I deal with dead people all day; I actually do not like the living—except you, beautiful Frankie boy! A body does not lie, cheat, or steal; they always tell the truth. Okay, handsome, if your guy got pumped full of roofies and was involved in a big struggle it might be enough activity to leave just a trace of Rohypnol, nothing more. But like I said, there are enough low-hanging criminals, Frank. You can catch ten of them while you try to figure out the masterminds. Hey, if you do catch one of those guys, remember I want to do a brain pan on one, so don't ruin the body with a lot of bullets, okay?"

"Like I said, Jean, scary."

"Okay, I got bodies piling up to cut on, handsome. That's all the time I have for you."

CHAPTER THIRTY-ONE

Avi next reads the dossier on Evan Woods:

Philanthropist of the arts and many charities throughout the San Francisco area. Single, most likely gay, but probably not ready to step out and embrace it publicly. He has been seen in the company of many men. Took home $20 M from the sale of Qualtrax, and still works there in this first post-sale year. Lives at 615 Castro Street. Qualtrax Systems office is at 1115 Harrison Street.

Avi likes San Francisco. Very nice city, tolerant and cosmopolitan, like some of his favorite European cities. He starts with his usual routine. Who is he? What does he like to do? Where does he work?

Avi is back in his California home-away-from-home, The Beverly Hills Hotel, starting his due diligence on Evan online. His room faces Crescent, one of the few rooms with a balcony. Avi prefers the rooms to the bungalows. The staff knows who is in which bungalow in case they need to sell a story involving someone. Most of the time, it's the star's own publicist who sells the story to give the star a little more twinkle in an otherwise dulling career. Avi's friend at the bell stand had told him about that scam on another occasion. Avi likes to come and go unknown and unnoticed. He tips the staff very well to stay low. He manages his environment with a little help from his friends.

So, Evan is gay and, shock of all shocks, living in the Castro. After a little digging around, Avi finds Evan is not necessarily interested in settling down; it appears he likes to go out on the town and find his way around.

Avi has played this card before, many times. It is amazing what one sometimes has to do to make it in this profession. Avi makes no judgment on people being gay or not gay. In fact, it's interesting how Avi sees the world. He is tolerant and cosmopolitan, probably what many would call liberal. He likes Europe, particularly France, Italy, Austria—mostly socialist countries. He is super-affluent, he likes his amenities, and he doesn't really have to pay for the safety net as he lives outside the system.

Avi realizes he is going to need to spend some serious time in San Francisco on this job. Just playing gay wouldn't give him a slam-dunk way in, although it does help. So how does he meet Evan?

Avi checks out of the Beverly Hills Hotel and takes another drive—like his recent trip to Vegas—this one up to San Francisco. He breaks the trip up with a night in Pebble Beach, enjoying Monterey and Carmel. The next day he checks into the Westin St. Francis, a large hotel where he can come and go without any fanfare. He takes the 20 or so minute walk over to Evan's office address just to hang out.

He notices the End of the Line Bar, a late-night place. It is close to Evan's work and looks interesting. He makes a note and walks down to a park near the warehouse-looking office building that houses Qualtrax Systems.

CHAPTER THIRTY-TWO

"This is going to require more time," Avi tells Viktor.

"I don't have more time. I need this done right away. This whole thing is taking too long," Viktor says, then remembers to whom he is speaking. "I mean, I know you are doing your work the way it's supposed to be done. I'm just under a very difficult time constraint."

Deciding that killing Viktor would not be a good long-term solution for now, Avi lets it pass. "I will proceed as fast as possible to make sure it works as it should, but it will require another 50. I will expect it tomorrow."

"Okay, very well. Thank you." Very few people unnerve Viktor, but Avi is one of them.

Viktor continues to stress about how long it is taking Avi to finish the jobs. Viktor did not realize how much pressure he would be under as a hedge fund manager. It was fun managing his own money as a young man in Bosnia. It was even fun working with various firms on Wall Street for a few years after graduate school at Columbia, cutting his teeth in the asset management business. He enjoyed making the trades and speaking to brokers and traders. Now he has become so successful he is mostly making payroll and dealing with employee issues instead of managing the money. That is when the investment returns began to fall— once he stopped managing the money and started managing the business. He has made himself rich but has continued to buy more toys and needs even more money to maintain a billionaire lifestyle on a millionaire's finances.

Avi is becoming a problem for Viktor. He needs the deaths to make the returns, but he can only push Avi so far or Viktor might end up dead. As a stand-alone investment this project is astronomical in returns, but as part of his portfolio it does not yet show up in a major way, but his vision is to roll out a much more robust program once he gets the math and the activity more down to a science. He has a list of all the CIA hit men he drove while in Bosnia and envisions rolling it out on a larger scale once he gets the bugs worked out.

Avi heads down to Bryant Street to have a coffee. He has his laptop in a messenger backpack and is wearing a baseball cap, designer jeans, and a t-shirt; he looks like every other thirty-something-year-old tech guru in the coffee shop. He checks on his investments while he waits to see if Evan goes to lunch. Half a day shot to hell for nothing. He thinks of how much better it is working for the Company. They are great to work for. He remembers when he worked for them in Kuala Lumpur. The call would come in and they'd say, "Be at the corner of Whey and Kearin in 15 minutes. The subject will come by on a small scooter wearing a red helmet." Bam, just like clockwork, there he would be. You follow him along for a while, and he is completely oblivious to what is going on until you ride right up beside him. When he realizes the people he was working for have just betrayed him, he looks at you in terror and then he's dead. You ride off. They have a car waiting for you. You are whisked away to another city before anyone even knows the guy is dead. Solid professionals, not like Viktor. In some ways, Viktor is still like the kid in Belgrade. In one sense, he's a lot like the dictators who need work done. Messy and ill-prepared. You have to do all the footwork for them and cover your own ass every step of the way. Still, they pay big money—and after all, it is a job.

Back to the CIA. They're very professional and have an unlimited budget. They cover the infrastructure with no expense spared, but they pay less. Overall, though, a great employer.

Avi walks back to Harrison Street to wait for Woods to leave work. He has a good description of Woods—5'10", 220 lbs. A fairly big guy carrying a little computer game-playing gut.

He sees Evan head out of his building, walking the block or so to 7th and Bryant to board the train to the Castro, or at least that is what Avi presumes. Avi also gets on the train. He goes over to stand near Evan. Evan notices Avi, and Avi gives him the "yes, I am one of your people" smile. Evan smiles back. Avi goes back to his newspaper but is aware Evan is checking him out.

Evan gets off the train, as does Avi. Avi takes the lead as

he walks toward Evan's address and stops off at Twirl, a wine-tasting bar. Evan follows him in.

Avi turns to greet Evan, "Hi, I'm Philippe."

Evan replies, "Can I buy you a glass of wine?"

"Sure."

They begin to chat. "So, Philippe, I haven't seen you here before."

"No, I just took a job here last week. I'm staying in a hotel nearby and haven't decided where I want to live, but this area looks pretty good to me so far," says Avi, eyeing Evan seductively.

Evan takes the hint. "I live just around the corner from here. It's really a great neighborhood. Lots to do; many friends to meet."

"Really? Do you have many friends?" Avi asks.

"Sure, lots."

"Do you have a roommate?"

"Why no, I don't. I have my own place."

"How close are your friends?"

"Well, they're around if you want to meet them."

"Actually, no, I would really prefer not to. I'm kind of a loner. I mean, I like to have friends, but only one at the time."

They both grin. They order another glass of wine. More small talk and then they head down to Harry's Bar for another drink. Avi can put away drinks, at least it appears so. He puts them away by spilling them on the floor when no one is looking so he can stay sober and order drink for drink with his hard-drinking friend. Once Avi appears drunk, he can spill drinks as a drunk which allows him to even drink less. The obvious spills are Evan's clue that Avi has had too much, which at this point is probably Evan's plan for Avi.

"Philippe, would you like some oysters?"

"Sure, I'd love some."

They work their way down the street toward Anchor. It's a small oyster bar and Avi, seeing the size of it, believes he will be remembered.

"Hey, didn't you say you lived near here? No oysters required."

They walk back to Evan's place. Evan opens the door to a very spacious condo with windows opening out onto Castro Street. Avi slides over to the curtains and closes them. Evan reaches out and pulls Avi close and kisses him. They move to the bedroom and begin to get undressed. Avi dresses down first while Evan views his beautiful body. A scar here and there from past mistakes but just enough to make him look rugged. Once Avi is naked, he approaches Evan, putting both arms around his shoulders and turning him around. He reaches back, supposedly for a condom, and peels a crumpled plastic bag out of his jacket pocket. He pulls out a chloroform cloth and covers Evan's mouth and nose. Evan struggles briefly before he goes down. Avi then shoots Evan with a syringe of bee venom and waits for the venom to be pumped throughout his system. After a few minutes, he places Evan in his bed. Nothing like an allergic reaction between friends. It will look like an allergic reaction even if he is not known to be allergic. The coroner will be happy to have something to pin Evan's death on quickly so he can move on to other dead bodies.

Two hours go by. Avi checks Evan's phone—password-protected. Darn. But he can see no texts since 5:30. It is now dark.

Avi wipes down the curtains where he touched them, cleans the knobs on the inside and out as he leaves. It's dark, and there is no one to see who is leaving Evan's house this evening. Avi pulls his baseball cap on and walks down the street. With Evan's reputation, Avi plays the odds no one will be looking for him for a few days thinking he has found a new friend to hide away with.

CHAPTER THIRTY-THREE

As Ralph Hartman, Avi makes a call to Lloyd at the rental place in Tucson where Lloyd still has a day job, barely. The call comes through the switchboard, not to Lloyd's cell.

"I need a cable access van for six hours on Tuesday, with the usual premium."

Lloyd is taken aback by the call and shows some alarm. "Ah . . . oh . . . it's you. Oh, okay."

They hang up. Lloyd calls Agent Cavuto from the office phone. "I just got a call from the dude about the van."

"Good boy, Lloyd. We will take it from here," says Cavuto.

Sipping an Earl Grey tea, and enjoying the English aroma, Avi knows he has just set a trap.

Lloyd lays out their usual plan to the FBI—he rents a cable van from his friend at the cable access motor pool and leaves it at the UPS store on Romouth; Ralph leaves $5,000 for Lloyd in the store in Box 16. They each have a key.

Avi orders room service, locks the door, and puts a chair under the knob. He knows anyone can pick the flip lock. He goes to sleep.

The next day the FBI walks into the UPS store. Cavuto shows a badge to the owner working in the store. "Box 16, we will watch it from here, and please let us know if anyone opens the box."

Lloyd waits until the day of the job to go to the box, and the cash is already there. The FBI missed the drop. Hartman must have dropped it off before the call, or he works at the UPS store.

The van is still in place. No one has reached out to pick it up.

Cavuto has another chat with Lloyd. "How did the UPS box come about?"

"One day, this guy came to me with a request for a specialty vehicle. I told him I would help, and he told me how to do it."

"Who is your contact at the cable access place?"

"A friend of mine I knew from school."

"Ralph did not set him up for you?"

"No."

"What does Ralph look like?"

"He's 6 feet tall and around 180 pounds. Middle eastern maybe . . . I don't know. . . Brown eyes, black hair, regular build."

"Great, that sounds like one-third of the men in the world! So, what about the box?"

"He gave me cash to rent the box, and I gave him the extra key."

Avi listens to the entire interview from across the street in a rented car. He watches the two FBI guys drive off as their newly-bugged car shows up on his iPad app. He drives past Lloyd's house where he sees two more FBI guys staked out. Jeez, how many people are on this detail? He keeps driving.

Lloyd goes to the sub shop near his office to get lunch. Ralph comes up beside him in line and says, "Don't point me out. I know they have you. Nod if you want to escape them."

Lloyd nods; Ralph leaves. Lloyd says nothing about the lunch encounter to the FBI.

Lloyd still has full surveillance on him. It looks like an 8-man rotation in 4 teams. Ralph Hartman has done nothing illegal as far as the FBI knows and they are spending about $15,000 a day on stakeouts. After four weeks of round-the-clock, the FBI gets bored with Lloyd. They suppose Hartman's onto them or he's just a pervert sneaking into houses. Since he never picked up the van, they know he must know Lloyd squealed on him. $100,000 of Uncle Sam's money spent with nothing to show for it.

CHAPTER THIRTY-FOUR

Rachael is filling out her application for employment at Diversified. From what she could tell from the staff with all the models, she already has what it takes to get a job there. The application is going to be a problem— "former detective at Tucson PD investigating possible homicides at viatical companies" may not help get her a job. Rachael calls Roger at her old office.

"Tucson PD."

"Janice, it's Rachael."

"Rachael?"

"Rachael Lopez. Remember? I was just there last week?"

"Oh, sure, Detective Lopez. How are you?"

"I'm fine. Can I speak to Roger?"

"Let me check, Rachael."

Rachael waits on the line for a minute or two. Finally, Roger picks up.

"Rachael, I'll say this for you, you have some nerve calling me after what we just went through. What is it?"

"Roger, I'm sorry we had words. I am far too outspoken and I know that."

"Well you've already quit, and anyway, you would need to talk to my replacement if you wanted to beg your way back on to the force."

"I'm not calling to beg . . . Wait, where are you going?"

"New York. I have been offered a captain's position at the NYPD."

"Wow, Roger, that's great. Congratulations."

"Now, what can I do for you?"

"You may not be able to help me since I am a private citizen now, but I am still working on the McCally case and I need a favor."

"You are really something. You know that?"

"Roger, you know me. I know I'm a hard case, but my gut tells me something is here and I have to finish this."

Silence from Roger.

"Roger?"

"I will live to be 100 and never understand you," says Roger. "As I said, you have good instincts, but you have some serious social skills issues."

Rachael remains quiet, which is not in her nature, but she needs something from Roger.

"Roger, look, I know. I had a strange childhood and have problems with men. I've heard it before, and someday I will have to deal with it, but you know I'm good at police work. Now, I really need your help so I can break this case open."

"What is it?"

"I need a backstory so I can get a job with this group in Grand Cayman I think is the mastermind behind all this."

"And you want me to fabricate a backstory so you can go in undercover?"

"Yes."

"There's only one problem with this I can think of—you are no longer a cop."

"Oh, but I am for two more weeks because I'm on vacation until I use up my vacation pay."

"Fine, Rachael. I will give you a backstory. Hell, it doesn't need to be too far from the truth. You are a rogue agent who shot a cop and got fired. Blackballed out of the business. How's that?"

"I'll take whatever I can get, but that works fine. I'll need some dates and times that work, and the firing happened last week."

"That's easy enough. After all, I'm a short-timer here. This can't blow back on me anymore," says Roger.

"I know we've had our differences, Roger, but you're a good cop. NYPD will be glad to have you."

"Rachael, going undercover like this requires some experience, which you do not have. Only a seasoned agent gets this kind of assignment in the real world. You may be in over your head, but I know that's how you operate. In any event, watch your back out there because you are absolutely on your own. I have no way to stop you or to help you. I sure as hell don't have any jurisdiction in the Caymans, and you are not an FBI agent."

Roger stops talking but Rachael doesn't say anything. After a couple of moments, Roger speaks again.

"I needed to tell you so maybe you would change your

mind about this theory and drop it, but I know by your silence you're going head first into this. Anyway, if you're right about this guy, you're dealing with some very bad people. And Rach, if you're wrong, you're better off being just a private citizen. A cop pulling this kind of shit is a really serious offense. Not to mention the fact it would likely taint any arrest. Neither is a very good option. Anyway, I've had my say. Oh yeah, and don't show up in New York City to apply for a job!"

"I understand all this. Roger, thank you."

Rachael gets her backstory straight and after a few days goes to a job interview at Diversified Financial Services. An Eastern European model shows her to a conference room where a tall, thin man enters.

"Hi, I'm John Menuso, Head of Statistics and Actuary Research."

John had a bout with acne in his youth that left a few scars on this very white man with thin, grey-blond, slightly receding hair. He is about 6 feet tall.

"Hi, John. Rachael Lopez. I'm pleased to meet you."

Rachael notices John looking at her legs—they may not be really long or Eastern European, but they're competitive.

"Uh . . . Oh . . . Well, we have a very fast-paced business here, and well, frankly, it is hard to get someone with your background to relocate to Cayman. I mean, everyone loves it, but most people like leaving at some point. I do have a little concern about the police shooting thing in your background."

"Oh yes. Well, that was, of course, an accident, but my boss didn't like me and well, John, can I be honest with you about it? My boss and I were having an affair and he had it in for me."

John looks a little nervous but intrigued.

"Oh, I see. That kind of thing does happen. I mean, you know when people work together and get close, I mean."

"Of course, it does," says Rachael, "I don't know how many times it's happened to me."

"Well, Viktor will need to make the final call on this Rachael, but you've explained what I had an issue with."

"I've had my fill of the big city, for now, John. I'm looking to slow the pace down some," she says.

"So, you came here on your own?" John fishes for a boyfriend connection.

"Yes, I'm here all on my own to find a new life, new friends, and my way around. Have you been here for some time, John?"

John thinks about the question. His quick mind processes back to how he got here.

John Menuso met Viktor Ludvidz at a math symposium in Princeton, NJ. John was calculating statistical analyses in his head for fun. It was a symposium for quantum mathematics. Viktor knew what he needed, and the symposium was the place to find it. Viktor gets to know John; they have a few beers at the bar in the evening, and a friendship develops. John is hired. Viktor is not big on details. They work together for years as Viktor manages his hedge fund and develops a reputation for delivering great performance.

"I've been here 10 years, and I know every inch of the island and most of the Caribbean," John states enthusiastically.

"I will keep that in mind," Rachael says playfully.

CHAPTER THIRTY-FIVE

John meets with Viktor about Rachael and the job. Viktor has an office you don't find in regular Fortune 500 corporate America. It is the entire back of one floor of the building. It has three walls of one-way glass windows that show the best views in the Caymans—the blue water and the beachfront beyond the Ritz, so one can see all the bathing suits on Seven Mile Beach. There is a telescope positioned strategically (of course), a conference table for eight (just for show—he has a real conference room down the hall), and a nine-foot-long couch (this is not for show) with three club chairs surrounding a very nice coffee table. Viktor asks Emily to bring John and him some coffee, small cups of European espresso which hold about two ounces but are supposed to take four hours to drink. Emily brings in the coffees and smiles at Viktor.

"Well, at least she can make coffee," Viktor laughs with John as she leaves. "Now, John, you know I really don't give a shit who you hire for that job as long as you continue to handle the actuarial breakdowns by policyholder, but what is this lady's story?"

"That is what I wanted to talk to you about. I think she would be a great asset to our firm. She was a cop."

Viktor comes to attention. "A cop?" he asks.

"Yes, I'm not sure of all the details, but she shot another cop and it seems her boss, whom she was having an affair with, had it in for her—at least that is what she told me."

"Interesting. I take it she got fired from the cop job?"

"Yes."

"I think you are right about this one, John. A former cop with some bad feelings toward other cops might come in handy."

"What do you mean?"

"Never mind. What else do you know about her?"

"She seems really talented and sharp," John replies.

"What does she look like—a cop girl?" asks Viktor.

"I heard you met her when she came in to pick up her application. She was sent to your office by mistake."

"Oh, damn! That Latin chick who was in my office? Shit, she's fine!" Viktor looks at the application and the report from the background check that was run on her. "You think she can do the job then? And she's got the bad cop vibe going and had an affair with her boss, huh? Well, she does seem like our kind of girl, especially since she shot a cop. That could come in handy someday."

"I don't know what you mean, Viktor, but while she does have some past issues, we don't usually get candidates like her here. You know how hard it is to hire someone really talented unless we bring them in and even then, some get bored being around the same people on this little island and go back to their old lives."

"Good work, John. Sounds like you think she's a good candidate, Go ahead and hire her if you'd like." Viktor stands up indicating the meeting is over. John is not quite up to par with his interpersonal skills and does not pick up on Viktor's signal.

"You can go now, John," Viktor finally says, and John leaves Viktor's office.

CHAPTER THIRTY-SIX

Viktor's assistant speaks through the intercom. "Sir, Ho Hin Guong is on the line."

Viktor grabs the line. "Good morning, sir," he says.

"Viktor, it appears the fund's returns have declined over the last 6 months," says Ho, not one to stand on ceremony or pleasantries.

"Yes, they have, Ho. At some point, things have to come back to earth. We have done 75%, 65%, 41%, 38%, and 38% for the past 5 years, while everyone else was in decline or had minimum increases."

"Yes, but for the last six months only 4.88%, Viktor," says Ho.

"There has just been a lull in our reallocation. I have made significant improvements in investments over the last year that are finally beginning to pay off. We are up about 8% this week," replies Viktor.

"This week?"

"Yes, sir. Your monthly statement will reflect this movement, sir."

"Very well, Viktor. Ho hesitates for a moment but continues. "With this news, we would like to add another $100 million to the fund, but I need to feel comfortable the returns issue has been addressed."

"Ho, I can assure you the returns issue has been addressed."

"I certainly hope so. I have people to answer to, Viktor."

Little does Viktor know, Ho has the same problem he has. He cannot find returns for all the money pouring in, and he is reaching by adding to Viktor's fund. Viktor does not know that Ho has $3 billion a week of new money he has to invest somewhere.

"Okay, Viktor. I will authorize another $100 million to go into the fund with another $100 million reserved if the numbers you have projected come to fruition."

"Great, I'm sure you will not be disappointed."

They hang up. Viktor feels the stress of having another $100 million to invest with another $100 million waiting in the wings.

The world of an investment manager has a couple of constant challenges—how to make the money currently invested grow consistently and how to continue to produce big returns so investors will continue to add money to the fund. Another problem can be too much money in the fund. Once investors have confidence in a fund, they pour money into it to the point where it becomes harder to mimic the superior performance that attracted the money in the first place. It's a catch-22 for the manager.

Viktor frets constantly about the inflow of money into the fund. He cannot be happy. He understands that while he's generating amazing returns, he will have a difficult time replicating them with an additional $100 million of new money. This is a problem across the entire investment industry: becoming a victim of one's own success.

Viktor calls all of the current managers overseeing Diversified Financial Services' investments to give them the same hell he just got from Ho and also to offer to place additional funds with them. They jump at the chance to manage the new money since their personal compensation will go up with the new money invested, but they have no real idea where to invest the new money either. More money¬—more big money—chasing fewer and fewer quality investments makes the prices of those investments go up,

Viktor goes to his office for a shot of El Corazon tequila.

CHAPTER THIRTY-SEVEN

As Frank Holland sits down at his desk, Detective Bill Smith comes over to him.

"Frank, it looks like we're getting a new boss."

"Who is it?" Frank asks.

"Some guy from out West. It seems the old guard was concerned about how clubby it was getting around here since 9/11 and thought some new management would break up the staleness. It came about after the sexual harassment case. The mayor had to figure out how to cover his ass. Seems three females are coming in as well as this guy from Tucson, Arizona."

Frank and Detective Smith walk to the coffee machine in the break room as they talk.

"Tucson! Jesus, what is he going to do in Manhattan? Not a lot of people swimming in illegally from Jersey!"

"Yeah, the nerve of those guys," says a voice Frank doesn't recognize. Bill turns around and makes an introduction.

"Frank, meet Captain Roger Emanuel," he says.

"Oh, hello. . . uh, sorry about the comment, Captain."

"I would probably feel the same way, Frank. Call me Roger. It's got to be tough watching someone leave who has been there for you in the past and having a new guy come in from out of town. Guys, this is a pretty big move for me. I don't mind telling you, and you can probably imagine, that I must have some skills to be placed in charge of such an esteemed group of professionals, but I'll need your help to make this transition smooth and to make sure you get the resources you need to get the job done. Not sure how 9/11 impacted you guys, but I am here now. Anyway, that's probably more of a speech than I will give to the whole department tomorrow at roll call."

"Roger, seriously, welcome to the 35th," says Frank.

"Thank you, Frank. Tell me about yourself."

"Boss," says Bill, "Frank is true NYPD blue through and through. His dad was a cop, and he works 24/7 for the department."

"Bill, stop it," says Frank.

"You know it's true, man. You solve the tough ones around here. Why don't you tell him about the one you're working on now—it's not even a murder."

"Bill, really, that's enough," Frank says.

"Frank, my office is always open, and I look forward to hearing from you in the next few days about what you're working on and how I can help."

"Thank you, Roger. I think it'll be good to have some new blood around here."

CHAPTER THIRTY-EIGHT

Rachael starts her new job at Diversified Financial Services and backs off dating Rick in order to concentrate on finding out what John knows and how this whole thing works. With the limited number of "live aboards"—or rich locals on Cayman—she will probably be back to Rick once she has made the rounds. The Caymans are a small rock, and everyone knows everyone.

"So, here's your cubicle, Rachael. You'll be doing statistical analysis, or basically tracking pools of funds to determine payouts. It's almost an accounting function so we can track payouts to the fund. It's somewhat difficult as we are at the mercy of Wisconsin Viaticals and several other US firms to report payouts accurately since we really do not know who dies when."

"That seems like information you'd need to know to make sure you're not cheated."

"Correct! In time, we get a fund report with our overall payouts so we can monitor our performance."

Rachael goes to work. She learns fast. She begins to see

how this viatical settlement game works, but only vaguely. She gets tons of emails from tracking agents, who are sort of like the mortuary guys of the life settlement world. They check social security numbers for deaths, make calls to people, and email are-you-dead-yet correspondence to the insured.

Rachael begins to learn her way around and is now getting the notices that show the gross amounts paid to the funds, the number of deaths, and the payouts on a monthly basis.

"So, how large is this fund?" Rachael asks John. "You have all these people working here, and the death list I get is huge. I mean, these people are dropping like flies. How do you keep up with whether the firm gets the proper payouts? Couldn't the insurance companies short you the proceeds without your knowledge?"

"Rachael, you're a quick study. I mean really sharp. We don't usually get the top of the line here in the Caymans. I mean, many really sharp people come here but they just can't cut it. They think they'll move to paradise, but after a while, it becomes just a small rock and gets old. To answer your question, the insurance company could just short us the proceeds, but I developed a way we can audit the pools. Most of the people working here are doing just that. We receive death notices and payout notices, and we have ways of checking the pools to make sure the insurance companies don't cheat us."

"How do you determine if you are being cheated?" asks Rachael.

"See all those people out there? They all do different functions for this massive effort. This piece of the fund primarily invests in viaticals and life settlements."

"What's the difference?"

"Viaticals are on clients who have terminal illnesses, and life settlements are just on old people."

"What about young people?"

"Life settlements on young people are low-return vehicles because young people don't die that often. But I have noticed in some of our pools, some younger people have been dying more recently. Statistics don't lie, so I guess Viktor just has a feel for how to buy the right pools."

That could be, Rachael thinks, especially if the young people in those pools are being killed.

CHAPTER THIRTY-NINE

Avinash is concerned about the pace of his current business with Viktor. At 6 to 8 contracts a month, he hardly has time to relax between assignments.

"I'm taking a sabbatical," he tells Viktor.

"We are already behind," says Viktor. "The process needs to accelerate, not slow down."

"We are pushing too hard. With each additional transaction, the risks go up."

"So will the returns."

They hang up. Avi may have to kill Viktor.

Rachael soon develops a routine, staying an hour or so later than most people. Viktor leaves at 3:30, John at 4:30, and everyone else at 5:00 pm sharp. This is the Caymans—no one is going to work more than necessary except security.

Rachael can find out next to nothing on her computer. It appears John and Viktor have everything compartmentalized so no one can see the whole picture. She gets gross settlements, another department gets death certificates, and another gets the names of the deceased to cross check with the proceeds from the pools. No one is to know who is in which pool; the insurance companies go to great lengths to keep this information a secret. This way, they can play with the pools of funds and make sure they do not get screwed in the process.

"Hey Rachael," says John late one afternoon. "Want to go out with the gang for a drink?"

"Sure!"

It's an easy walk to the Brasserie from the office, so she and John walk over together. They have a nice chat on the way.

"So, John, tell me about Viktor."

"What do you want to know? He's been good to me. He has a great business, and he's a really smart man."

They reach the Brasserie. A couple of Wall Street types eye Rachael as they enter.

"This is an interesting place," says Rachael.

"Well, it's kind of like Harry's in New York City. Did you know Grand Cayman is the fifth largest financial center in the world?"

"No kidding! So that's why this place is full of those guys."

"Yep."

"So, where's the rest of the office?"

John, embarrassed, says, "Well, . . . uh, I didn't actually invite them!"

"You need to learn to shoot straight with a woman if you want to get to first base, John."

"Okay. I'm sorry, Rachael. Are you leaving?"

"Relax, John. I'll stay for a drink."

"Okay, okay."

"How did you and Viktor meet?"

"He was interviewing for actuaries at Princeton, where I went to school, and he encouraged me to go to this math conference his company sponsored. That's where we got to know one another."

"Just like that?"

"What do you mean 'just like that'? I'm good at what I do."

"Oh sorry, John, I didn't mean to imply anything."

"Sorry Rachael, it's just Viktor is always surrounded by beautiful girls, and sometimes he's not so nice to me . . . I guess I get a little self-conscious."

"You have no reason to feel that way, John. You seem very accomplished to me."

They have several more drinks.

"So, John, where do you live?"

CHAPTER FORTY

Frank comes home, pops a beer, and picks up a copy of the USA News. He opens the paper to the money section and begins to read an article about a real estate guy in California.

Multimillionaire-to-bankrupt deceased Chester DelGotto is in the news again. This time it's because of his life insurance policy. The big news is the parties to the lawsuit between Hartley Life and the current contract insurance owner, Diversified Financial Services, have reached a settlement for an undisclosed amount.

Frank sits up on the couch and studies the article a little closer.

The ongoing saga of the larger-than-life builder mogul to bankrupt, murdered businessman Chester DelGotto continues to play out with a great deal of publicity he would have enjoyed. His life insurance policy, which many believe to have been for $10 million, was, in fact, sold to a hedge fund in the Cayman Islands. Prior to his death, it appears DelGotto sold his life insurance policy to a viatical settlement fund, which resulted in a lawsuit between the settlement fund and the insurance company that wrote the policy, Hartley Life. Now Hartley Life has agreed to pay the claim, although the amount has not been disclosed.

This is exactly what Joe Stein was talking about, thinks Frank. He takes a phone call from the office to investigate an incident in the Village. He finishes his beer and goes to the crime scene.

CHAPTER FORTY-ONE

John lives on Seven Mile Beach near the Ritz Carlton. Rachael follows him in her rental car, and as she drives up to the estate, she thinks she's picked out the wrong guy. He has to be in the club with Viktor. This place makes Rick's house look like rent-controlled housing.

"John, what the hell is this place?"

"It's where I live."

"Jesus, is everybody in Grand Cayman filthy rich?"

"Oh, this belongs to Viktor, but he has a place at the Ritz Carlton and only uses this for parties. So I live here and get to go to great parties sometimes—sometimes not."

"Wow, that seems really cool."

At this point, they are greeted by a man. "Good evening, Mr. Menuso."

"Clifford, this is Ms. Lopez."

Clifford leans forward in a bowing gesture to Rachael.

"Clifford, nice to meet you."

"Shall I make you drinks?" asks Clifford.

"Yes, please, Clifford. Rachael, what would you like?"

"What would be a good Cayman drink?"

"How about a stingray?"

"I don't know what that is."

"It's kind of a rum punch." "Okay. Sounds good."

"The usual for you, Mr. Menuso? Baker's #7 bourbon, two ice cubes, and ginger ale?"

They have a few more drinks, and John is beginning to get pretty drunk. Rachael decides this is a good time for her to keep things light but friendly.

"John, this living arrangement of yours is one heck of a perk! What else do you do for Viktor?"

"I'm the chief actuarial guy at the firm."

"It seems like you're being rewarded for more than just accounting, John."

"Well, I did something that catapulted the company's returns. I'm very talented, you know. I was the one who broke the life settlement code."

"What does 'broke the code' mean?"

"After the deaths, we get all of the death notices, and no one knows who is in which pool. I figured out how to dissect the pools so we can see who is in each pool. This makes it possible for us to buy pools with a better mortality profile. I can tell you who's in which pool—insurance, age, everything."

"Wow, John, that is big. No wonder you're so valuable."

They have yet another drink. Even with the ginger ale, John seems to be getting pretty drunk, and that's good for Rachael. She has decided John is not in on it. He's just a pawn, but a very smart pawn at that.

Rachael has to get a look at John's computer. That must be where the goods are. She looks around John's place while she waits for his return from the restroom. She goes to his top desk drawer and finds a notebook. She opens it, flips through a few pages. One page is marked "PW". Oh, John, she thinks to herself, and takes a Post-It note from his desk and writes down his password.

When John returns, Rachael finishes her drink and says goodbye. John, while disappointed, feels somewhat comforted since he can actually consider this a date.

CHAPTER FORTY-TWO

Rachael works as a very good Diversified employee for the next few weeks, extending her stay at the Comfort Suites and feeling a little panicked about running out of money while developing a plan to get access to the data. She takes a phone call from Sheila.

"Okay, what are you doing in the Caymans for this long? I understand your needing a vacation after everything that happened at work, but when are you coming home?"

"I'm not sure."

"Oh, Rachael, who is he?"

"Nobody. Remember me mentioning the case to you about the woman who fell in her bathroom?"

"Yes, the one you got fired over for investigating. I remember."

"I did not get fired. I quit."

"Oh right. Sorry. You quit after you had a knock-down drag-out fight with your boss in his office."

"Okay, fine, I get it."

"Okay, so what? Did you find out something?"

"Yes. She was murdered by this guy in the Caymans."

"What?"

"Yes. He runs this fund and he must have had her killed for the insurance money."

"Rachael, can you prove it?"

"Not yet, but I'm working there and I'll get him sooner or later."

"What do you mean, you're working there?"

"I took a job at his hedge fund."

"What the hell are you doing at a hedge fund?"

"Mostly looking pretty and keeping my head down so far. This guy is a creep. He is surrounded by models so I kind of just fit in without any issues."

"Get back here now! This is crazy! What if you get caught and this guy is who you think he is? He will kill you."

"Yeah, I've thought about that, but I only need a few more days and I'll have enough information to get someone to follow up on this case. I have to run, love. I'll see you soon. Don't worry."

One evening, Rachael works late. Viktor leaves as usual with Victoria at 3:30, John at 4:30, and everyone else at 5:00. Rachael is alone with security. The guard makes rounds and checks on Rachael on his way by. Rachael times him: 17 minutes. He stops to talk as he comes back by her.

"I'm Mike, with Security."

He is dark, about 5 feet 9 inches tall with a build like a fullback; he probably weighs 230 pounds but carries it very well.

"I'm Rachael."

"You're new."

"Yes, I was brought in for statistical analysis working with John. I hate to be rude, but I need to finish this report—I have to be somewhere later."

"Okay." Mike moves along on his rounds.

Mike is a stand-up guy. Bad guys admire good guys and like to employ them because they know they can trust them, to a certain point. Mike was born son number three to a single mom in Kingston, Jamaica. Jamaica has a very strict class system, and it's difficult to move up from one class to another and stay on the island.

Mike resumes his walk around the building. Rachael decides now is the time to go into John's office and try the password she found at his house. It works and she's in. She writes down the names she sees in a random pool, but then decides that will never work. Instead, she types in "Donna McCally." The message reads FILE CLOSED. Bingo! They had a file on her. It was a hit. Still, no way anyone is going to believe this yet. Mike is back and has seen her in John's office.

"It's great that John has a printer in his office," she says to Mike.

He looks at her suspiciously. She grabs something off the printer and goes back to her desk. Mike lingers. Rachael has to get back into John's office to delete her search but can't with Mike hanging around.

"How long have you worked here, Mike?"

"Five years."

"Are you from Cayman?"

"No. Jamaica."

"Where is the best Jamaican food on the island?"

"Down at West End."

"Oh great! I need to try it."

Mike looks at Rachael suspiciously but walks on. As soon as he is out of sight, Rachael goes back into John's office, deletes the search, and as she turns to leave she runs into Mike.

"What are you doing, Lady?"

CHAPTER FORTY-THREE

Rachael tells Mike, "I had to pull data from John's computer to finish my report because I didn't have access to it on mine. What time do you get off work, Mike?" Rachael asks, trying to distract him.

"Lady, I'm married," says Mike. He eyes her suspiciously and then moves on again.

The next day Rachael goes to John's office to meet with him about a couple of issues.

"Mike tells me you were on my computer last night."

"Yes, for some reason mine was moving slowly, and I wanted to finish some things before I left."

"I'll have a tech check your machine out today," John says. "I noticed you erased your search history."

"I thought it would be more secure that way."

"From who? Me? Listen, Rachael, I don't know if you are just nosy or if you are up to something, but I really like you. Trust me, everything is on the up and up here. It's pretty simple: Viktor runs a hedge fund which invests in life insurance settlements along with a lot of other things. I've seen the whole operation top to bottom. Now, what are you up to?"

"Well, I'm new here and I'm enjoying getting to know you, John. I don't want to put you on the spot, but I guess I'm just a little nervous about you and me and how it may affect my job. I want to do a good job and earn my way up."

John calls a tech to do some work on Rachael's computer and sends her back to her office. John is beginning to believe Rachael likes him romantically. He missed the ruse about her computer. He sits back at his desk and tries to figure out what he should do next.

Later in the day, John goes to Rachael's cubicle. "How did it go with the computer tech?"

Rachael smiles alluringly and says, "He was very helpful, John. Thank you for sending him by. So, John, what are you up to tonight?"

Distracted from the issue at hand, John is pleased she just wants to work hard and be with him.

As they drive back to his place, Rachael thinks about her life and where this is leading. She decides to compartmentalize and think about her case. She pours herself a double Baker's, no ginger.

"I think we can excuse the butler for the evening, don't you, John?"

"That will be all for now, Clifford. Good night."

"Good night, sir."

Rachael pours a second Baker's, neat, and saunters over to John. She takes his hand as they look out at the beautiful moon and stars. The moonlight is so bright the stars pale.

John leans over and kisses Rachael's neck. It feels nice to her. He is a nice guy—gentle, sweet, and, like most men, very interested in her. She turns to him and they have a nice, long kiss—civilized, venerable, intimate. Rachael takes John by the hand and leads him toward the bedroom right off the pool. She moves with him, feeling like a kindred spirit. Somehow each alone although together, sensing a closeness Rachael has not felt before.

In the bedroom, they leave the doors open to the pool and the ocean. The moonlight follows them into the room. Van Morrison's voice breathes out across the warm air, drifting in from the pool and through the house, singing in the background, "It's a marvelous night for a Moondance, with the stars up above in your eyes." Van is like a ghost Rachael and John cannot see but know very well.

CHAPTER FORTY-FOUR

John comes into Rachael's office the next day to see about plans for the evening. "I have to go to an off-site meeting today at 4:00, Rachael, but I'd like to meet you later for dinner if you'd like."

"Why don't I just come out to your place and you have the chef prepare something for us there? Say around 7:00?"

"Let's make it 7:30. I'm not sure how long this meeting will last."

"Even better. I can use the time to catch up here at work."

They awkwardly embrace and then John leaves her cubicle. Rachael works at her desk doing meaningless tasks just to look busy until the office empties out a little after 5:00. As soon as no one is around, Rachael makes her way to John's office. It is very quiet and all she can hear is the hum of the office air conditioners, which are constantly running in the Caymans. She sits down at John's desk. Still not another noise. No Mike making rounds. Nothing.

Rachael punches John's access code into his computer.

She's in. She pulls up John's file search and types in "Chester DelGotto." The search runs and says, "FILE CLOSED."

"You certainly are ambitious for someone on the islands, Rachael."

Rachael jumps back from the computer, and her chair rolls over toward Viktor. He stops the chair's momentum with his foot.

"Viktor! Oh, hello, you scared me!"

"I have that effect on people," he says.

"I was just checking on some closed files to make sure we hadn't missed any collections."

"Oh, really?" Viktor says.

Viktor moves in closer. "You know, Rachael, the only real way to move up in this company is through me." He moves even closer.

"Oh . . . uh, well, I think I'm finished for the day, Viktor."

Rachael tries to build some distance between herself and Viktor but has a hard time getting away from him.

"Good. Then the night can start right now." Viktor brushes his hand up and down Rachael's shoulder.

"Actually, I have someone waiting for me, and if I'm not on time, it would reflect badly on our company. It's an attorney who wants to do business with us."

"Why would you have anything to do with that?"

"Well, I don't really. I just thought I could introduce him to you sometime and…"

"We have plenty of attorneys. Come here and sit down next to me."

Viktor pulls Rachael over to a small couch in John's office.

"Viktor, I really…"

Viktor grabs her, pulling at her clothes. She stands and pulls away from him, but he has a firm grasp on her blouse. Rachael slips and falls to the floor and her blouse tears in Viktor's hands. Mike steps through the door.

"Is anything wrong?" Mike asks as he walks into the office and over toward Rachael.

"Mike!" yells Viktor, "get back to work! Nothing is wrong."

Rachael says "Mike, hi! I was just leaving, and I fell. Viktor was helping me up when I slipped and tore my shirt. Right, Viktor?" she says as she pulls her blouse closed to cover herself.

Mike stands squared off in a confident stance in front of Rachael, facing Viktor. Mike does not like what he sees here. Viktor takes the hint, even though he is not the least bit concerned about how this looks to Mike. He just knows he does not want to get into it with Mike. Viktor would likely be the one to get hurt, and he wants to keep Mike as an employee.

Mike walks Rachael to the lobby. She is obviously upset about the encounter with Viktor.

Mike asks, "Are you all right?"

"Hell no, I'm not all right! No one treats me that way."

"Rachael, Viktor is very powerful and dangerous here in the Caymans. I would watch myself if I were you."

Mike walks back into the building, locking the door behind him.

Rachael reaches the street and remembers she left her phone in John's office.

Rachael is somewhat shaken, but she is able to pull herself together. She's been here before in her life—growing up on military bases, she found herself in this situation more than once. She needs to calm down so she can figure out what to do next. She puts her jacket on over her torn blouse and drives to the Ritz to have a drink to calm her nerves. At least, that's what she tells herself. She sits down at the bar and orders a martini as Rick walks over.

"Hey, stranger. Long time, no see . . . whoa, Rachael, what's going on? You look like you just saw a ghost or something."

"Hi, Rick. Sorry I've been out of touch, but I did just the opposite of what you advised me. I took a job with Viktor."

"What? Rachael, I told you to stay away from that guy. He's trouble—I know what I'm talking about here."

"Well, guess what? You were right!"

She slams her drink down her throat, drops a 20 on the bar, and walks out. Rick follows.

"Rachael, wait. I'm sorry. I didn't mean to sound like an I-told-you-so kind of guy. How can I help you?"

"Rick, what do you know for a fact about Viktor?"

"I don't know many things for a fact; it's all only what I have heard. I've had a few conversations with other lawyers who have asked me about various goings-on, and I have been on teams that have created documents for off-shore companies like Viktor's, but that doesn't necessarily mean he has done anything illegal."

"Then, Rick, you cannot help me at all." She walks to her car.

"Rachael . . ."

Rick watches as she drives away.

CHAPTER FORTY-FIVE

Viktor sees a cell phone in John's office and picks it up. It's locked. He uses the office phone to make a call and one of his tech guys answers.

"Gill, meet me in my office in 10 minutes. I need you to open a phone for me."

He takes the phone to his office and pours himself a drink while he waits. Gill comes in, takes the locked phone and switches it off. He presses down on the button until it comes back on. He uses a few codes to get access to the phone to make it think it needs to be in recovery mode.

"What's the social of the owner?"

"How the hell should I know?!" Viktor yells, sitting in one of his club chairs with a drink, looking out at the Cayman water.

"I need some info on the user," Gill says.

"One moment," says Viktor. He calls the human resources number, but everyone has left since it's now around 7:30 pm. The only reason the IT guy is at work is that he needs to work on updates when everyone else is gone.

"What fucking time does everybody leave around here?!" Viktor yells. "Take this phone down to HR tomorrow and get the info you need on Rachael Lopez, then unlock it and bring it to my office. Do not give or show it to anyone between now and then except Grace in HR. As a matter of fact, give it to me. Come here tomorrow morning at 8:30 and pick it up from me to go to HR."

"Yes sir," Gill says as he hands the phone back to Viktor and leaves.

Viktor opens his safe and places the phone inside. He decides to look at footage from the cameras in John's office for the last few days. He and one security guy are the only ones who know about all of the cameras in the office and at Viktor's house where John is staying. He sits down at his computer and pulls up the footage from 5:00 pm until 2:00 am for each night since Rachael started working. He watches her slip into John's office almost every night after the first two nights to access his computer. He sees her interaction with Mike from a few nights ago. He also looks at footage from John's house over the same time period. He sees Rachael and John having drinks, and he sees where it goes from there.

The next day Gill picks up the phone and brings it back to Viktor, unlocked and ready to use.

Avi's bat phone rings. He recognizes Viktor's number but does not speak when the phone is connected.

"Are you there? It's me," says Viktor.

"Yes."

"I am going to call you back in one minute from a

different number," Viktor says and hangs up.

Avi's phone rings again a minute later. He answers it again without speaking.

"This is the girl's phone. I'll send you the dossier."

"Have you made sure this phone is clean?" Avi asks.

"Yes, I had it completely checked and it's clean."

Avi turns on the system and triangulates the number and now has Rachael's phone bugged for audio and location. "Got it. Hang up," he says to Viktor.

Viktor hangs up and deletes the call to Avi's number from Rachael's phone.

CHAPTER FORTY-SIX

Avi is still not happy with Lloyd ratting him out, so after four weeks have gone by, he decides the FBI probably will not spend another week waiting for him to surface. He shows up at Lloyd's regular bar two hours before Lloyd usually stops by. No goons. He waits until Lloyd comes in and then approaches him.

"Lloyd, you got to run, man. They are all over you."

"What?"

"It's me Lloyd, Hartman."

"Oh man, I didn't recognize you."

"That's the point, man," says Avi, mimicking Lloyd.

He gives Lloyd an envelope and Lloyd peeks inside finding a one-way ticket to Mexico and a stack of hundreds that looks like about $5000.

"Wait, man, what do you mean run? I live here, man; I can't run."

"It's just for a few months until the heat goes away. You and I have done nothing, except for your little drug business, which they will come back to eventually. You need to run for a while and lay low."

Lloyd still looks as if he is not convinced.

"I'm the only friend who can help you out of this, man. Listen to me. A car will pick you up two blocks north of here in one hour."

"Oh, man, I don't know. I could sure use the money though. And a vacation would probably make them forget about me. I guess that makes sense. I can lay low in Mexico with this cash for a while."

"It's a good plan, Lloyd."

Avi gets up and leaves. Lloyd waits the one hour, then walks the two blocks and gets into a car driven by a tall, blond man.

"Hey, man, take me to the airport," Lloyd says.

The driver says, "Yes sir," but drives Lloyd out toward the desert instead of the airport.

"Hey, man, you missed the turn to the airport right there! Hey man, what gives? Where are you taking me?"

"Lloyd, calm down; it's me," Avi says from the driver's seat.

"Oh, man, I didn't know what was happening!" Lloyd begins to calm down, but in the back of his mind questions what is happening. Finally, he sees the desert approaching and civilization disappearing and asks, "So, where are we going?"

"Lloyd, I need to take a leak, man. I'm pulling over here for a second." Avi gets out of the car, walks to the back door, and opens it for Lloyd to get out. Lloyd takes off running into the desert once he jumps out of the car. Avi just stands there looking at Lloyd in disgust. He finally sees Lloyd stop running as he has given out from being so out of shape.

"Lloyd, what are you doing man?" says Avi. "I already gave you five grand, If I were going to kill you I would have done so before I gave you the money, man."

Lloyd is still not sure what is going on until he gets back to the car and sees the bully club in Avi's hand. Avi hits Lloyd twice in the head, and Lloyd goes down easily after the two strategic blows. Avi props Lloyd up in the front seat beside him and drives further out into the desert. He pulls off the road behind a dip in the landscape and drives further from the road. He stops, takes Lloyd's clothes and passport, and dumps his body in a shallow grave. Avi knows Lloyd's body may be found once the birds of prey show up and begin circling the scent in a few days. He would prefer Lloyd not be found but does not have time to dig a deeper grave or cut off Lloyd's feet, hands and head to prevent the authorities from identifying him.

Avi drives to the airport and parks the car in the long-term parking deck. He changes into Lloyd's clothes and takes his passport. He ducks into the airport restroom with his make-up kit and quickly makes himself look more like Lloyd. Then he boards a flight to Mexico.

"Hey, Cavuto, looks like your boy Lloyd is fleeing to Mexico," says Special Agent McGhee as he gets an alert in his email.

"What?"

"Yep. He just boarded a flight to Guadalajara, Mexico."

"That little shit. You think he's running on his drug charge or is he running from Hartman?"

"We don't have anything on Hartman except he rents a van from Lloyd and pays him cash."

"I guess we better pick Lloyd up. Who do we have in Guadalajara?" asks Cavuto.

"Well no one, since it's in another country! Do you seriously want to fly an agent or agents down there to pick up Lloyd?"

Cavuto weighs his options. "I guess not. I mean, he will probably make his way back here. According to his sheet, he has never lived anywhere else."

"What about relatives? Does he have anyone here who might know about his activities?"

"Not really, just a sister in another city. Is anybody with him on the flight?"

"Doesn't appear to be. He booked the ticket alone. There's a lady from Detroit in the seat next to him. Looks like she is traveling with two people sitting behind her."

"How about the Mexican authorities? What if we have someone down there pick him up for us?"

McGhee looks at Cavuto with astonishment and says, "I can't believe you would even entertain that idea!"

"Ok, fine. Let's just leave him out there and see if he shows back up at home sometime. Knowing that dummy, he's probably down there working on a drug deal. Let's leave a BOLO in the system for Hartman. I want to know if he pops up anywhere."

CHAPTER FORTY-SEVEN

Despite knowing she has put herself in a dangerous place, Rachael plays it head-on in usual Rachael style, going to work the following morning at Diversified. She is met at the door by the receptionist.

"Rachael, please come this way."

The receptionist takes her to an empty office where her friend Mike and Grace from HR are waiting.

"Rachael, Viktor has decided to make a change in your employment," Grace tells Rachael as Mike stands by. "I have your final paycheck. It is very generous of Viktor to add severance to it even though he owes you nothing but what you are due. If you sign this release, you can have this check."

Grace has a box of items which are apparently Rachael's things from her cubicle. Rachael rifles through them.

"What about my phone? I left it in John's office yesterday."

Grace looks at Mike. "Let me check on it for you," he says and he leaves the office.

Rachael and Grace sit in uncomfortable silence as

Rachael looks through the box. In about five minutes, Mike is back with Rachael's phone.

"Is this it?" he asks.

Rachael looks at the phone, dials in her code and it comes to life.

"Yes. This is mine."

The release is a hold-harmless for the company and Viktor, but criminal activity is criminal activity. Knowing full well she cannot be forced by this piece of paper to hide criminal activity, Rachael signs it. Grace hands her an envelope with a check inside. Rachael opens the envelope and looks at the check—$10,000. She swallows hard when she sees the amount.

"Like I said, Viktor is most generous," says Grace.

It is against Rachael's instincts to stay quiet, especially after what happened to her yesterday, but she somehow manages it. She stuffs the check into her bag and picks up the box of her belongings. Mike walks her out of the building.

"Rachael, I'm sorry about this."

"Mike, it's okay. I know you have a family and a good job here. You did what you could, and I am grateful for that."

Rachael is relieved to be out of the building with no Viktor in sight, holding a box of stuff she mostly does not recognize and a check for $10,000 for three weeks work. She sits in her car smiling, but her instincts tell her this is not over.

Above, Viktor watches the whole scene unfold from his office through the secret cameras.

John answers his office phone.

"John, Viktor would like to see you."

"Of course."

John leaves his office immediately and walks to Viktor's office.

Viktor is at the office door when John arrives. "Have a seat," says Viktor.

John sits in one of the club chairs, and Viktor takes one just across from him.

"I hope everything is okay with you, John. Listen, I had to let Rachael go. She has been secretly sneaking into your office to access your computer, and I can't have people around we can't trust. Is there anything else I need to know about her?"

"I don't think so, sir. She seemed to like the work. I don't know what could have come over her. I thought she was working harder to get promoted."

"How did she get your access code?" asks Viktor.

"I don't know."

"Has she been spending time at your house?"

"Yes, she has been over a couple of times . . . What could she be looking for? We don't have anything to hide," says John.

"That's true; we certainly don't. It's just unfortunate. Let's put it behind us now though, John. Shall we?"

"Yes, sir."

"Let me know if she tries to contact you."

"Okay, and Viktor, I am really happy with my work. I enjoy being here."

"I know you do, John, and I enjoy your friendship as well."

When he gets home that evening, John calls Rachael's number. No answer.

Viktor's phone chimes and he checks it. It's an email saying John has called Rachael.

Frank continues to dig into the Chester DelGotto case that Hartley, the insurance company, settled. So, a hedge fund that owns a pool of life settlements got the money. Hartley decided to pay off the policy. Frank decides to check the NYPD mysterious deaths file. He finds out there isn't one. It seems police everywhere are overwhelmed, and budget cuts don't help. Police departments, which are underfunded anyway, cannot keep up with the workload. The quicker a case can clear, the better. When in doubt, it's an accident or a natural death. So long as no one screams too loudly, everyone simply moves on.

Frank goes to the best source of information he knows— Google. He types in "mysterious deaths" and finds lots of blogs and posts. He wonders how he can narrow down his search. Even on the world wide web, Frank cannot find an accurate list of deaths that are open or suspicious. It's a who's who of witch hunts and speculation, but nowhere does anyone show a record of anything. Frank is dismayed, but not surprised. Cases close.

CHAPTER FORTY-EIGHT

Rachael takes her $10,000 check to the bank and cashes it. After all, this is the Caymans, cash is king. She pays off her hotel bill and moves to the Villas of the Galleon Hotel. It's nicer, has security, and is off Seven Mile Beach where Viktor and company hang out. She has to develop a plan.

With no other way to go with these new leads, Rachael puts in a call to her old boss, hoping he will at least hear her out.

"Detective Garcia, Homicide."

"Garcia, It's Rachael Lopez. May I speak to Roger?"

"Rachael, he took a job in New York City. What do you care and why are you calling?"

"Oh, that's right, he told me he was moving last time we spoke. I may have a lead on something for him. Can I get his number?"

"Hold on. Beth, pick up on 1."

"Beth Johnson."

"Beth, would you give me Roger Emanuel's new office number? I need to give him a lead on a homicide."

"Who is this?"

"It's Rachael Lopez."

"Okay, hi Rachael. His number is 212-555-1212."

"Okay, thanks." Rachael hangs up and dials the number.

"Roger Emanuel."

"Roger, it's Rachael. Please don't hang up. I know we've had our differences, but I know you're an honest cop. As you know, I've been working the McCally case, and it turns out there's a life insurance angle after all. I think you are going to want to see how this scheme works. If you'll give me 15 minutes to lay it out for you and you think I'm right, you may blow the lid off of something big. If you still think I'm crazy, you will have only wasted 15 minutes of your life."

"Where are you, Rachael?"

"I'm in the Cayman Islands. This thing goes international."

"Then why not call the FBI or the CIA? Why me?"

"I can't even get you to listen to me. How am I going to get the FBI to? Roger, please, just give me 15 minutes. I can come to your office, whenever you say."

"Rachael, I just got here. I'm staying in the damn Penta Hotel; I don't even have a decent place yet. I am not in the mood for more of your bullshit."

"You're a good cop, Roger. I know you are. Maybe you don't like me, but I know you want whatever is right to prevail. I'm just asking for 15 minutes in your office."

"Oh hell, fine! How about we meet next Tuesday at 3:00."

"I'm not sure it can wait."

"Well, it's going to have to."

"Okay, I'll see you then."

They hang up. Avi also hangs up. He has Rachael's phone bugged, but at this point has no contract from Viktor. He is amused by the call.

Next Tuesday seems like it's an eternity away for Rachael on this little rock called Grand Cayman Island. There are not many places to hide. So, she decides a few extra days in NYC is better than hanging around the Caymans—no reason to give Viktor any ideas.

Two days later, Rachael catches the 2:15 pm to LaGuardia. She arrives at 9:30 pm and stays at the Hampton Inn by the airport.

Viktor, who saw the transcript from Rachael's call to Roger, calls Avi. "We have a problem with Rachael and this Roger Emanuel character."

"We do not have a problem; you have a problem," says Avi. "I read the dossier and the data from one of her calls. She may be an undercover cop—she called an NYPD cop."

"I know; I was listening as well."

"Well, I still do not have a contract, so my working without one has already cost you more."

"Can you make my problem your problem for $150,000?" asks Viktor.

"For two cops, $300,000 is what it takes to become my problem," replies Avi. "Send me what you have on the Emanuel guy."

"Okay. I will wire funds to your Cayman account tomorrow."

"Okay, I'll start tomorrow then," says Avi.

"You have already started," says Viktor.

"No, I have been entertaining myself with this, but I will stop thinking about it until tomorrow."

"Wait, I can't send any money today; it's too late."

"Ok, I'll start today, but for $350,000 tomorrow. I will check my account at 7 am."

"Fine! It will be there."

CHAPTER FORTY-NINE

The next morning, there is a meeting at the NYPD where Roger is formally introduced to the department. He meets with the detectives one by one to discuss how he rolls and what they are working on. It is Frank Holland's turn.

"So, Frank, what's up?"

"Well, we have a couple of homicides on the East Side and a few robberies. You know, the usual."

"Anything interesting?"

Frank thinks about giving him his theory on Sodkoff but decides not to discuss it.

"No, nothing really interesting."

"Frank, the word is you're the hero of this precinct. I want to be a friend and I want to help. Hopefully, you'll feel you can trust me once we spend more time together. If it's okay with you, let's meet weekly for a while."

"Sure, Captain."

"Call me Roger."

"Okay, Roger. Thanks."

Avi makes a call to an operative he has used in New York for Company jobs. They meet and he assigns her to drug a target. He hands her a two-page dossier on Roger Emanuel and brings her up to speed. He gives her an envelope with $10,000 in cash and instructions that what is about to take place never took place.

Roger goes to his room at the Penta Hotel (now the Hotel Pennsylvania). While it's been upgraded slightly, it's still a discount rental by New York City standards. One of the advantages of staying there is it has underground connections to Madison Square Garden and the subway. Macy's is right across the street, and thousands of people flow through the hotel daily.

Roger walks into the bar, orders a double Jack Black, and strikes up a conversation with an attractive woman. She's tall, African-American, and he cannot take his eyes off her. She has deep green eyes and long thick hair.

"Looks like you've had a long day," she says.

"You have no idea. I just moved here from Arizona, and there are more people in this hotel than there were in the town where I worked."

"I know what you mean. I'm from Georgia. I work for a law firm downtown. Just moved here myself. I'm Grace."

"I'm Roger."

"So, Roger, could I buy you another drink?"

"Sure, why not? A double Jack Black."

She orders his drink and a cosmopolitan martini for herself.

"I hate to admit this, but I have a 50-year-old man thing and I've got to step out to the men's room," says Roger.

"No worries, I'll be right here when you get back."

As Roger walks off, the drinks arrive. She picks up Roger's drink to move it to his place, sets it down, and spikes it with a sedative.

Roger returns, and they continue to chat as they have their drinks. After a while, his head begins to nod, and he realizes he's quite worn out after these first few days in his new job.

"Grace, I think the jet lag and new job are beginning to get to me. If you'll permit me, I'll excuse myself and go to my room."

"Certainly. It was nice to meet you, Roger."

Avi watches the whole encounter in the bar while reading a paper.

Roger goes back to his room and passes out, snoring quietly.

Being the prepared, accomplished assassin he is, Avi has a knack for using people's own weapons against them. He has used bombs in guns in many places. It's an easy fix. It's not used often because of the difficulty of getting access to someone's weapon, especially in war zones or areas with high terrorist activity. People often sleep with their guns and never let them out of their sight.

Avi was taught the gun trick by the DRS (the Algerian CIA) in the Congo when he was taking out a bad guy who carried multiple pistols everywhere. He had three or four on him all the time. They used this same technique, setting him up with a beautiful woman who put a mickey in his drink to give them time to go to his room and build a hand bomb in the pistol grip.

The only issues Avi has to consider are Roger's gun type and the size of the explosion. Roger likely has a .38, a .45, or possibly a .357. All three have the same stock assembly, so Avi knows he has room in the handle for his device. It is difficult to determine how large a charge it will take and how it will react once it has been placed in the open space in the handle though, so he brings two sizes with him. He is careful as he walks through the hotel with the detonator in one side pocket and the C4 in the other. He has to keep the detonator dry. Without a detonator, the C4 is just like clay, not a bomb. Combined, however, anything can happen and usually does. Avi has brought a small roll of screwdrivers, pliers, and tweezers to do his handiwork on Roger's gun.

Avi is a master with locks and hotel doors are easy prey. He has several universal keys to unlock most hotel doors on a card security network. He has a swipe on his phone which will renew the signal to his card right from the hallway. He only needs someone to use a key nearby to give him the digital footprint of the hotel code. He can break the room code once he has the hotel code. The pesky part of breaking into a hotel room is the security latch some guests put on from inside the room before retiring.

Avi gets on the elevator with a couple and gets off at their floor. He follows them down the hallway and keeps going when they reach their room. He turns his phone toward their lock as they place their key in it and gets the digital footprint of the key. He moves to a door as if to enter it, waits until they go into their room, and then walks back to the elevator to go to Roger's floor. As he approaches Roger's door, he takes a plastic "do not disturb" sign off an adjacent door. He opens Roger's door but finds Roger has remembered to flip the security latch. Avi pulls the door almost closed and uses the plastic sign to push the security latch back from the door. He is in. Roger is snoring away; the asset has done her job.

Avi goes to the drawer of Roger's bedside table. No pistol. The closet. No pistol. The desk drawer. Pay dirt. He disassembles the handle, places 2 ounces of C4 into one side, replaces that side loosely but firmly enough so it won't fall off. He removes the other side, puts in the detonator and connects it to the C4. The C4 has BB gun pellets throughout to create a small claymore mine effect once it explodes.

Now the tricky part—keeping the chemicals from heating up and going boom while he is assembling the bomb. He plugs in the micro-blasting cap and starts the timer on the device. He reassembles the handle plate, places the fully-loaded pistol back into Roger's holster, and puts the holster back into the desk drawer.

As he leaves Roger's room, Avi takes the plastic "do not disturb" sign and puts the end of the security latch into the hole of the card. He brings the door almost closed while he maneuvers the sign to bring the latch back over the metal piece. He pulls the sign out and places it on Roger's doorknob. No one the wiser.

CHAPTER FIFTY

The next day Roger Emanuel appears in the doorway of Frank Holland's office.

"Frank, I've got a former colleague, although I hesitate to call her that, coming in. We had an accidental death case out in Arizona she cannot let go of for some reason—some kind of insurance angle in her mind. Anyway, I would like for you and me to meet with her at 3pm. I don't want to see her alone. Can you do that?"

"Sure, Roger. You know it's interesting you should bring that up because we have a case right here that seems to involve an unusual insurance angle."

"Really? Well, maybe she's not such a nut case after all."

At 2:30 pm, Frank is interrogating a suspect on a robbery charge on the 2nd floor when he looks at the time. He steps into the hall and calls Roger's office.

"Emanuel here."

"Roger, I'm downstairs in an interrogation that is going to take a little while longer. Can we meet at 3:15?"

"Sure, no problem. That will give me time to eat lunch."

Roger puts his gun on his desk as it is digging into his side and calls down to reception.

"I have a 3:00 pm with Rachael Lopez. Can you hold her until 3:15?"

He takes a call from another detective. Meanwhile, his gun is ticking away silently counting down: 45:00, 44:59, 44:58 . . .

When Roger finishes his phone call, it's 3:05. He is sitting at his desk on the 10th floor, about to eat a late lunch. He looks at his sandwich and starts to take a bite when he realizes he does not have any water. He gets up to get a bottle. At 3:10, he returns to sit down at his desk and eat and . . . BOOM! A large explosion fills the squad room with glass and smoke, causing everyone to jump and duck for cover. Glass falls from the window panes, and many think it is a chain reaction of explosions down the hall. The alarm goes off, and the sprinkler system comes on throughout the building. Panic sets in and chaos ensues even though this is NYPD—after all, a bomb is a bomb. A couple of cops fire a few rounds at the explosion area in panic. No one knows what has happened. There are smoke and fumes from a gas leak that occurred after the explosion, and the smell spreads through the whole 10th floor.

The captain is nowhere to be found.

On the 10th floor, someone yells, "Everyone calm down! Do not fire your weapons! Make your way to the stairwell in an orderly fashion immediately."

The floor is being evacuated and, once people reach the stairs, there is no room for additional people to enter. The stairs are completely full of personnel evacuating from higher floors. Firefighters and the bomb squad begin to make their way up to the 10th floor. They carve a small path upward on one side of the staircase. The police touch each firefighter and bomb squad member on the sleeve or shoulder as they pass. This city has been here before. These brothers and sisters in arms go to work when most run away.

CHAPTER FIFTY-ONE

Knowing how long it takes a civilian to get through police procedures for a meeting, Rachael arrives at the NYPD at 2:45. The front desk tells her the meeting has been changed to 3:15. After filling out some paperwork, she gets a visitor's pass and then goes through x-ray. She still has a few minutes, so she stops by the women's room in the lobby and finds a line of women waiting. Give me a break! When will we learn there need to be more women's stalls than men's? While she is in the restroom, the lights go out, the sprinklers come on, and the fire alarm sounds. What the hell? Everyone in the restroom head for the exit.

The building is now on alarm status and has to be evacuated immediately. No one has any idea what or where the explosion came from, according to a woman with a radio jogging from the bathroom. All hell breaks loose as everyone tries to exit the building at once—it's total chaos.

The first report is the damage seems to be limited to the 12th floor. No, the 10th floor. No one is sure.

The New York Fire Department takes over the scene,

evacuating the building floor by floor. They narrow down the site of the explosion to the 10th floor, call up their ladder trucks, and enter the floor through the windows and up the stairs just like they did the World Trade Center on 9/11.

The word from the 10th floor is the explosion was limited to one squad room. Two people are wounded, and one is dead. They turn off the alarm, turn on one elevator, and bring up the medics. They remove the wounded and dead, and then they check the building floor by floor.

It seems as though an officer's pistol exploded right in the holster in his office. With that kind of firepower, it acted like a hand grenade. It took out his office and all the glass, and it killed him; it just so happened he was alone. The word spreads among the police it was the new guy whom only a few had gotten to know—Roger Emanuel.

Rachael stands outside with members of the NYPD. She tries Roger's number over and over, but it goes straight to voicemail each time. As a civilian, she can't get any information. Scared, she takes a cab to go find a hotel room in the city. She finds one and pays cash.

Hours later, Frank Holland finally makes it to the 10th floor to see the clean-up. He learns about Roger's piece. He turns to a detective and says, "That's really weird. I've only heard of that happening in combat, and usually when heat or some other elements are involved. Very strange."

The next day, Rachael reads a description of the accident that killed Captain Roger Emanuel in the Times. Now she's really frightened. She wonders where she can go that would be safe and what she should do.

Avi also reads the Times and finds the accident only caused one death. Where is that girl? No mention of another victim. Only one dead, so far?

He orders Eggs Benedict from room service as he looks out over Central Park from his Park Lane Hotel suite. The breakfast arrives and it's a little cold. He should have known better than to order Eggs Benedict since it's impossible for room service to get the order upstairs quickly enough. Avi has opted for the Parkview Junior Suite. It's basically a big room with a sitting area. He knew what he was in for at the Park Lane. Nice but cheap by New York City standards. The décor is basic beige and there's no minibar. He reads on about the incident.

Details are sketchy so far, but the rumor is this was an accident with a firearm in one of the offices.

Avi is pleased his efforts have produced the proper effect. He finishes his cold breakfast and begins his workout routine.

CHAPTER FIFTY-TWO

Frank has to come up with a plan. He wants to treat Roger's case as a homicide, but he's getting tons of grief, and it's an uphill battle.

Captain Barnes discusses it with Frank. "If this is a homicide, then it must be a terrorist act—and if it's a terrorist act, we've got to call in the Feds."

"So, tell me how you want to play it," says Frank.

"Look, man, it happens. It's freaky, but it happens. Pistols blow up. No way we need Homeland or the FBI inside NYPD jamming up the works! I mean, if it's a terrorist, then it's got to be an inside job. How could somebody pull this kind of thing off from the outside? Plus, we didn't really know Roger. I mean of course the guy was vetted nine ways from Tuesday before he was hired but maybe he was harboring some bad streak."

"You know you don't mean that."

"Frank, help me out here, man. You want to tell Homeland we have a terrorist working at the NYPD? Then we'd all go bat shit crazy because every guy will think the cop in the next cubicle is out to kill him. Damn, man! Even if it's true, we can't take that kind of risk! If it's terrorism, then this is a freebie. We would need confirmation, and confirmation would mean closing down the whole building for 5 to 10 days. I'm sorry, but I don't know any other way to play this. We have to agree it was on this one guy with his own piece. Frank, we didn't even know the guy. Maybe he was sloppy with his piece. Let's just see what comes back in his autopsy before we jump to any conclusions. Frank, I have to tell you, I'm in no rush to investigate this death even if it shows up bad. Poke around a little if it will make you feel better but don't push it any further until we get his results back. Okay?"

Frank goes home dejected. He knows Captain Barnes is right about the consequences but believes sweeping it under the mat sends the wrong message.

"She has gone to ground, Viktor. That's all I can tell you. She came in straight from Grand Cayman, got in at 9:30, stayed at the Hampton Inn by the airport, and somehow vanished after that," says Avi. "Your bug is not working."

"If she missed that meeting at the NYPD, she knew something—and now she really knows something. Stay on it."

"Stay on what? She's in the best hiding ground in the world, surrounded by 8 million people who don't know her and don't care to. I don't know where the phone signal is—she must have cut it off. She must be on to us. I'll give it 10 more days at $10,000 a day. Send the money now. Goodbye."

Avi hangs up.

CHAPTER FIFTY-THREE

Rachael is now fully aware she is in danger. Someone killed Roger, and she would be dead as well if she had made the meeting. Someone must have known well in advance to set something like this up. But how? How does someone pull something like this off? Is she just paranoid and this was a coincidence? She takes a look at her phone. It was locked when she picked it up. She forgot to plug it in yesterday and the battery is dead. She plugs it in the charger.

Rachael is holed up in her hotel room trying to develop a plan that will, first, not get her killed and, second, bring in the bad guys. It seems too big. I wonder if Roger told anyone about our meeting? He must have since I had a visitor's badge waiting for me. She turns her phone on but it does not have enough of a charge to make a call. She turns it back off and picks up the room phone to make her call to the New York Police Department.

The NYPD receptionist asks, "Who's taking calls for . . ."

"For who, Grace?" Frank asks.

"For Roger Emanuel, the new guy who . . ."

"Who is it?"

"It's Rachael Lopez. She said they had a meeting scheduled."

"Let me have it!" Frank picks up the phone. "This is Detective Holland."

"Detective Holland, Rachael Lopez. I think Roger may have been murdered by the same people I was planning to talk with him about."

"I'm listening."

"How do I know I can trust you?"

"Same here, lady? Maybe you did it."

"Okay, you're all I've got. I have to take a chance on you."

"What do you mean?"

"I'll tell you at Starbucks near St. Patrick's Cathedral on 5th in 15 minutes. How will I know you?"

"I'm 6'2", 225 pounds, African American, and will be wearing a blue sports coat. And you?"

"I'm pretty easy to notice. You'll figure it out when you get there."

Frank hangs up the phone and heads out to Starbucks. Fifteen minutes later, he enters the Starbucks and spots an incredible looking Latin woman who looks right at him for about 15 seconds. He walks over and sits down with her. "You were right," he says. "I figured it out."

"It has been a blessing and a curse to look this way," says Rachael.

"It does make it hard to blend in, I guess. Okay, Rachael.

A public place, good idea. What do you have?"

"For the past four weeks, I have been working for a hedge fund belonging to a man named Viktor Ludvidz in the Caymans. Turns out some recent fatal accident victims had policies that were owned by Ludvidz's Diversified Financial Services."

"How many?"

"I don't know. I got fired before I could get more than two."

"But you got two?"

"Yes, two recent victims of accidental deaths I knew about had closed files."

"Wait. Is that all you have? An offshore insurance company with two closed files?"

"Well, yeah. That and a dead guy whose piece blew up at the time of our planned meeting in your office building."

"Well, you do have that on your side as evidence. I wanted to open a homicide case, but my boss explained to me why it had to be an accident whether I believe it to be or not. Had you been killed as well, I might have had something to work with."

"Sorry to disappoint you."

"Don't worry. If you had been killed, we'd both be dead. Roger had asked me to be at your meeting. But Rachael, I just don't know how to move forward on this. We don't have enough information. Everyone will think we're crazy. We need more to go on."

"I'm going back to my hotel where I'm registered under an assumed name I'm not telling you. If I'm still alive, I'll call you in two days."

"Two days! Listen, Rachael, if you're right about this, we may not have two minutes. We have to think of a plan and move fast."

"I need to check something out first, Frank. Give me your cell number."

CHAPTER FIFTY-FOUR

The next day, Frank calls Joe Stein, Adam Sodkoff's attorney.

"Joe, thank you for taking my call. I have just one more question about Adam. The insurance policy that was sold, who bought it? "

"Frank, it's interesting you would ask me that because I have been thinking about all of this—I mean, about Adam's insurance and his death—and I've done a little digging myself. The policy was sold to Wisconsin Viatical Settlements Group. They, in turn, sold the pool of policies containing Adam's."

"Well, who bought the pool?"

"A company called Diversified Financial Services.

Rachael's dot shows up on Avi's laptop in his hotel room. Got you. Rachael's phone is moving by the Rainbow Room, between 49th and 50th. Avi runs downstairs, hops on his rental bicycle, and dashes down the bike lane on 5th Avenue toward 49th to try and pick up the trail. He has linked his phone to his laptop map. The phone dot is moving toward

6th Avenue. Avi bikes back up 49th to 6th and spots someone who fits the description and photo. He follows her to the Courtyard Marriot Hotel. He watches her enter the hotel, and then he stops at a crosswalk just above the hotel. He gets off his bike and steps into the paved front area of an office building. He sits and waits to make sure Rachael wasn't just checking for a tail by ducking into the hotel for a minute. He waits 10 minutes but there's no movement. She is staying put. He hops back on his bike and returns to the Park Lane Hotel.

Rachael is completely spooked by Roger's death. As a detective, she is having a hard time figuring out how they could pull off something like this. Clearly, she is in over her head. The only common link between her and Roger was her cell phone. She looks at her phone. It has to be bugged somehow. Destroying it or cutting it off will give the bad guys an edge. They'll know she is onto them. What is the best play?

Rachael knows she does not have enough evidence to convict anyone. She needs to find additional proof of Viktor's activities. She decides the only option she has is to call John.

She leaves her phone in the room charging and goes downstairs. Out the front door of the hotel, she walks to a nearby phone store and purchases a prepaid cellular phone.

She calls John.

"John here."

"It's Rachael."

"Rachael, what happened to you? Where are you? Are you okay?"

"John, I've probably put you in danger by calling you. I'm sorry. Please go to a pay phone and call 212-555-6400."

She hangs up and John calls the number from his cell. Rachael answers the burner phone.

"Outback Steakhouse. How may I help you?"

"Uh, I'm sorry. I think I . . ."

"John, it's me.

"Outback Steak House? Do you work there? What's going on? . . . Rachael, there's only one pay phone left in Cayman and it's at the airport. I'm on my cell."

"John, you probably just killed us both," says Rachael.

"What do you mean? You're talking crazy. I can't follow you. What happened between you and Viktor that caused him to fire you? He seemed really upset after you left, and he had a talk with me about loyalty."

"I'll explain everything to you, but we can't talk on your cell phone. Go to the airport and call me back from the payphone. Please, John. This is a matter of life or death."

"Okay Rachael, I'll do it."

They hang up again. About 20 minutes later, the phone rings.

"Ok, I'm here at the airport on the pay phone. Now, what is this all this about?"

"John, you think you are confirming deaths, but Viktor is using your program to find out who is in the insurance pools and is having someone kill them. That's why he's so good at picking the pools—he's creating the deaths. Your program is helping Viktor kill people to collect on their life insurance."

"That's not possible; I don't believe it."

"Think about it. How is he so good at picking pools? How do deaths occur so often in the pools? You're in danger by having this information."

"Rachael, that's just too far-fetched for me to believe. Why would he do that? He's already rich and powerful."

"For the money—for the returns on the fund. You know how he treats you. He needs this information and your program more than anything. John, listen, I need some definitive proof this is going on."

"And you want me to go into the office and build a case for you based on your crazy ideas? Rachael, it doesn't work that way in my world. Viktor just would not be mixed up in anything like this. Now I know why he fired you."

"You have to believe me, John. Look at the evidence— look at the people who are dying at least. Pick someone who has a big policy and see if they have just been killed. He's swinging for the fence. It's an easy trail for you to follow. These policies are for millions of dollars. John, you are not like Viktor; you are a decent and honest, hard-working man. But if I'm right about this, he will drag you down with him, and I will not stop until I am dead or Viktor has been caught."

"Rachael, I have to go."

John hangs up the phone in a daze. Part of him knows she is right. He has seen the big policies being paid out and knows about the DelGotto settlement, but he cannot admit it to himself. John decides to check it out on his own just to prove her wrong.

After the call to John, Rachael is scared, but something finally clicks. She now knows exactly what she's up against—these guys are professional assassins! They are calculated killers and are killing people relentlessly.

She takes a walk to regain her composure. She calls Frank Holland on her burner phone.

"I may have screwed up; I called John Menuso at Diversified Financial Services."

"You what?" asks Frank.

"I don't think he knows anything, but I'm sure his phone is tapped. He's Viktor's right hand at Diversified and lives in Viktor's mansion. I tried to turn him and get him to get me the information we need to convict Viktor."

"Did he give you anything?"

"Not yet."

"Well, I have something for you. The guy whose death I looked into on Long Island was in the pool sold to Diversified Financial Services. I think with Diversified owning the policy I ran down, your two names, and now Roger's death, we have enough to go to the FBI."

"I hope so. I know everything we have is still circumstantial but hopefully, they will think we have enough for someone to follow up on."

"I'm on it. Want me to call you back on this phone?' "

"Yes, I think my other phone is hacked. I'm still going to need to use it so they think I don't know."

"I don't mean to be a wet blanket. I know the Roger

Emanuel thing must have been a hit, but the phone tap? The other murders? My Long Island guy? I mean, we really don't have anything to tie it all together. Are you sure they would go to the trouble to hack your phone?"

"No. I don't know, but I can't think of any other way they could have known about Roger."

"I'm just saying, maybe they didn't know about Roger. Maybe Roger was an accident or something unrelated."

"Frank, I need to run. Get back to me when you arrange a meeting."

They hang up.

Frank calls a friend at the Bureau.

"Hey, Bill, it's Frank Holland. I need a meeting on a possible global insurance murder case, and it needs to be up the chain."

"Give me some more, Frank. I can't just stick my neck out on some wild goose chase."

"It appears some hedge fund guy is having life insurance policyholders killed after he buys their policies so he can make a buck. So far, we've connected several cases, but I think I need to bring in a witness to this and go over it."

"Okay, I think I can get someone to meet with you on it. How solid is it, Frank?"

"Not really sure. The pieces fit together perfectly but so far it's circumstantial."

CHAPTER FIFTY-FIVE

Rachael's dot has not moved in four hours so Avi stakes out the Courtyard. No bicycle this time. It's difficult to run a stakeout in New York since you can't just stand in front of a building for hours at a time. Everybody is moving, walking somewhere. Almost the only way to stand out is to stay still. There are a few benches on the sidewalks, but most are by the park. Checking into the hotel is the best way.

Avi uses his Ralph Hartman credit card and checks in. He sits in the lobby reading the paper for two hours. No sign of Rachael. Her dot is showing she is here, or at least her phone is here—that's the problem with only having one bug. Avi would have preferred to have her clothing or a handbag bugged as well. Once people figure out they're bugged, finding one bug is usually enough to make to believe they have solved the problem. He goes up to his room on the 8th floor, a height Avi can escape from if required. Rachael appears to be on the 22nd floor.

She uses her cell despite suspecting it is bugged in order to flush out the killer.

"Detective Holland," Frank answers.

"Frank, it's Rachael."

"Rachael, good, I have a meeting set up for you and me with the FBI."

"Where and when?"

"The Federal Building downtown off-Broadway—tomorrow at 10:00 am."

Avi now knows the FBI is meeting with Rachael. He could walk away and let this fall on Viktor, but since his own reputation is at stake, he will finish the job. The situation with Viktor is becoming untenable. The stakes are even higher now—he may have to kill the Holland guy as well as a few agents in the process of cleaning this up, although Rachael is still the most important. Avi wrestles with this entire affair.

This will require a more elaborate plan. A drive-by shooting of two cops at the Federal building will drop a net on the whole city. Avi does not see this as an option. It would be effective, but not elegant.

Frank has a car drop him at the Federal Building just off Broadway in downtown Manhattan. He goes inside the building and waits for Rachael to arrive. Soon, she appears and they both get guest passes, x-rayed and photographed. They take the elevator to the 48th floor. The receptionist looks over her glasses at Frank.

"Detective Holland and Ms. Lopez, here to see Special Agent McKinley," says Frank.

"One moment, please."

In a few minutes, a young man comes out to meet them.

"Detective Holland, Ms. Lopez, I'm Agent Todd. Please follow me."

They walk down the corridor to a conference room which looks out onto the Brooklyn Bridge over the East River and NYPD downtown headquarters. A few minutes pass and Agent McKinley enters the conference room. Introductions are made.

"What can we do for you?" asks McKinley.

"Special Agent McKinley, what we have to tell you may sound unbelievable, and until two days ago I would have felt the same way, but I really believe events have transpired that need your attention."

Agent McKinley remains silent.

"A few weeks ago, a guy I ride bikes with, Adam Sodkoff—a CEO in the city—died of a heart attack, but there were traces of Rohypnol in his bloodstream. I thought it was suspicious he had a date rape drug in his system, but I didn't have enough to follow up on until I heard from Rachael. Her old boss was Roger Emanuel—my new boss. He was killed at our office two days ago in what I believe was a murder."

"I know about this. His piece went off or something like that, right?" asks McKinley.

"That's right," says Frank.

"Okay, but this isn't making any sense to me yet, Frank. How are these two deaths related?"

"Rachael," says Frank.

"Agent McKinley, I had an accidental death case at my

old precinct in Arizona that led me to the Cayman Islands to work for a guy named Viktor Ludvidz. He is buying pools of life insurance policies and having the insured people killed so he can collect the death benefits for his hedge fund. Diversified Financial Services. His firm is collecting insurance policies by purchasing them in life pools. They have a computer guy who has figured out how to dissect the pools, and Viktor has the insured murdered so he can make money for his fund."

"Wow, that's some story. You both have done some heavy lifting to pull this together. What evidence do you have that this is taking place?"

"We have the deaths of four people, three of which were in Diversified Financials portfolio of insureds, and one dead cop who was supposed to meet with me to discuss this," says Rachael.

"But tell me, have any of these cases been reopened?" asks McKinley.

"No. They're all still closed."

"Then you don't have a crime so far as I can see, just a strange coincidence."

"Agent McKinley, are you serious? Roger and I worked together in Arizona. I had a meeting scheduled with him to discuss this case at the exact time his piece went off!" says Rachael. "After all this, you're telling me the FBI does not see enough evidence here to at least follow-up?"

"Ms. Lopez, we get cases every day, and most of them have a real crime associated with them. Someone is actually killed—a coroner tells us a person has been killed. We follow up on murders, not on suspicion of murders in closed cases. I'm sorry, but I need some hard evidence a crime has been committed before I can put any resources on this. What did you find while you were working for the Ludvidz character?"

"I found these closed files meaning those deaths were in his pools."

"Closed files on all these people? They were all in his closed files?"

"I only found two. I got caught and he fired me."

"How many lives in one of these pools?"

"I couldn't tell."

"I suspect there are more than two lives in each pool, wouldn't you say? Let's just say its 100. 2% seems reasonable, even likely."

"Well, I also know the guy who broke the code on the pools to allow Viktor to see into them and kill off the highest valued policies."

"You know these were the highest valued policies in the pools?"

"Not for sure."

"Even the Emanuel case, while strangely unlikely, has been closed as an accident," states McKinley. "I'm sorry, but the FBI will not be able to help you unless you bring us some hard evidence or a few murders in the same pool that are not accidents."

McKinley stands, indicating the meeting is over. McKinley shakes hands with Frank and turns to Rachael, who is leaving the room without a goodbye. She stands in the hall outside the conference room steaming. McKinley leaves the room while Frank waits for the young agent to escort them out of the office.

In the elevator, Rachael speaks, "I just don't believe that guy. I mean, whose side is he on? How dumb do you have to be to not believe we have something here that needs to be investigated?"

"Rachael, I have to admit, it does sound far-fetched, but I definitely agree with you we are looking at murders. I'm sure if we have more data, it will point to the obvious."

A cab pulls up in front of them, and Frank opens the door for Rachael.

"Let's split up and go back to your hotel. Have the cab let you out about six blocks away from the hotel at 49th and 6th. I'll be there to follow and see if you're being tailed. Call me when you get to your room. I'll wait across the street until I hear from you."

"Fine."

Rachael does what he told her and calls him from her room. "I'm here." Frank walks over the two blocks and goes to her room.

"Looks like you were clean—I didn't see a tail. Either they have you tagged with a bug and do not need to follow you . . . or no one cares, and this is all just a wild goose chase."

"Frank, these people are for real. Looks like they have developed the perfect crime. I guess the only way we can prove these crimes are real is to get some incriminating evidence from John . . . that or maybe if they actually try to kill me—I guess that's what we need. I think I'll try to flush them out. I'm tired of this cat and mouse shit! I need a gun, and I need to stir the pot some more."

"Rachael, let me remind you that if you're right about this, we're likely dealing with professional hit men."

"Ok, theory one is they have a bug on me. If so, it must be my phone. I'm going to keep using my phone. If they do care about me, we'll find out soon enough. Now, how do I get a gun?"

"There are a couple of problems with that. One, it requires a special permit you won't be able to get because no one believes our theory. Two, it's illegal to conceal and carry once you get a permit, so the permit is useless anyway."

"Fine, I'll go it without a gun if I have to. Let's set up a trap."

"I don't think that's the way to go. Like I said, these people are professionals. We will likely end up on the wrong end of the gun ourselves." He walks to the window where Rachael has closed the blinds. He is silent for a minute before he speaks again.

"I have a few guys who may be willing to listen to me on this. Let me make a few inquiries, and let's follow up together later this evening or tomorrow. You could probably use some rest."

"I'm not getting any rest while this deal is still going on."

"These guys are too smart to show their hand by coming after you. We can't prove anything. All they have to do is wait us out. I'll call you in three hours, and we'll talk about it some more. Don't poke anyone in the eye while I'm gone to stir up the pot, please."

"I can't promise anything, Frank, but I'll try."

CHAPTER FIFTY-SIX

Viktor uses cameras all over his operations. Using a remote, he can turn off any camera whenever it is convenient for him; after all, he does not want to film himself anywhere. He learned the hard way from Bosnia. He goes to the film library on his personal laptop and pulls all of his "John M" footage. The videos show John in compromising positions with several very young-looking girls. Viktor transfers the footage to his phone for viewing later that evening. He calls John.

"John, I would like to have dinner with you tonight. Let's have something prepared out at the house, and I will join you around 7:30. Does that work for you?"

"Sure, Viktor, of course. That would be very nice. I'm glad we can have some time together because I wanted to ask you about . . ."

"That's great, John," Viktor interrupts. "I'll see you at 7:30."

John paces around the house and by 7:00 pm, his nerves finally get the best of him and he has a double Baker's while waiting for Viktor. Finally, at around 7:45, John hears the Ferrari growl up the driveway. Viktor hops up the steps and acknowledges the houseman.

"Clifford, once dinner is served, I need some private time with John, so make yourself scarce."

Clifford acknowledges Viktor's request with a half bow. Viktor strolls into the house like he does not have a care in the world.

"John." He reaches out with both hands to shake John's hand.

"Viktor, I'm glad to see you. Thanks for having dinner with me tonight."

"Think nothing of it."

Clifford hands Viktor a Vespa Martini, the kind James Bond drinks, in a very chilled glass.

"Thank you, Clifford."

"When would you like dinner served, sir?" Clifford asks Viktor. Viktor downs the martini.

"Let's eat soon. I'm starved. How about you, John?"

"Sure, of course."

"And, Clifford, set the table by the pool for dinner," Viktor commands.

"Certainly, sir," Clifford says as he steps over to a cart and pours another Vespa into a chilled glass and hands it to Viktor. He knows Viktor's first martini disappears rather quickly.

"Ah, right on time."

"So, John, have you heard from Rachael?" Viktor asks, knowing the answer.

"Yes, she called me last night. It was very strange though. She had me call her at a different number and then said I had killed us both by using my cell. I don't know what she meant by that."

"That's really strange. Sounds like she might be crazy. Listen, I have a special project for you. I need you to go to New York. But first, let me show you something."

Viktor hands John his phone and presses the play button on the video he downloaded from his office.

"Viktor, what is this?"

"John, this is for your own benefit."

John looks at the videos of himself with some of Viktor's young Eastern European friends, both in the Caymans and in Europe. John turns pale and sits down as he hands Viktor back the phone. He holds his sides and rocks back and forth.

"None of these girls is over 17, my friend."

John continues to rock back and forth silently.

"Come now, John. Don't worry. I did this because you are my friend, and I need you to be in this with me. I have taken care of you and I will continue to. This is just so I don't have to kill you."

John stops rocking and looks at Viktor.

"I really like you John, and now I can trust you as well. This Rachael thing has gotten out of hand. I need your help addressing this issue. Just go to her and offer to help her, and I will take it from there."

John sits completely still, staring at the pool.

"I don't understand."

"John, you are so naive. Business is full speed ahead all

the time. Our returns must be excellent at all costs. Sometimes, we have to break some eggs. The code source you broke has allowed us to elevate our returns to another level. With this strategy, we can be one of the biggest hedge funds in the world. No one can compete with this type of exclusivity. You're a part of something great here."

"So you're using my data to kill policy insureds?"

"John, we are only expediting the payout on their policies by a very short time. All of these people were going to die sometime anyway. Your program just allows us to take advantage of the most opportune times for their deaths, that's all. This is just the beginning of a very large opportunity for us both, partner."

John cannot believe what he is hearing. He knows Rachel was right.

"John, you're upset."

As if on cue, and it was on cue, Elmba, an attractive associate of Viktor's, and two of her friends saunter out to the pool and move to embrace John.

"John, just relax here by the pool with me and my friends for a while. Eat something. You need to have some food in you tomorrow when you fly to New York. You can take my plane and take Elmba. She needs a trip away as well."

Elmba tries to get John interested in her, but even in his slightly intoxicated state, he moves away from her.

"John, don't be that way. It's not her fault you don't live in the real world with the rest of us. Come on, I need you to step up here and be a team player."

Viktor watches closely for John's reaction to the truth.

"John, where are you on this? I need to know."

John walks over to the pool bar and picks up a Baker's bottle and turns it up for about two seconds.

"All right, my man," says Viktor as John comes back over and begins kissing Elmba.

CHAPTER FIFTY-SEVEN

Avi may have made his first mistake by underestimating the FBI investigation of Ralph Hartman. The FBI database has vastly improved since 9/11, especially in New York.

"Hey, Sam. We have a hit on an Arizona suspect in New York City—Hartman, Ralph. Any updates?"

"Let me check . . . I don't see anything for the last eight weeks on Hartman," says Agent Daniels. "Looks mild-mannered enough—a few credit card charges. I wonder what they want this guy for? . . . Looks like he just checked into the Courtyard Marriott."

"I'll send this info to the Arizona field agents to follow up."

In Arizona, FBI Agent McGhee is talking to Cavuto, "Hey, they got a hit on Ralph Hartman in New York. He was dark for eight weeks."

"Any word on Lloyd?" asks Cavuto.

"Nothing. Has not shown for work in weeks, and no credit card charges in Mexico since he got down there. I doubt he has that kind of cash—you think Hartman got to him?"

"Probably. Lloyd did hang him out," says Cavuto.

"Let's have Hartman picked up as a murder suspect and see where it leads. Reach back out to Agent Daniels in New York," says McGhee.

Cavuto calls Daniels' number, and he answers on the first ring.

"Special Agent Daniels."

"Daniels, it's Agent Cavuto from Tucson."

"Yes. What can I do for you? I got an email from your group about one of my BOLOs."

"You may have my man Hartman in your fair city. Someone used his credit card to check into the Courtyard Marriott; that's all I can confirm. If he's around, we'd like you to pick him up on a suspicion of a murder charge."

"Do you have a description?" asks Daniels.

"6 ft, 180 pounds, brown hair."

"That really narrows it down for me—that describes half the agents in my building!"

"I know it's not much to go on, but you guys know how to roust a guy in a hotel without him knowing you are there," replies Cavuto.

"What else can you tell me about Hartman?"

"We've actually never seen the guy, but we think he killed an operative of ours here in Tucson."

Cavuto raises his eyebrows at McGhee who nods his head.

"I'm definitely going to need some paperwork on this,"

says Daniels. "The other side of the Patriot Act is starting to bite us in the ass here for bouncing too many people who don't need to be bounced. You get me?"

"I do, I do. It's on the way now," answers Cavuto.

"I can't promise you guys anything on this. I mean a suspicion of murder. That's pretty weak for an across the country grab, man. I'll send a couple of guys over to the hotel, have a chat with him there and if he is suspicious or resists, I'll bring him in for questioning. But you need to have something pretty strong so I can hold him for you longer than a few hours."

"Understood. Thanks, Daniels."

They hang up.

McGhee speaks to Cavuto, "You know, we really don't have anything on the guy. For all we know, he's some person who rents cable trucks and Lloyd has just gone dark. Hartman didn't even show for his last rental van, although he did leave the five grand for Lloyd. I'm just not sure we want to stick our necks out on this guy."

"You know something, McGhee? I think you're right. I'm going to call the guy back and tell them to leave him out there and we'll reach back out when we have a little more to go on."

"Sounds like a good plan. If he really is our guy and he's in New York, he's probably not going anywhere. He probably does not even know we have him marked. He will keep until we have more."

CHAPTER FIFTY-EIGHT

Rachael tosses and turns but cannot sleep. It's 3 am. She calls John.

"John, it's Rachael."

"Oh, hi, Rachael. Are you okay?"

"Yes, I'm fine," she answers. "John, go and buy a one-use cell and call . . ."

"Rachael, it's 3 am here, and I'm not going anywhere. You don't need to worry, though. Everything is just fine. In fact, I'm going to be in New York tomorrow. Can we get together?"

Rachael hesitates then says, "Sure, John, is this number good to call you on?"

"Yes, Rachael, this number is fine."

"Okay, how about dinner tomorrow? Call me when you get here."

"Okay sure. Goodbye, Rachael."

Rachael gives Frank a few hours to sleep and then calls to tell him about her conversation with John.

"Frank, he sounded comatose."

"It was 3 am and he's flying to New York today. Maybe he was just sleeping."

"Okay, maybe. But we have to figure out how to bring the FBI in on this."

"Unfortunately, me and a couple of guys are all we have. I'm not sure how to play it."

"Well, I've been chasing down this group of bad guys for months, and I'm seeing this all the way through. If I go down, at least you'll have something to take to the FBI. Anyway, I'm going to suggest we meet at the Oak Room, and I doubt he'll try anything there. Can you wire me up for this meet and be my back-up?"

Frank sits silently for a moment.

"Frank, talk to me."

"Ok, we'll wire you, and I'll put two plainclothes guys in the Oak Room—I can't let you go in there alone. I'll be across the street listening from a squad car just in case one of the hitters has been trailing you and saw us together. Hitters . . . shit, Rachael, just saying that makes me want to take you into custody, but you'll just do this alone if I don't help you."

"You got that right. I want this to end—one way or another."

CHAPTER FIFTY-NINE

"He's on the way to New York City," Viktor tells Avi over his cell phone.

"I will mark him when he lands," replies Avi.

"You should be able to track him with all the devices I've planted," says Viktor.

Avi hangs up with Viktor and puts his phone on vibrate to let him know when he has secured John's beacon signal. Viktor has three bugs on John—in his shoes, clothes, and phone. That is how Avi likes it: three bugs.

Avi is sitting in the lobby reading a newspaper, waiting for John's plane to land so he can pick up his signal when he sees two agents walk into the Courtyard Marriot Hotel. They stand out from everyone else by their attire—cheap jackets and slacks made of synthetic material and comfortable shoes—and the bulges on one side of their jackets and one pants leg. Detectives usually carry a backup piece in their pants leg. Oh, of course, Ralph Hartman. Avi curses himself for using that card—a rare slip-up. No matter, Ralph will not be returning to the Courtyard anytime soon.

Avi notices the agents move to a table. An African American man, nice looking and almost certainly a cop, joins the agents. They are cordial like they know each other. They sit together and talk. Avi decides they are not here for Ralph but are there to help with Rachael. They are setting something up. Avi moves closer by going to the guest coffee pot and pouring himself a cup so he can detail the two agents and the other taller man. He has them marked; he knows their features, but when they see him again, they will not know him.

Viktor's Gulfstream 5 arrives at Teterboro Airport carrying only John at 12 pm. Elmba did not make the trip after all. Viktor, in a rare acquiescence, allowed it. A car meets John to take him to the Pierre.

Avi picks up the signal and tracks John. No deviations. Good boy, John.

He arrives at the Pierre around 12:30 and calls Rachael.

"Hi Rachael, I'm here. Shall we have dinner?"

"John, are you okay? I don't like this, you showing up in New York City to meet with me after I've been fired. You and I both know something's up."

"Listen to me, Rachael. Everything's fine. I just happen to be here, but it's important we meet. You will feel better after—I promise."

"Okay, I hope we're close enough that I can trust you."

"You know you can. I'm at the Pierre."

"I'll meet you at the Oak Room at the Plaza at 6:30."

Avi listens to the conversation.

CHAPTER SIXTY

Knowing he has six hours before the operation at the Oak Room, Avi heads over to case the place dressed as a successful business executive in a designer suit, shoes, shirt, and tie to have a Wall Street type of drink—just your average-looking Manhattan millionaire having an early afternoon cocktail. He enters through the side door, notices steps down to the men's room, and goes there first. He scans the stalls and the shoeshine station just down the hall. He sees a locked storage cabinet in the men's room with a Carlyle maintenance emblem on it. He makes a mental note to bring his Carlyle key when he returns.

He heads back up to the Oak Room for his businessman's drink. He walks in, looks left into the restaurant, and is greeted by a hostess.

"Good afternoon, sir. How many for lunch today?"

He looks at her for a moment and says, "Oh, sorry, I'm just here for a drink. I'll go to the bar."

"Very well, sir."

Avi looks around the restaurant and then heads over to

the bar. He takes a seat at the bar. To his left near the door is where the wait staff goes to order drinks for their table guests in the restaurant. He scopes out the bar—tables by the windows with a view of the street and more seating by the wall away from the windows. He notes the bar has a couple of pieces of fixed furniture that could provide places to hide.

"Good afternoon, sir." The friendly, but not too friendly, bartender says to Avi.

"Hi." Avi uses his Midwestern accent. It's so neutral he could be a radio DJ. "I'd like a cosmopolitan martini, Grey Goose, please."

"Right away, sir." The bartender loves these rich Wall Street guys drinking at noon. He figures he'll order two or three of these high-end cocktails, be drunk by 4 o'clock, and leave a big tip before he rolls out to some fancy dinner.

Avi spills his first Cosmo onto the rug near his seat while the bartender is not looking. A few minutes later, the bartender comes back and smiles when he sees Avi's glass is empty.

"Sir, would you like another?"

"Yes, thank you. I would."

They both smile; all is going according to plan for the bartender. Avi, on the other hand, has seen enough. He has also made himself nondescript by being typical. He drinks the second martini and then tells the bartender, "Hey man, I've got to run. I need to settle up with you."

"Very well," says the bartender, slightly disappointed but also pleased to have sold $48 worth of martinis on a slow afternoon. Avi slips him $70 in cash and walks out knowing everything he needs to know about the Oak Room.

Next, he heads to a costume shop in midtown many actors use for plays in New York City. He buys makeup, some blow-up cushions, a pair of platform shoes, and other miscellaneous accessories he needs to improvise his next persona. He finishes at the costume shop and takes a cab to Steinway Street to buy an extra-large Kurta, an Arab shirt, in a nondescript dark color and a taqiya to wear with the rest of his outfit. He pays cash for his purchases.

Avi heads back to the Park Lane and begins his transformation into a large, Arab-looking man with a beard, thick hair under his hat, and sunglasses.

He relaxes in the room, doing one of the many things he does well—waiting. Avi gets into character standing in front of the mirror speaking to himself in an Arabic accent.

He watches John's dot. The dot begins to move from the Pierre up 5th Avenue and then right onto South Central Park toward the Plaza.

CHAPTER SIXTY-ONE

Avi makes his way to the Oak Room after giving John a 10-minute head start. He walks in the side door as before. With platform shoes and padding, he looks about 6'3" and 245 pounds. He is noticed, even though the good people of New York City try very hard not to notice. He waits while a waitress places an order with the bartender at the wait stand. When her order is filled, she turns to see a big Arab man standing behind her.

"Oh, excuse me, sir," she says. He looks at her with an angry scowl. She stares at him for a moment, a little frightened, and intentionally looks away as she moves into the restaurant.

In his best Arabic accent, Avi demands of the bartender, "You, bring me a fruit drink, now!" He speaks loud enough that the room of patrons pause their conversations and look at him.

"No problem, sir. Right away," says the bartender, giving the guy a look while rushing to fill his order.

Avi sees this is a different bartender than the one from

lunch, likely here for the evening shift, but still friendly but not too friendly. Avi has most of the room, including the bartender, a little on edge with his behavior. A minute or two passes without further commotion from Avi, and the scene returns to normal. Almost everyone here will remember a big Arab guy who was mad at the bartender. He spots the two cops from the Marriott about 25 feet away from John and Rachael who are at a table by a window. Both are perfectly positioned for a drive-by shooting, but Avi is in the bar and in character for a straight-ahead slaying—the most dangerous way to accomplish his job, but it's hard to set up a drive-by without multiple operatives. Even then, you may or may not get the shot you need to finish the job. Head-on will be much more effective.

Avi is unaware Frank is outside listening to Rachael and John's conversation. The waitress comes over to their table.

"Hi, what can I get you?"

"I'll have Baker's neat—two doubles, please," John answers.

"Two doubles?" asks the waitress.

"Yes, 5 ounces in one glass is fine if you don't mind, with ice."

"And for you, miss?"

"I'm fine for right now, thanks," replies Rachael.

"Suit yourself," says the waitress, slightly annoyed she only has one drinker at a two-person table.

"I'm glad to see you," says John.

"You too, John. I know Viktor is into some stuff, and you're probably as much a victim of this as I am. What are we going to do?"

"All I know is Viktor wanted me to meet with you and tell you he has put all of this behind him—he says there are no hard feelings on his end."

"That's easy for him to say but I can't let this go. I'm a cop, John."

The waitress interrupts the conversation. "Here you go—a tall glass of Baker's with ice and a glass of water."

"Thank you," says John. The waitress moves to wait on others.

John continues, "Rachael, Viktor and I both know that. Viktor knew from the very beginning. That's why he hired you. We know you shot another cop, too. He just sees you as another person he will need to pay off. That's the world he comes from."

"Let me get this straight—you think you're here to tell me Viktor is putting me on the payroll as an extortionist and plans to pay me to keep quiet about what I know?" Rachael asks.

"That is how he sees it, Rachael."

"Holy shit, John, now I have heard it all! You came here to negotiate a settlement? John, do you actually believe that?"

"No, not really, but it was the only option I had to get to see you face to face, so I went along with it. Viktor has me where he wants me. He has me all the way; I have no way out with him now except one. I can't believe I was so taken in."

John reaches out for Rachael's hand and shows her a small object. "Take this and get out of here." He hands her a flash drive. "It has what you need to do your job if you're still a cop."

"John, turn states evidence and let the police protect you."

"They cannot protect me from Viktor or protect me from me. I did this to myself, Rachael. I'm done here."

Rachael takes the flash drive from John's palm. "You're a good man," she says and leans across the table to kiss him on the cheek.

Avi sees Rachael move toward John. He suddenly screams at the bartender, "There is alcohol in my drink, you infidel!"

Avi pulls his gun and shoots right into one of the seated cops. He then turns and shoots twice, hitting Rachael with both shots. The momentum of the slugs knocks her back under the table by the window, and her body slides down onto the floor. John sits silently, not moving at all, with his eyes closed. Avi believes he has finished the job on Rachael. She is not moving, and blood is gathering under her.

Everyone in the bar seems to be held in suspended animation. No one moves. A few people begin to rush toward the side door away from the shooter and many follow. Finally, everyone left in the room scrambles.

Avi moves into the room and takes aim at John. He assassinates him from about 10 feet with two quick shots, leaving John's lifeless body leaning over the table. Avi takes cover behind one of the fixed tables in the middle of the bar. People are running in every direction, so it is difficult for the second officer to get off a shot without hitting a patron.

Finally, he pulls the trigger in Avi's direction. Avi feels the shot go by his head and drops back to the side of the bar to take cover and fire another shot at the officer. Using the bar as cover, Avi shoots a patron who is in the path of the police officer to give him a clear line of fire. He fires a round into the police officer who goes down and stops firing. Avi debates walking over to Rachael but it would blow his cover to do so. She is not moving.

From the subway entrance across South Central Park Street, Frank hears the shots and commotion coming from the Oak Room. He sprints straight toward it, running across South Central Park Street. Seeing broken glass on the sidewalk under a window, Frank leaves his feet and dives right through the broken window into the Oak Room. Avi sees Frank, and in an instant recognizes him as the handsome man meeting the two cops at the Marriott. Avi takes aim as Frank slides onto the table. Avi shoots from beside the bar, using the bar to steady his hand, and hits Frank in the left arm. Frank rolls over onto the floor and crawls quickly under one of the fixed oak tables in the middle of the room. He tries to get off a shot without killing any of the panicked people racing out of the room.

Avi rushes out the side door. He goes down the stairs and into the restroom, where he opens the storage closet with his Carlyle key. He takes off his Arab suit, revealing a Carlyle maintenance uniform underneath. He dumps part of his disguise into the locker, checks to see no one is in the restroom and flushes the smaller suit pieces down the toilet.

He disables and disassembles his gun and drops a few of those pieces into the toilet as well. He pulls off the beard and wipes off as much makeup as he can, and pulls a baseball cap down over his face. He leaves the restroom with a red nametag that reads "Vince." Avi now looks like a skinny Mexican-looking floor cleaner with a small mustache.

He runs back into the hallway to wait for the police to rush into the Plaza. He takes the stairs two at a time and screams in the direction of the police, "He ran into Central Park! A big Arab guy."

The police, who just made it in through the crowd, turn around and head right back out toward the park.

Avi walks swiftly down a hallway that ends at another set of stairs. He climbs the stairs and comes out in the Plaza's lobby. He leaves the scene through the 5th Avenue exit. He circles back onto 58th, walking fast to the back entrance of the Park Lane. No one notices the Mexican guy in a maintenance uniform. People are flooding in and out of the Park Lane; no one knows exactly what to do. The word on the street is there is a terrorist in Central Park. Avi acts panicked like everyone else and takes the elevator up to his room. He gets off at his floor and looks around to make sure there's no one in the hall who can identify him. He waits in the hall for a few seconds before entering his room, just in case he needs to play his role as a nondescript maintenance man.

CHAPTER SIXTY-TWO

Frank gets to his feet and goes to Rachael and John. John is dead. Rachael is unconscious but breathing. In the background, Frank hears fire trucks and sees people being trampled as they try to get out of the room. He stays with Rachael. Eventually, firefighters are on the scene along with paramedics and the NYPD. They come straight to Rachael and Frank, who is bleeding himself.

Frank checks on his guys who were at the table. Both shot; both dead. Avi does not leave professional witnesses if at all possible. People are still in a panic all over the hotel, but the Oak Room is empty except for the wounded, the dead, and New York City's finest. Finally, the FBI shows up.

Frank follows Rachael's stretcher out to the ambulance.

"What hospital are you taking her to?" he asks the paramedic.

"Hold on!" says the paramedic, seeing blood on Frank's shirt. "It looks like you've been hit too. What's your name?"

"Frank . . . Officer Frank Holland."

"Officer, let's take a look at that arm . . . Jesus! This is a mess."

As the adrenalin leaves his system, Frank stumbles. The paramedic catches him and lets him down easy onto the ground beside the ambulance. Frank is finally feeling the bullet in his arm.

"Ok, big fellow. Off you go," the paramedic says as he loads Frank into the ambulance with Rachael. Then, with sirens blaring, it speeds both victims to the hospital where surgery awaits both if they are lucky.

New York City is turned upside down once again due to a large Arab man opening fire at the Oak Room. He is thought to most definitely be a terrorist.

Viktor sees the news on CNN and does not know what to think. No one can say anything other than a Middle Eastern man with a large build opened fire in the Oak Room, apparently killing several patrons. The police have killed a large Middle Eastern man in Central Park.

CHAPTER SIXTY-THREE

Frank sits beside Rachael in the ambulance.

"Hang in there, girl," Frank says to Rachael as they bounce. He knows she is out of it, but he speaks to her anyway, hoping somehow she can hear him. Frank watches as the two paramedics work to stabilize her vital signs with IV fluids. Frank can hear the heart monitor beeping in the background.

Frank asks the paramedics, "how does it look?"

The paramedics just keep working.

"Guys, I need to know something!"

"Sir, we gave you something for your arm, and we'll be arriving at the hospital shortly. I'm sure when it's time, you'll get an update from the doctors," says the paramedic in charge, and then he puts his stethoscope back on Rachael's chest to listen to her heart. Frank pulls one of the earpieces out of the man's ear.

"Listen," Frank continues, "this was not just some nut job shooting. This is an issue of national security, and she is vital to stopping what looks like mass murder here in the

US. I need to know something!"

"We're doing everything we can to stabilize her, but she looks to have been shot at least twice and has lost a lot of blood. It's touch and go."

Frank sits silently listening to the siren and the beep, beep, beep of the heart monitor.

"Hang in there, girl. You got this," Frank says again, but this time it's more of a prayer.

The ambulance arrives at the hospital and is met by two doctors and two nurses as the paramedics pull Rachael's stretcher out of the ambulance. They hand her off to the hospital team with all of the devices and fluids attached. She is rushed down the hall and straight into surgery to try and save her life. Frank stands by the ambulance and the head paramedic walks over to him.

"Well, you made it with her," Frank says to him.

"She's got a chance, man. She made it this far. Now, go and get that arm fixed, and I don't want to see you in my ambulance again, okay?"

"Thanks, man."

Frank walks toward the Emergency Department entrance under his own power with his arm in a sling. He sees a crowd gathered by the entrance and notices cameras and microphones. He walks right by the bank of reporters.

"There's Frank Holland!" one reporter yells out, and they make their way over to him. They give him a round of applause as he is placed in a wheelchair and pushed into the hospital. He gives the nurse his name, and after a brief examination, he is taken to the Operating Room.

"One bullet to the upper left arm," a nurse calls out as they take Frank into the room. A surgeon awaits him, prepped and ready.

"Let's have a look," says the surgeon. "We need to go in and take this bullet out, my friend. I don't see any bone issues on the external exam, and you do not seem to be in as much pain as you would be if there was bone involvement. You're going to take a little nap while I work on you."

"Doc, I need a local. I cannot be asleep for the next few hours. We have a situation going on in the city."

"Well, officer, someone else is going to have to pick up where you left off. I need to take care of your arm, and you are going to feel it if we do it without general."

"Look, Doc, I have to stay awake. It's a matter of life or death for others."

"Well, it's your arm and your pain. Nurse, shoot up the wound and give the officer a couple of painkillers so we can get this done. You will probably sleep a little anyway, but not for very long."

Frank reluctantly takes one painkiller since he needs to get back out to the scene as soon as he can. The surgeon goes away for a little while to let the local anesthetic and pain medicine take effect. Frank drifts off into a light stupor while the surgeon works efficiently to remove the bullet, clean and suture the wound, and check to make sure he doesn't have any other injuries. Frank has cuts and bruises everywhere from the window at the Oak Room and from the fall to the floor. Moving quickly, the doctor bandages up the wound, leaving the IV in for fluids and antibiotics, and they roll

Frank out of the OR into a recovery room. He is already beginning to wake up a little and can feel some pain. He holds his arm and winces.

"Easy, Handsome," says a nurse. "You just had surgery, and I need to look at your anesthesia protocol."

"I didn't have any anesthesia; I have to get out of here and go back to the scene," Frank says, pulling at his IV.

"Orderly!" she yells out, and a man comes over to hold Frank down in the bed while the nurse straps him down.

"Hey, wait! I have to get back to the scene! I need someone to help me!"

A doctor comes over and asks, "What's going on here team?"

"We've got a wild one, Doc. He just came out of surgery with a bullet wound," the nurse says.

"Doc, I have to get back to the scene. I told the surgeon no anesthesia so I could get back out there."

"Who are you, Superman? You just had surgery!"

"I'm Detective Frank Holland."

CHAPTER SIXTY-FOUR

"Frank Holland! I guess you are Superman—you're a national hero! You stopped the terrorist from killing everyone in the whole bar—I mean, jumping into the line of gunfire!"

"Terrorist? Doc, what are you talking about?"

"It's been all over the news. People on the scene said you jumped through a window and shot at the terrorist, and he ran out into Central Park and they got him. He was shot dead at the scene! You must have really messed up his plans when you dove into that window."

Frank lays back down on the bed, and the orderly does not try to restrain him any further. Then Frank gets out of the bed quickly, staggering a little.

"Whoa, big fella, where are you going?" asks the doctor.

Frank pushes the doctor away and regains his balance. He tries to run but ends up walking sideways around the recovery room with the nurse and orderly following behind to catch him in case he passes out. He stops, breathes in and gets his bearings, and then begins to walk out of the hospital, wheezing with fatigue. The IV pole follows behind until the needle finally falls out of his wrist. Frank stops and notices the blood dripping from his wrist. The doctor and nurse catch up with him and bandage the IV site, trying to stop the bleeding.

"I think he just checked himself out," the doctor says.

Frank gets to the front entrance of the Emergency Department.

"Frank, I wish you would stay and let us finish treating you."

An NYPD cop sees him standing outside with his arm in a sling.

"Frank," the young cop says, "what are you doing out here, man?"

"I need to get back to the crime scene."

"But you've been shot, dude."

"Kid, do you have a car?"

"Yes sir, right over there."

"Let's go! It's an order."

"No problem, man. We're gone!"

They hop in the squad car, and the young cop hits the siren and whisks Frank back to the Oak Room. Feeling drowsy, Frank dozes while the officers move the barricade at the Plaza so they can make their way to the scene. Frank rouses and steps out of the squad car. People see Frank and recognize him from his picture, which has been all over the media as "the man who stopped terrorism in its tracks." A cop on the scene sees Frank coming and pulls the tape up so he can walk under it.

"Go right in, Hero," the cop says to Frank.

Two FBI agents are listening to the bartender give his account of what happened as Frank walks up.

"Guys, it was a big Arab guy. He was impatient from the very beginning—he wanted a fruit juice—can you believe that? In the Oak Room? Complete bullshit! He knew what he was going to do. I'm just glad he was such a bad shot— he was shooting at me and shot right over my head. I am still scared shitless, guys, I'm telling you. He said I put alcohol in his drink. I mean, he stood right there and watched me make it." The bartender indicates where the man was standing.

"These fucking terrorists, man, just shooting people in the wrong place, wrong time," says one of the detectives.

"I want to work the scene with you guys," says Frank.

"Frank," says the FBI inspector, "I know you're a national hero for stopping this guy from killing everyone, but we're in charge. This is a federal matter now."

"You're damn right it's a federal matter! If I could have gotten you guys to do your job two days ago, we wouldn't be here cleaning up this scene right now! You could have stopped this!"

Frank walks off in a huff, approaching one of the NYPD detectives still there.

"Frank," says the detective, "this guy gets four or more shots off. You get off two but he wasn't hit. Funny thing, for a crazy Arab—he shoots your guys plus the woman and the other guy at that table."

"There were a lot of friendlies in here who were not hit

as well," Frank says defensively.

"Hey man, I'm not saying anything about you. You clearly saved the rest of these people from being on a gurney, but this guy looks like he came here for a reason and accomplished that reason. But the Feds want to play terrorist bad guy games so they can make a big splash out of this."

"The FBI owns the scene, Frank," Tony, an NYPD detective, says as he walks up, "but look, I found this flash drive on the floor. Do you think it's evidence? Should I hand it over to the Feds?"

"Probably not, Tony, but I'll take it and see," replies Frank.

"Yeah, probably not. Fucking Feds."

CHAPTER SIXTY-FIVE

"Who's the head FBI person here, anyway?" asks Frank. "Maybe I can get through to them."

"He's over there," Tony answers, nodding toward a man standing across the room. "I think his name is Miller."

"Thanks, Tony."

Frank walks over to the other side of the bar near the restaurant. As Frank approaches him, Miller says, "I thought you were at the hospital. Thanks for your work! You're a hero!"

"I guess. What about the victims?"

"Four KIAs here: John Menuso, according to his wallet ID. The girl and the other two guys were all shot twice. One man bled out here and the other died at the hospital from a headshot. The girl—you were at the hospital, right?"

"Yeah, she's in surgery but it doesn't look good," Frank replies.

"The guy also shot two more patrons, but they will survive; probably just happened to be in his line of fire. You never know what will set these guys off. A bad drink—

maybe the alcohol—but he didn't even kill the bartender."

Frank can't decide if he should lay it out for Miller or go back to the deputy director now he actually has something to go on. He needs to get a look at the flash drive. He regrets telling Rachael that if she were to get killed, they would have something to go on.

"Frank, you were here when all this went down, so let me tell you, I have a couple of problems with this scene," says Miller. "By my count, our terrorist gets off at least 11 rounds which actually hit people, you included; so he's carrying a 15-round clip in a nine millimeter? And he's a terrorist? He has a Glock? Who's paying for this shit? Saudi Arabia? Did you notice a round or clip extension on the pistol?"

"No."

"So, he has one gun with a 15-round clip? Not a stretch, but a fatty?"

"Yes, I didn't see a second gun, but once I hit the window, he shot me and I dove under this table. That was the last I saw of the guy, so I can't be sure he didn't have a second pistol," answers Frank.

Miller continues, "So we have a fat Arab guy, mad at the bartender, who basically assassinates Menuso, drops two slugs into your girl and two into each of the policemen in the bar, hits two civilians—one shot each—then hits you with one. We are up to 11 shots with no misses so far, from one gun, and everybody in the bar is in chaos except for this guy with a fat pistol holding 15 rounds. I've got to tell you, Frank, this guy seems like a better shot than Lee Harvey Oswald, and he killed the President in a moving car from a sixth-story window and wounded another guy with one bullet. I'm calling bullshit on the random Arab guy going nuts here."

"You're right, Inspector. This was an organized hit on Rachael. I'm just not 100% sure why, but maybe I will have more to tell you by tomorrow."

"Frank, fuck 100%, tell me something!" demands Miller.

"This guy came here to kill Rachael and John. The rest of this stuff is window dressing to distract everybody."

"Frank," says Miller, "I'm as willing to listen to a conspiracy theory as anyone, but what do you have for me to go on besides what I am seeing right here on the Oak Room floor?"

Frank starts to feel a little dizzy and almost falls down. Tony helps him stand back up and holds him steady.

"Whoa, Frank," says Tony, who then turns and yells across the bar. "Officer Daniels, I need you to take Frank home, please." Then, to Frank, Tony says, "Frank, go home and get some rest. It's an order. Better yet, get back to the hospital."

CHAPTER SIXTY-SIX

Frank leaves the scene with his arm aching in the sling and feeling pretty shaken. When he gets home, he calls his ex-wife.

"Hi," he says into the phone.

"Hi yourself, Hero, sounds like you're still alive."

"Yeah, I think so. The real hero is lying in surgery and may not make it. She has been on this thing since day one, and no one would listen to her until she got herself almost killed. She may die yet—she's not doing very well."

"Well, I saw where you jumped through a window to thwart a terrorist attempt and got yourself shot; that sounds like a hero to me."

"I guess."

"So how are you doing, Hero?"

"Actually, not so good," Frank says slowly into the phone.

"I saw the news and I was scared for you. I'm relieved to hear your voice. I always will be; I just can't help it. But it's not okay for you to call me only when you're not doing well.

I'm glad to hear from you, but I'm mad at you at the same time. I was not sure how you were doing, I mean, you were taken to the hospital after being shot! What am I to think? This is just the way it was when we were married. You didn't even call me when we were married until you started thinking about you, not me."

After Camille has her say, they are both quiet for a few moments.

"I'm sorry. I just wanted to talk to you," Frank says.

"I know that, but that's the point. I can't very well be there for you when you can't be there for me."

Frank is quiet on the line again for a moment before speaking. "You're right. I'm sorry—I mean it. I know it's not fair."

"So, you called and we have had our regular say. Now, what's up?"

"I could probably use your help. My arm is in a sling and kind of hurts."

"If you say it hurts then it must be falling off. I'm coming over, damn you."

"No, Camille, don't. It's not fair to you. I'm okay. Really. If I was really bad off, I would ask you to come over. I promise."

"Frank, you did just ask me."

"I'm sorry. I may be a national hero, but I've had a pretty rough day and just wanted to hear your voice."

"It's nice to hear yours as well. I'm sorry I got so upset. I don't know how to take care of myself around you, Frank."

"Hey, it's okay. I understand. Well, I guess I'll hang up now, Camille. Okay?"

"Okay . . . I . . . Be, uh, take care of yourself, please, Frank?"

"Okay, I will. I promise. Hey . . . thanks. Good night."

"Good night, Frank."

Frank knows it wasn't terrorists, but he can't get over the same feeling he had after 9/11.

Frank looks over at his computer and remembers the flash drive. He plugs it in and his computer opens the application. The screen comes to life with pools of life settlements owned by Diversified Financial Services. The files are listed by the names of the insured, their ages, policy amounts, and cities. Holy cow, these guys knew which was the most valuable life policy in each pool! Frank searches the pools and cross-references the names found in these pools with Google news.

Donna McCally...obituary, Tucson Arizona; Rev. James Shook...obituary, LA; Chester DelGotto...obituary, S. Cal.; Adam Sodkoff...obituary, NYC; Evan Woods...obituary, San Francisco; Max Lester Banks...obituary, Oshkosh, WI; William Presfield...obituary, Philadelphia, PA; Frederick Kin...obituary, San Jose, CA; Heiress Rolanda Reid...obituary, NYC.

Frank sees two other names in the pool of insured, Rachael Lopez and John Menuso. Diversified bought life insurance on each. Frank now has what he needs to go back to the FBI and make the case. John had to die to provide this to Rachael—Frank hopes Rachael doesn't have to die as well.

"Is she dead?"

"Viktor, I don't know," answers Avi.

"What do you mean you don't know?"

"She's at the hospital. It doesn't look like she will make it."

"But she is still alive! Still alive is alive!"

"Sorry man, you'll have to take it from here. This place is terror central. Very hot," says Avi. He hangs up. Viktor calls him right back. "Wait."

"Okay, I'll hang out here a little longer and see if she lives. It's too hot for me to try to leave anyway. But know this—this is now not my problem. The fact is, this is all your problem. You've gone too far, and I told you to back off."

"I really need your help," Viktor says. "I have provided a nice living for you, and now that I really need you, you are going to treat me this way?"

"From the first day I met you, I knew all along it was all about you," says Avi. "I should have killed you before now, but I always had a soft spot for you since you grew up in Serbia and were treated like shit like the rest of us. But you've fucked up. I'm done here, and you're done."

CHAPTER SIXTY-SEVEN

Frank calls the precinct. "I need to get back to the hospital."

"No problem, Frank. We'll send a car for you."

Frank gets into the squad car and makes a call to FBI agent McKinley on the way to the hospital.

"Agent McKinley's office," a voice answers the phone.

"This Is Frank Holland. I need to speak to Agent McKinley."

"Did you say Frank Holland?"

"Yes."

"Oh, you're a . . ."

Frank interrupts her, "Yes, I know, a national hero. That's all the more reason I must speak to Agent McKinley."

"Let me see if I can locate him. I think he is in a meeting down the hall. One moment, please."

Franks holds on the line.

"Frank," says Agent McKinley warmly, "great job at the Oak Room. If you are ever interested in big-time federal crime work, I think we can find a place on our team for a guy like you."

"Thanks, Agent McKinley . . ."

"Bob, please, Frank."

"Okay, Bob. I need two people on Rachael Lopez's room at the hospital ASAP. This thing is a long way from being over."

"Hold on, Frank. We killed the guy; I spoke with our people at the scene. This case can close."

"Close! Your guy told you about the 11 shots and 11 hits from a fat Arab guy who was mad at a bartender?!"

"Yes, freaky, huh? I guess when you have a roomful of targets it's harder to miss than to hit. Although you seemed to have missed him when you shot, Frank. He didn't appear to have any bullet holes in him at the park until after the SWAT team caught up with him. But if you tell me you hit him, I can add that to the report. He was shot up so bad that I guess it's possible you had a slug in there somewhere."

"McKinley, this conversation is going nowhere. I'm just arriving at the hospital now, but I need to come in and meet with you ASAP."

"Frank, anytime. You're a hero and part of our team as far as I'm concerned. Come by after you finish at the hospital."

They hang up. Frank gets out of the car and walks in the hospital, getting another hero's welcome from the medical staff. He walks down the corridor to the intensive care unit. In reality, Frank feels lost and is uncertain about how to proceed. He's making enemies in high places for pursuing the truth. He could tell McKinley has no interest in the truth around this. He has his case made. Frank knows he has to keep pushing for this to come out. Sweeping Roger Emanuel's murder under the rug actually provided a path for this guy to kill Rachael, or at least attempt to kill her.

"Dr. Rich, this is Detective Frank Holland!" a nurse says. Frank's arm is still in his sling.

"Let's take a look at that arm," says Dr. Rich. "I heard you checked yourself out last night before anyone could take care of you properly."

Frank sits down in one of the open partitioned patient areas, and the doctor takes his arm out of the sling. Frank winces at the movement.

Dr. Rich pulls the dressing from Frank's wound. "This doesn't look good. You busted some of the stitches and bled more last night. I can't tell how much blood you've lost, but it fortunately stopped and you're still alive, so I guess we'll just move along with IV antibiotics and fluids."

The doctor motions for a nurse to come over, writes some notes on a pad, and says, "Bring this back to me so we can start him on it right now, please."

The nurse scurries off to get the supplies the doctor has requested.

"Doc, how is Rachael doing?" asks Frank.

"She lost a lot of blood, and I had to take out her spleen as well as patch a few holes in her. She was shot twice—once through her right breast. We removed that bullet and, if anything, that gave her a better fighting chance. The second bullet was another story altogether—it hit her in the side, went into her lungs, and tore the lining of her stomach before coming to rest in her intestine. It was a mess in there.

She had numerous tears and substantial internal bleeding. We will need to go back in for another round of surgery since all I could do the first time was to stop the bleeding and remove the bullets—minimal repair work. It will be touch and go with her for the next 24 hours. If she stabilizes, I will be able to go back in to clean up, I hope, but that is if she can stabilize on her own. We're in a wait-and-see mode right now."

"Thanks, Doc."

Frank can hardly get the words out. He feels like he set her up for this. The doctor notices Frank's blood pressure falling a little as he patches his arm.

"Hey Frank, if you had not gone through the window like you did and scared that guy off, no doubt Rachael would be dead, and probably a whole lot more people as well. So, whatever guilt you may be feeling, do not beat yourself up with the "if only I had done this or that." You did more than anyone else to save Rachael's life and a lot of other people's lives. Hey, whether you believe it or not, you're a hero, man—heck, a superhero!"

"Thanks, Doc, but as you said, it may be too little, too late."

"Well, at least you've given her a fighting chance."

"You too, Doc . . . Hey Doc, I'm not sure her life isn't still in danger."

"Of course, it is. I mean, she's nowhere near stable, like I just said."

"No, I mean . . . uh . . . we will need to place police on her while she is here."

"I don't understand, Detective. What am I missing?"

"Sorry, Doc, that's all I can tell you for now. Just keep an eye out for anyone suspicious until I can get her police coverage. Okay?"

"Frank, this is a hospital. While we try, it's not the most secure facility in the world."

"I'm just saying, whatever security measures you have, can you double them until I can get some people here?"

"Sure. I'll call the hospital administrator and have a few more security brought in."

"Not sure that's a good idea, Doc. Just ask everyone to check in on her more often. The guy who may be after her plays for keeps, and I don't want to put anyone else in harm's way."

"Frank, now I'm alarmed."

"Just let me out of here and take down my cell number. Call me if anyone suspicious shows up."

"How about staying another 15 minutes so I can get enough fluids and antibiotics into you to possibly hold off infection from your escape from here last night. Chalk it up to protecting us by waiting on your bad guy."

"Okay, Doc. I guess I can do 15 more minutes, but no pain medicine—just antibiotics, right?"

"Right!"

CHAPTER SIXTY-EIGHT

Frank arrives at Agent McKinley's office in another complimentary car from the NYPD. Frank could get used to the hero thing with the free rides. He walks into the reception area.

"Hi, I'm Frank Holland . . ."

"Oh, you're . . ."

"Yes, that was me. I'm here to see Agent McKinley."

McKinley comes out to the lobby to greet Frank personally this time.

"Frank, welcome to the FBI Special Crimes Unit."

"Agent McKinley," says Frank.

"Call me Bob. You're a national hero!"

"Yeah, they keep telling me that," says Frank.

They walk down to McKinley's office, and on the way, McKinley tells his secretary, "Two coffees, please, Doris."

"How do you want yours, Frank?"

"Black, I guess."

"Okay. How's the arm?"

"Sore."

"Yep, I bet. I've never been shot, Frank. Can you believe it? I guess most of the time it's investigative work on our end, and we prefer to bag the bad guy with no shots fired if possible."

"Yeah, that's how we try to do it as well, Bob."

"Of course, it's just you guys at the NYPD seem to find a way to fire more often than most, although certainly not in your case. No one would think your shots weren't justified."

"That's a relief."

"Look, Frank, let's just start over; shall we? I'm sorry about the other day. You were right; we should have followed up with you on this thing, but we really didn't have anything substantial to go on."

"You had Roger Emanuel's death, which I told you was this same guy."

"Frank, the NYPD closed that case."

"I know. I went along against my better judgment, but I'm not going along now."

"Okay, Frank. Tell me what you've got."

"Bob, this is not terrorism. It's about money."

"Money!? A guy shoots up the Oak Room for money? I didn't see a ransom note or any money change hands. It looked pretty clear what was going on."

"What was going on was the assassination of Rachael Lopez and John Menuso."

Bob does not take the news well, as he is ready to close the book on this case and chalk one up for the good guys. Listening to Frank will not be easy, but he owes him the courtesy.

"Frank, let me bring in a couple of special agents to hear your story so we can determine a course of action. I hate to do this to you, but I have another meeting. I will join you when I'm finished. It will take a while to pull our guys together. We need to get the complete lowdown on your theory."

"Theory? God damn it, this is not a theory! I have an agent shot up and dying in an unguarded hospital bed, I'm shot, two police detectives are dead, my boss is dead, and there's an assassin on the loose in New York City—probably just waiting for the chance to go in and finish Rachael off for good."

"Calm down, Frank. I hear you. Let's walk down to the conference room where you can wait for the team to assemble. I'll be right down once I've finished. Doris will get you whatever you need while we pull everybody together."

Frank gets the regular run around—so much for a hero's welcome. He waits. Unbelievable. He may very well be at the hospital finishing Rachael off right now, and I can't get anyone to pay attention. I'm losing my mind! While wondering why no one will listen to him, Frank is also feeling the effects of adrenalin, medications, and the gunshot wound.

Finally, the suits come into the conference room. It's full FBI—everyone who's anyone wants to be seen with Frank. There is a lot of handshaking, greeting, and commenting on Frank's hero status. He is really getting tired of people telling him he's a hero.

"So, Frank, talk," says Agent-in-Charge McKinley, who

has now returned from his meeting.

"I have evidence I received from a Diversified Financial Services employee, the employee who was killed in the Oak Room, that implicates his company's hedge fund in a murder-for-profit scheme. It seems the fund has been buying life insurance pools, dissecting the ownership, and killing the insured policyholders for the proceeds. The data provided by the employee matches up with a long string of deaths mostly classified as accidental. In some cases, these accidents paid double. The employee, John Menuso, was at the Oak Room to give this information to Detective Lopez." "Whoa, Detective Lopez?"

"Yes, she had worked with my new boss, Roger Emanuel, in Tucson, and his death is also part of this elaborate murder-for-profit strategy."

"Frank, slow down. All of this is connected to the insurance deal you described?" McKinley is sounding a little annoyed with Frank for raining on his parade. He wanted it to be simple—good guys win, bad guys die. Black and white. Case closed with TV shots and promotions for everyone. "This is going to take some background work and some digging."

"We don't have time for background work or digging, God damn it!" shouts Frank, briefly overcome by all that's happened to him. "As I told you before, there is a detective lying in a hospital bed, unguarded, who could easily be killed at any moment. Rachael knows information on all the players' whereabouts and account records. She was a mole inside their organization. She was on to them. They knew it and put out a contract on her. She's also on their list as an insured. The firm bought insurance on her knowing they were going to kill her. And, I repeat, the employee who provided this information was killed at the Oak Room. It was set up to look like a terrorist job, but it was their assassin doing all this."

"Frank, this is outrageous. Do you have what we need to make the case across the board on all of these guys?"

"I have a flash drive."

"Let's see it."

Frank holds up something that looks like a flash drive.

"Bob," Frank says a little too forcefully, and the room shows some discomfort with Frank using his first name. "I'm not letting this out of my sight until you get a team on Rachael and show some interest in catching the killer."

"You know I'm going to have to pass along the flash drive so we can develop a game plan, Frank. We've got to push this upstairs. It's not my call. You're throwing a lot at us right off the bat here. This is the FBI. We don't just go running into something without having some facts to go along with it."

"Don't I know it! I don't know why I'm here. Many more people will probably die while you guys get your facts straight. Do you think this group is just going to wait for you to make your move on them? This is business as usual for them. I have of list of at least 10 US citizens Diversified has killed—this is mass murder, guys, on your watch. How many more facts do you need before you'll act? I know this screws up your tidy little 'we caught the terrorist' scenario—

and who knows who the poor slob you guys murdered in the park was! He was probably just minding his own business when a SWAT team chased him down and killed him."

"For your information, he had a sheet . . ."

"Oh yeah, he had a sheet! Jesus! You guys could make it look like he killed Kennedy if you wanted."

"Frank, you're out of line! I know you're upset, but you need to calm down and let this go through the usual procedures. If you're right, we'll catch all of these guys, and it will be by the book—not jumping through some window during a covert op." The room is completely quiet for a moment.

"When a team is in place covering Rachael at the hospital, I will give you the flash drive."

McKinley nods to two agents. "Go to her room at the hospital and sit on her until I can get a team in place."

The agents leave to go to the hospital and guard Rachael's room.

Agent McKinley pushes an intercom on the conference room phone and says, "Doris, I need to order an official 24-hour watch on a federal witness to a terrorist act. Please set it up for me to start as soon as you can get the paperwork through."

"Yes, sir. For whom shall I make it?"

"Rachael Lopez, at Columbia Hospital." McKinley turns to Frank. "What room Frank?"

"She's in the ICU, room 7B," Franks says.

McKinley pushes the intercom button off and looks at Frank. "Satisfied?"

"No, but it will do for now," Frank holds the flash drive out to Agent McKinley. "Please copy it and give me back the original."

"This is evidence, Frank. It has to stay in the file."

"I'm not giving it over without getting a copy back. Nothing personal, but I've read too many crime novels to not cover my ass, Bob."

McKinley pushes the intercom button again. "Doris, please come in here and bring a laptop with you."

Frank gets up and walks over to the coffee service and pours himself a glass of water. His adrenalin level is decreasing again, and he is feeling fatigued.

He sits back down with his water, and Doris comes in with a laptop. She puts it down in front of McKinley. Frank slides the drive over to McKinley, he plugs it in and presses save and download. While it is downloading, both men sit quietly. After a couple of minutes, he hands the flash drive back to Frank.

"Thank you," says Frank.

McKinley says nothing in response. Then, finally, he says, "Is there anything else you wish to discuss?"

"Not right now. Let's just see where this goes with your team. McKinley, don't let me down on this. I'm counting on you to do the right thing. We have to close these guys down and put some people in prison."

CHAPTER SIXTY-NINE

"Viktor, it's Mr. Guong."

Oh shit. Viktor picks up the line. "Good morning, sir."

"Viktor, we have a problem."

"Oh? The reports for this month are ready to be posted to your share file today. The numbers are good."

"No, it's something else. I need you to come to Beijing to discuss this in person. Tomorrow would be best. I suggest you leave tonight. I look forward to seeing you tomorrow. 3 pm. A car will be waiting for you at the terminal."

"Excellent. I look forward to seeing you." They hang up.

Viktor knows it is totally out of character for Ho to invite him to Beijing. He has only been once, and they treated him like a chauffeur. Viktor, normally a master of information, is in the dark for once. Viktor has had no word from Avi. John is dead, and Rachael is in the hospital, barely alive but alive. Viktor has to make the call whether to travel to Beijing tomorrow or not.

Checking the news, Viktor learns all hell is breaking loose in NYC. It seems they have killed a terrorist in Central Park.

They killed Avi! Viktor is really freaking out now.

Viktor goes to the safe in his office and takes out all its contents: eight large hand-sized pull-string bags and four passports. He opens one of the bags and dumps the contents into his hand to inspect—25 clean, white cut diamonds. Viktor puts them back into the bag and puts all the bags in his briefcase. All told, these bags contain about $20 million in diamonds. The safe also has a Desert Eagle .50 pistol, which is more like a hand cannon as it is one of the highest caliber pistols in the world. He pulls out a soft-sided gun case bag, four clips with 9 rounds of ammo each, and two boxes of bullets. He stuffs the Desert Eagle into the briefcase along with the extra clips and bullets. He also adds two prescription medicine bottles, and his emergency exit bag is ready to go.

"Marko, call Dmitri and have him get the plane ready to fly to Europe. We're leaving now. Bring the car around."

"Sir," Marko calls Viktor back, "Dmitri says he cannot fly for five more hours; he has had alcohol."

"Bull shit, he and Visili better be ready to go in one hour."

Viktor dials Anna. She answers the phone, sounding groggy. She usually works second shift with Viktor.

"Yes, hello?"

"Get ready. We are leaving. Get Biljna and Filipa. Don't say anything to anyone else. I will pick you up in five minutes."

"I need at least 30 minutes to . . ."

Viktor hangs up. He takes his grab bag and goes down to

the waiting car. He is leaving the Caymans. He hopes this is not his last time here. It is a fabulous place to live and be wealthy. He is known by all the restaurants' employees and by the service staffs who help maintain his toys all around the island. It's a good life. Oh sure, those New York assholes do not recognize him as a renaissance hedge fund manager on the cutting edge of financial discovery, but if he can get through this little issue, they will know him soon enough. Ultimately, he will be teaching them how to design cutting edge investment portfolios with alternative income features, similar to what he has developed with Avi for millions of dollars in fees. He just doesn't want to get caught here and not be able to leave. He has his driver take him straight to the girls' compound, which is past the airport. Viktor pours tequila on the drive over to calm his nerves, and he begins to relax a little.

The drive to get the girls takes 15 minutes, but they are still not ready. Viktor goes inside and grabs one, half-dressed, and forces her into the car. The other two follow quickly in different stages of readiness.

Dmitri punches in the code so Viktor can ride in his Maybach sedan right up to the plane. Viktor boards the plane as it is still being refueled, while the girls are still finishing getting dressed in the car. Visili, the copilot, is supervising the refueling, while Dmitri, the pilot, boards the plane to talk to Viktor about the flight plan.

"Sir, I have to . . ."

"You can file the flight plan in the air. Let's go."

"Sir, I have to file something just to get us off the ground."

"Very well. The Azores."

"The Azores. Yes, sir. Thank you, sir."

Dmitri files the flight for PDL, San Miguel, Azores. Then, he quickly rechecks the plane and speaks in Russian to Visili who has finished the refueling inspection and is now in the copilot seat going through his checklist. Dmitri rushes his preflight check with clearance to the Azores. The Gulfstream quietly nuzzles its way from the terminal onto the tarmac as Dmitri awaits the final go authorization. They wait. Anna has brought Viktor a shaker of martinis. She places the cold silver container on a tray by Viktor's chair with a chilled glass. She smiles at him and moves over to the lavatory, closing the door behind her. She pulls out her makeup bag and tries to build a mask of happiness from her already beautiful features.

The waiting is driving Viktor crazy, even though they have only been on the tarmac a few minutes. Viktor pours a martini from the shaker and looks around admiringly at his beautiful Gulfstream G 450 superjet. No one else Viktor knew from Serbia, no one at the embassy, his friends, or anyone he went to college with has their own Gulfstream. He tries to use this moment to calm his nerves, but he fears the worst is yet to come with Avi and John Menuso dead. He is not sure about Rachael, but he needs her dead as well to keep his life from falling apart.

Back in New York, Frank enters the richly paneled executive offices of the FBI to meet with the Deputy Director and a host of other agents from his office. An assistant comes in to offer a round of coffees and recognizes Frank.

"Oh, Detective Holland," she says excitedly, "can I get you something, sir?"

"Just water, please," Frank says. He is still wearing the sling, but it is beginning to bother him. He takes his arm out of the sling, but then winces and puts it back in.

"Frank," says one of the agents at the table, "are you sure you don't need to go back and have that arm checked out again? It's been a pretty busy 24-hour period for you, hasn't it?"

"I appreciate your concern, but what I really need is to speak with someone who can move on this evidence right now so no more people are killed." Frank says this in a loud voice, hoping to show he is a lot more than just a little frustrated with all the bureaucracy.

They all get settled while they wait for the deputy director. Five minutes later, the deputy director comes in. The power game begins.

"Deputy Director Todd, this is Detective Frank Holland of the NYPD."

"Yes, the terrorist stopper?" asks the Director.

"Well, sir, yes and no. That's why we're here," states Agent McKinley.

"Go on," the deputy director says as he sips a hot coffee placed in front of him at the head of the conference table.

"Frank, please bring the deputy director up to speed," requests Agent McKinley.

"Sir, this whole deal is not about terrorism. This started with financial transactions in which a madman in the

Caymans hired a killer to assassinate life insurance policyholders for the payouts. He is running a hedge fund down there. Rachael Lopez, the woman shot at the Oak Room, was on to this entire plot. Roger Emanuel, the new hire at the NYPD whose gun 'accidentally' exploded the other day, is in fact now believed to have been murdered in his office as part of this same plot, as were a host of citizens who sold their life insurance policies to an investment fund and then began to be killed one by one so the fund could collect the proceeds of the policies."

"Frank, you're not making any sense. How can someone pull this kind of thing off? It's far-fetched," replies the Director.

"Sir," Frank continues, "that is exactly why it worked. It is totally bizarre. I have a flash drive given to Rachael by John Menuso, who worked for the hedge fund, and that's why they were shot at the Plaza. It was not an act of terrorism. It was just made to look that way."

"Well, it was a good day's work when we got the guy in the park."

"Sir, I'm afraid not. That was just some random guy."

"Detective Holland, our intel on the park guy shows he had ties to an organization with straight links to terrorist activities."

"Maybe you just got lucky with him, but the actual assassin is a major player in the global killing world. He must also be a master of disguise. In all likelihood, there may be a team of these assassins out there handling all of these killings. If just one guy is responsible, he has killed people all over the country, and we are up against a real professional. Most of these killings have looked like accidents. Most of the deaths are now closed cases, and the insurance proceeds have probably been paid out."

"Let me get this straight, Frank—you're not a hero, and an assassin has been hired to kill people to make a buck for some guy's hedge fund. Who is this guy?"

Agent McKinley answers, "We are still in the process of pulling all of this together, but it looks like it's a guy named Viktor Ludvidz, who runs Diversified Financial Services out of the Cayman Islands. I only have the data from the flash drive to go on at this point, but it seems to be in order. It was provided to Rachael at the scene by John Menuso, the Diversified employee who was killed at the Plaza, sir."

"Well, this is one hell of a mess! I'm not even sure which agency to report this to—the FBI? CIA? Homeland? First, is this an international crime with a domestic component? Second, who else is involved? Sounds like money laundering as well."

"I'm not sure about any of that, sir, but I do have the flash drive, which seems to show all the proceeds received from the insurance companies, and many of them match up with supposedly accidental deaths I have found in obituaries," says Frank.

"Accidental deaths. We will need to develop a case against this guy, who for all we know is not a US citizen, does not travel to the US, and is living outside our jurisdiction. You sure know how to ruin a guy's day. Frank, although this all sounds outrageous, in light of the current facts, I think we need to investigate this matter further. I'm meeting with the director this afternoon, and we'll take this all the way to the top."

To Frank, it seems going to the top is moving closer to nowhere than to stopping the murders. "Sir, with all due respect, this is the second meeting in which I have explained what is going on, who is involved, and how we found out what we know, and now it looks like I'll be heading to another meeting while a team of murderers is on the loose killing American citizens."

The room gets quiet.

"Detective Holland, I'm sorry you feel that coming to my office has been a waste of your time, but I can assure you the next meeting will not be, because you will not be there. We are the FBI. This is what we do. We will take this from here, and you will be informed through the proper NYPD channels as to what role we need you to play in resolving this investigation if any."

The deputy director stands clearly pissed at Frank for barking at him in front of his team. Frank stands and turns to leave as the director brushes by him, leaving the room first. At least Frank has an FBI team on Rachael now.

CHAPTER SEVENTY

In an even bigger office, with a bigger conference table and better coffee, a conversation begins to take place.

"Director Connelly, have you read the affidavit about the New York City shootings?" asks Deputy Director Todd.

"I have. It appears we have a guy running around killing US citizens for profit for a hedge fund. What do you have on the fund?"

"It is run by a Viktor Ludvidz in the Cayman Islands."

"Any records on this thing?"

"It is all offshore with offshore investors. No US investors that we can find. The set-up of this fund is brilliant. It is a limited partnership owned by a corporation registered in the Caymans through Guernsey Limited Liability Corporation."

"We will have a hard time dissecting this thing. Check with Director Ward at the CIA to see if he can shed any light on it."

Another day goes by and Frank feels he has definitely been cut out of the loop. He is no longer in the waiting frame of mind, but the wheels move slowly at this level. He cannot understand why they don't just call the Cayman authorities and at least have Viktor picked up.

"This thing is like a hot potato," says Director Connelly to his aide. "Hell, somebody has to take it and address it. Check with Secretary Ed Johnson at Homeland. This Holland guy is not going away and he probably has something here."

More time goes by and life in New York City seems to go back to normal.

A helicopter takes off from the South Lawn of the White House headed to Camp David for the weekend. Director Ward, of the CIA, watches from the White House lawn. He is approached by his undersecretary.

"Have you read the memo about the life insurance thing?"

"I have and I am still shocked by all this. This fund has been murdering people for the life insurance proceeds, and their largest investor is the Greater China Sovereign Fund."

"Yes, sir, that appears to be the case."

"This is a nightmare. How could this fund be investing in that type of activity? We have to take steps to punish them for this type of behavior. We cannot let this stand. It's almost terrorism."

"Sir, we do have another slight problem."

"Oh, don't tell me—another slight problem?"

"China is the largest single owner of US Treasury debt."

"You don't think I know that!? What the hell kind of

statement is that to make to me?"

The director composes himself and walks back into the White House with his aides following.

"What part did the Chinese play in this? Is this an act of war?" asks the director.

"Sir, we're not certain of many things at this point. This Ludvidz character, the fund manager, has scampered to Morocco. He was supposed to be in China yesterday. They may have been planning on ending this when he arrived, but he was too smart for that."

"Is he a US citizen?"

"No sir, not that we can determine."

"Well, that's good. Why don't you just go grab him and take him to Gitmo?"

"We don't have extradition with Morocco, and, as you said, he's not a US citizen."

"Clearly, this man is a terrorist. Grab him. There must be some money-laundering angle around this fund for terrorist activities. I mean, he is killing US citizens, that's terror if I've ever seen it."

"Sir," continues the aide, "the flash drive the FBI have shows he is profiting from this activity, but we don't have proof he is actually in on the killings. And most of these deaths have been closed by local police. Someone did kill his employee and tried to kill the detective from Arizona, so we have every indication this is all coming through Ludvidz."

"I don't give a damn! I want this cleaned up quickly. We need to reach out to the Chinese and see what their take is on this. We do not need an international incident developing out of some hedge fund guy making money. Get on it."

"Yes, sir."

CHAPTER SEVENTY-ONE

It is the next day, back in the CIA director's office.

"Sir, we have another slight problem."

"You know, this has become something more than slight, so you can knock off the 'slight' stuff."

"Yes, sir."

"Is this other 'slight' problem something I want to hear about?"

"Not likely, sir, but it could be an issue. The CIA may have some involvement in the killings."

In a very large office in the Dirksen Senate Office Building, Senator Spence waits for the CIA director to discuss the Ludvidz mess. This thing showed up at his office straight from the director of the FBI. The FBI is always looking for an angle to trash the CIA on anything. As the head of the Foreign Relations Committee, Spence knows it must really be big if he has to get in on it. It appears Ludvidz has both friends and enemies around Washington.

"CIA Director Ward is here for your meeting, Senator."

"Good, let him wait. I don't know how many times I've had to wait on the CIA, and I'm one of the people who approve their budget."

The senator is debriefed by his aide, Allen Strom, while Director Ward waits. Spence needs the story from his own people first to be able to recognize the spin the CIA director will put on it.

"Strom, I have read this dossier and am still not sure what we have here."

"Senator, we believe the Chinese government has a substantial investment in Ludvidz's hedge fund."

"I didn't see that in this dossier," says the senator.

"We felt it would be best to discuss with you prior to adding it to any official documents."

"I see. How about my friend waiting in the hall? Does he know about this?"

"It is likely, sir. Most of this information was on the flash drive."

"Ah, the infamous flash drive, recovered at the scene by our national hero, Detective Holland. Has anybody given any consideration to the fact this flash drive may not be accurate? I mean, how do we know for sure China is investing in this fund?"

"We did some preliminary research and it all checks out, sir. They are the biggest investor in the fund by a long shot."

"I see, but do we have any reason to believe they were in on any of these murders if they were in fact murders?"

"No sir, we do not."

"So, we need to go to the Chinese with this information,

let them refute it, and grab Ludvidz," says the Senator.

"We are just putting together the dossier on Ludvidz. He may have had ties to the CIA in the past," says the aide.

"Ah, damn! The question is, do we ask Ward about this CIA connection yet or will he volunteer it?"

Senator Spence speaks into his intercom, "Bridgette, show Director Ward in." Then, he says to the aide, "Let's play dumb on the Ludvidz connection for now and see if he shares it with us."

After sitting in Senator Spence's waiting room for 20 minutes, Ward is approached by one of the beautiful ladies on Spence's staff.

"Director, the Senator will see you now." He gets up from his seat, the perfect place to see Senator Spence's young female staff come and go about their duties, and walks into the senator's office.

"Director Ward, I'm sorry to have kept you waiting."

"Sir, it's okay. Your office is one of my favorite places to wait."

"Well, there needs to be some redeeming aspect to waiting," says the senator. "Ward, good work on tracking down this nefarious Ludvidz character. What a scoundrel! With that said though, Director, we need to tread lightly here. Many developments about this fund have just come to light. I'll need to know your every move on this. Keep an eye on Ludvidz while we investigate this further. I understand he has skipped to Morocco?"

"Yes sir, he is in Tangiers at a secure villa just outside of town. We have two people on him tasked with observing only."

"Good, let's make sure he doesn't move around on us."

"Yes, sir."

"We may need to grab him at some point once we have all the facts around this thing. Do you have a report for me?"

"Sir, we are developing this from zero, and we really only have the data from the flash drive given to the detective to go on at this point."

"What's your plan to capture this man?"

"Ludvidz?" Ward asks.

"Of course, Ludvidz! Who else am I worried about?"

"Of course, Senator. We are in communication with the Cayman authorities as we speak, looking into his business dealings there."

"Cayman authorities, what are they going to do? Buy him a drink? The guy is in Morocco, Ward."

"Senator, we don't have a grab plan for Morocco developed as of yet. They have generally not been cooperative when we have tried to develop joint strategies in the past."

"Get out of here and develop one, joint strategy or not, I don't care. At some point, the President is going to hear about this, and if he gets in on it, everything is going to go haywire fast. Hell, you're the CIA, since when have you needed a joint strategy to grab or kill anyone? Keep me informed of anything you get."

"Yes, Senator."

"Is there anything else?"

"Not at this time, sir."

"Very well, get on it."

The Senator stands to indicate the meeting is over. Ward steps out of the office and sees all the beautiful ladies again but is too nervous about the meeting to pay much attention.

Director Ward leaves the building knowing he is still sitting on the assassin piece of this puzzle. He almost gave it away with the Ludvidz question. Ward knows there are at least two people doing all these jobs, maybe more. His debrief shows Viktor Ludvidz may have been getting help from CIA asset #57. According to his confidential report, Viktor and asset #57 knew each other or came in contact with each other in Bosnia when 57 was working in Eastern Europe doing jobs for the CIA. Viktor was a driver in those days, and the team surmised that somehow they developed a relationship out of that meeting. That, sadly, is not all. Viktor has also been a contractor for the CIA in the past in Bosnia for guns and cash. If 57 has been behind many of the killings, he will have to tell Spence a CIA operative has been killing American citizens, but not for the CIA. How is he going to spin this so it doesn't bring the CIA or his budget into question? Who's going to believe him when he tries to disavow this activity?

CHAPTER SEVENTY-TWO

Frank goes back to the hospital to check on Rachael. She is still unconscious. Three days and one more surgery to go. Then he goes into the office, his first day back since taking almost a week of sick time off to work on the Diversified case. He goes into his new boss's office. As he walks into the squad room, everyone stops and stands quietly.

"Attention," Detective Suggs says to the group. "Detective Holland, we have a presentation for you."

Two detectives come over to Holland carrying a silver breastplate from a medieval suit of armor. It is inscribed, "Sir Frank, Nobleman of the Third Precinct, when rescuing damsels through windows, please wear me for protection." Suggs presents the breastplate to Frank, the squad room applauds, and a cake is brought out with a pistol candle on it.

"Frank, it's nice to have a hero on the team," says Suggs.

"All of you are heroes."

"Of course we are, but it's nice when the villagers recognize one of us for our efforts and don't show up with pitchforks. It makes us all look good."

Frank's new boss comes over to shake his hand during the celebration.

"Boss, I really need your help," Frank says to him.

"Sure, Frank. Come into my office after the celebration, and you can tell me all about it."

One by one, the squad personnel come over to greet Frank and shake his good hand. He is out of the sling but his left arm is still very sore.

Later, Frank walks into the boss's office and sits down.

"Frank, talk to me."

"The feds are going nowhere on this murder-for-hire deal, which has killed at least 10 people I know of, four of which were killed in our city and two were our very own people. I need some resources and a team to investigate this on our end and try to find the killer or put our hands on this Ludvidz guy."

"Frank, before we go jumping into this thing, let me check with the FBI myself and see if they will tell me anything about where they are and if we can help."

CIA Director Ward, FBI Director Davis, and both of their teams have come to Langley to put together a credible story to present to Senator Spence that will keep the peace and the money flowing to the various budgets across this spectrum. It is rare for all of these men to try to get on the same page. Ward is running the meeting since it is on his home turf.

After everyone has gotten coffee and settled into the conference room, Ward begins. "Has everyone here read the confidential memo about Ludvidz and asset #57?"

They all nod in agreement.

Ward continues, "We have a bad guy, Ludvidz, who has skipped to Morocco and a CIA asset who may have been killing US citizens for hire while still under the employ of the CIA to deal with. Plus, there's enough fall-out to bury all of us since this has been dangled in front of the FBI, the CIA, the NYPD, and just about every other agency for weeks to get someone to follow up on the Lopez and Holland show. It turns out they were both right, and we all look bad. We are here today to develop a plan so we can all look good. Let's start with Ludvidz."

"He has the China connection, and we need to keep China okay with our actions. Do they have an issue with him going out of business?" asks FBI Director Davis.

"Our intelligence shows China had a plan to terminate his services once we informed them of our knowledge of his little investment activity on their behalf," says Ward.

"So why not let China terminate Ludvidz's services without us?" asks Davis.

"That ship sailed when Viktor skipped to Morocco," answers Ward. "China has a few major infrastructure projects going on in Morocco. Viktor knew this and that is why he went there thinking China would not want the fallout of killing him in Morocco as well as the fact that the US does not have extradition."

"This Viktor sounds like a pretty sharp character," says one of the deputies.

"Apparently, he has stashed away about $240 million, as

far as we can tell, so he is not a lightweight. He has friends and he has money."

"But does he have an army?" asks Ward's deputy.

"We're not sure. We cannot get anyone in Moroccan intelligence to answer our request for assistance. We have not directly asked for anything but are just trying to establish contact to develop a plan. We may have to force a solution on Morocco at some point. At the very least, Morocco and China are trying not to ruffle each other. Viktor obviously has some connections in Morocco."

"Perhaps if we were to allow China to grab the $240 million, they would look the other way on our methods?"

"It's an idea, but should we bring in the White House around the $240 million? Or Spence?"

"It's a big piece of money, and we would look good if it were terrorist funds seized."

CHAPTER SEVENTY-THREE

Viktor settles in by the pool as Anna brings him a drink. The chef has prepared a feast on a large table. A white triangular umbrella shades the table for the luncheon guests. Viktor has been on the phone all morning with two associates in Grand Cayman.

"Viktor, like I said earlier, it's business as usual here. We have heard from no one, not the Chinese, not any investors. Everyone is just busy trading as usual. It looks like a pretty good market today in biotech stocks."

"Okay, just let me know how the day goes. Call me back by the end of the day or sooner if there is any reason to."

"Yes, sir. Thank you."

Viktor decides to stop working the phones. He realizes something is up because he has not heard from Ho. He was supposed to be in Beijing by now. The fact Ho has not called him tells Viktor Ho knew he might not show up. He must know about New York City, but how? Viktor calls Amina, his contact with the local company.

"Sabah Ilkir."

"Amina, it's Viktor."

"Yes?"

"I think I need more security here at my residence. Can you help me arrange it?"

"Of course, sir. What do you have in mind?"

"I need pros, Amina—big guys who can put out whatever fires show up."

"Let me put something together for you."

Viktor decides to move around until he has his security team in place at his residence. He calls in the driver, "Please get the car ready; I am going for a drive."

"I'm going out for a meeting," he then tells Anna. "I will return soon."

She smiles at him as he leaves, as she is expected to do, no questions asked. Viktor goes to his room and gets out a nine-millimeter pistol he took from his plane with a 15-round clip, not the Desert Eagle since the nine is more discreet and accurate. He puts it in a holster with his shirt tail out covering it. It tells anyone who is interested he has a gun but is discreet if anyone is not interested. Morocco has an Old West feel, meaning if you have means, you can do what you like. This is part of its charm for a man like Viktor. The driver pulls around in a black Toyota Land Cruiser with dark bulletproof windows and armor-plated side panels.

Viktor travels from his villa into town to meet with Amina.

"Take a left here," says Viktor.

The driver looks at him funny because this is not the way to the café.

"Take another right here."

He follows the directions. Viktor looks for a tail and sees nothing. "Ok, go to the café."

The driver drops him off at a café where Amina is sitting outside enjoying an espresso.

"Amina."

"Viktor."

Amina stands and the men embrace. A young waiter comes by, and Amina orders Viktor a triple espresso in Moroccan.

"I have made a few calls on your army," says Amina. "It will be in place within 24 hours."

"Did you pick these men yourself?" asks Viktor.

"No, but one of my lieutenants in the army picked all of them. He believes you will be pleased. He also requires payment in advance of the team's deployment."

Viktor tosses a small velvet bag onto the table. Amina looks at the bag and examines its contents.

"This is fine for me, but my lieutenant will require cash."

"Cash some of those diamonds and pay him."

Amina puts the bag back on the table and crosses his arms, signifying the deal is unacceptable.

"Okay, okay," Viktor says and hands Amina an envelope with US dollars about 4 inches thick. Amina smiles at Viktor, puts the cash in his pants pocket and the diamonds in his jacket pocket.

"Your team will be in place very soon. The head man speaks English, but I did not charge you extra for that."

"I feel I have paid extra. I forget how shrewd you traders

are with 10,000 years of experience. My skills have become weak from dealing with Americans so much."

Viktor smiles and so does Amina. They sit back at the table and enjoy their coffees.

The observers the CIA has tasked to follow Viktor call in. "We have movement on SB one."

"Roger that. Status."

"He has left the compound and did a few tail moves, which signifies he knows he is being tailed, and we lost him."

"Roger that. Go back to the compound and wait him out. If he does not return in five hours, phone it in."

"Roger. Over and out, mobile one."

CHAPTER SEVENTY-FOUR

"Director Ward, Viktor is on the move, and our team on the ground in Morocco has lost him."

"What is the activity level at his residence?"

"So far nothing different, sir. No packing up. Nobody leaving. It was just Viktor and the chauffeur who left. He did make a few tail maneuvers to lose our team. We had to let him go and give up the tail, once he made some moves. He would have known he was being followed if we had maintained our tail."

"This Viktor is crafty," states Ward. "He knows someone is after him. I take it the team is headed back to the compound?"

"That's correct, sir."

"Keep me informed. I want to know where he is and what he's up to."

Ward hangs up the phone and turns to his team. "We need to force a solution here, gentlemen. I need to make sure you have the decks as clear as possible when we attempt an extraction in Morocco. I just don't see this going any other way."

"Sir, what about asset 57?"

"I'll deal with that issue in due time. Let's not add any additional information about asset 57 to this file. From your resources so far, you have no knowledge asset 57 is directly involved, right? You only know he was chauffeured around in Bosnia by Viktor, correct?" asks Ward.

"Yes, sir. We have not verified any wire transactions from Diversified to asset 57."

"Trust me, you will not find any direct link. Even if there was one, I'm quite sure they both covered their asses on the wire. I would not even waste your time looking."

"Yes, sir."

CHAPTER SEVENTY-FIVE

Avi has checked out of the Marriott and the Park Lane and is moving back to the Ritz as Dr. Patel to have a profile that will be visible but discreet, as the Ritz always is. Bruce Springsteen could be staying at the Ritz and no one would know about it. Dr. Patel takes a park-front suite on the third floor where he can see down to the front door and also have ready access to the back stairs through the residences, which celebrities use to come and go discreetly. The back door has no camera but requires a special key card. Dr. Patel is, of course, a club level guest giving him access to five meal presentations a day as well as food and drinks without any accounting having to be done. He may be there, or he may not.

Avi is clean-cut these days with short hair and is nondescript Latin-, Nepali-, or Indian-looking—no one knows for sure—wearing a close-cut, expensive Ritz Carlton guest-looking suit that shows his physique. He puts a .25 caliber pistol in his right outside jacket pocket and a long stiletto knife in his interior coat pocket for a more discreet encounter should the need arise. He goes down to the lobby to read the paper and see if there are any suits or police around.

After an hour, he has not noticed anything interesting at the Ritz, so he goes back down to the Park Lane Hotel and sits on one of the couches in their lobby reading the Wall Street Journal for another hour. Nothing remarkable happens until a Carlyle maintenance man walks slowly through the hotel without a garbage bag or any equipment. Avi recognizes the look of a fellow hitter and smiles because the guy has no clue he just walked by his target. Avi has just figured out his previous employer has decided to terminate his employment.

Avi falls in behind the maintenance man as he leaves the hotel and walks down 58th and onto 5th Avenue. He is dressed to impress as he moves closer to the hitter to see if he recognizes him and to determine the threat level. Is he a rookie or a seasoned professional? The hitter touches his earpiece as he speaks into a microphone indicating to Avi he is an amateur. Avi lets him finish his call and sign off and then walks up behind him.

They are standing at the corner of 5th and 57th, right in front of Trump Tower. Everyone is waiting for the light to change when Avi sticks a sharp stiletto into the lower neck of the amateur hitter, quickly and discreetly twisting the knife back and forth to break the nerve endings in his spinal cord. The hitter slumps as all nerve activity ceases. Avi nudges the body forward into traffic and an oncoming bus slams into him. People scream, and everyone at the intersection watches as the bus hits the brakes and the body slides underneath the bus and gets caught between the rear wheels on the left back side. The bus continues on for 50 feet or so before coming to a stop. The hitter's body looks like a bunch of mangled up clothes caught between the tires.

During the distraction of the bus wreck, Avi slips the stiletto back into its sheath and into his lined suit pocket. Some blood seeps through the pocket and onto his shirt. The suit is dark enough not to show the stain. He turns and walks slowly and deliberately back to the Ritz's private entrance. He decides it is time to leave New York.

CHAPTER SEVENTY-SIX

"Sir."

"Yes, what is it?" CIA Director Ward asks.

"Asset 35 is down, sir . . . uh . . . way down at 57th and 5th. Looks like he was hit by a bus."

"Send four units to the area. Obviously, our man was there and took care of him before he could perform the hit."

In fifteen minutes, four black Suburbans converge on the block. When they arrive, the NYPD has already closed the scene down. There are firetrucks and ambulances, and police are on the scene taking statements. The Suburbans let out two passengers each and they spread out, combing the area for Agent 57.

Avi returns to the Ritz, gathers together his clothes, and calls the club level concierge.

"Good morning, Dr. Patel."

"Good morning. I need a car to drive me a few places today. I'll tell the driver where I'm going once I'm inside the car. Just book him for the day."

"When do you need it, Dr. Patel?"

"Now, or as close to now as you can make it."

"Yes sir, I will ring you back with the expected arrival time. We may have one out front who would be willing to take a whole day right now."

"Excellent. I'll be right down unless I hear differently from you. Thank you."

"It's my pleasure, sir."

Director Ward is in the situation room at Langley speaking to the agents on the ground who are searching for Avi.

"What do you have?"

"Nothing, sir. It's like a needle in a haystack. People are everywhere, and we don't know what disguise he may be using. I mean, hell, he could be one of these firemen for all we know, sir."

"Damn it, start checking them then. I want him neutralized, and I want it done discreetly. That city has been through enough."

"Yes, sir."

"Put two agents at all the airports and train stations in the city."

"What about the bus stations?"

"Those too."

"We may have to use NYPD to cover the buses as well."

"No, keep this in-house and discreet. Send one-man teams to the airports and bus stations."

"Sir, are you sure you want to split them up? We know what 57 is capable of."

"You're right. Don't split them up; keep two-man teams. We'll just have to take our chances on the buses."

Avi enters the black Lincoln Town Car in front of the Ritz and tells the driver, "I have a patient I need to see in Connecticut, but I would much rather drive than ride the train. For an extra $1,000, would you mind taking me?"

"$1,000? Man, for $1,000, I'll drive you to Boston!" says the driver.

"The only thing is, this patient is famous, so you'll need to keep this just between you and me if you can. It's really important. Tell you what, I'll throw in another $300 as hush money so you don't tell your friends about the big fare that fell into your lap. Deal?"

"Deal, sir. There was a bad accident over on 57th this morning, so we should probably go through the park to get out of town."

"Sounds like a good idea. What's your name?"

"Mike."

They travel through the park and head toward Connecticut. About four hours later, as they approach East Windsor, Avi speaks to the driver, "Hey Mike, it's not that I don't trust you, man, but I think I will get out at Bradley Airport and have my patient send his driver there to pick me up. It's nothing personal. I promise to give you a great write-up at the Ritz. I know how that works."

"I really would appreciate that, sir. I will never tell anyone about this ride or my passenger. As far as anyone has to know, I drove down to South Street in all the traffic and waited to take you to two other places before you sent me back, sir."

"Thank you, Mike. Hey, let me get your card so when I'm back in town, I can call and get you to take care of me."

"That would be great, sir." He hands Avi his card.

"Okay, Mike, just here at Bradley Airport is fine; departure area is fine. I'll see you around, Mike."

"Okay, thank you, sir."

Avi gets his luggage and goes into the terminal. He greets the smiling attendant with his US passport and his warmest Midwestern accent. "Hi, I need to get on the flight to Dublin. First class, if you have it."

Avi will check out of the Ritz once he gets to Dublin. With the "do not disturb" sign on his room door, he could go to China before anyone would know he wasn't in his room—especially if he orders room service and asks that it be left outside the door.

"What do you guys have?" asks Ward.

"Nothing, no spotting of anyone remotely close to his description—no one at the airports or train stations. He must have taken a car. It's been four hours and we have no leads, sir."

"Ok, come on in," says Ward.

"What now, sir?" asks his aide.

"He's out of town and out of our way for now. He will probably lay low until this Viktor thing goes away. He's a smart cookie. Give him a few weeks and we'll try to hire him for a job to see if he bites. His getting away is probably better for us anyway."

CHAPTER SEVENTY-SEVEN

By noon the following day, Tangier time, Viktor has an army in place guarding his compound.

The CIA observers call it in.

"It looks like Viktor has himself a small army now, sir."

"Shit, I guess we should have moved on him sooner. I really didn't think when it was all said and done Morocco would come to this guy's aid," says Ward.

"Boss, these guys are not regular army; they look like mercenaries to me, but they are fortified embassy style at Viktor's compound. It's something Bin Laden would have dreamed about having. Our job here—if there still is one, sir—just got a lot harder. We're not going to be able to snoop on this guy without satellite intelligence and more manpower. Once these mercs get wind of our presence, they may do more than just ask us to leave. We're pulling back to what I believe is a safe position for now to await your instructions. I think we can set up a follow team if he leaves but getting to him inside this compound is going to be tough, sir."

Back at Langley, Ward calls another meeting with FBI Director Davis and various other department directors without Senator Spence again.

"Gentlemen, our guest has fortified his position in Morocco to the point where it will take a scaled offensive to extract him."

"Here's the thing," says Davis, "and I think I speak for the domestic team—this is obviously your operation. It's overseas and he's a non-US citizen . . ."

"A terrorist," interrupts Ward.

"Okay, a terrorist, but it looks like you'll need to instigate this action through your channels."

"I wondered when you guys would circle the wagons and leave me out here to deal with this myself," says Ward.

"It's not that," says Davis. "I just don't see how I can help you if we are trying to keep this operation discreet and it's now not a domestic issue."

"The guy has been murdering US citizens on US soil—that's not domestic enough for you?" asks Ward.

Davis crosses his arms in a defensive posture and replies, "Well, what was that little accident this morning on 57th? I can count on one hand the number of bus killings in New York City, and we had one this morning. Were you out doing some cleaning up today? The man had no identification on him, and so far there's no record matching his fingerprints—or what fingerprints were left."

Ward does not respond to his questions. "Davis, I'm trying to grab this mastermind in Morocco and not interfere with your domestic issues, but if this thing goes tits up, I will not take the blame alone. Know that."

"What is it you think I can do to help you ambush some guy in Morocco? Or any of us for that matter? You need to run this op yourself. I would suggest a more covert plan. You're CIA—do some fancy CIA shit," says Davis.

"That is what I intend to do. I just wanted you all to be in on the information."

"Like we were this morning in New York?" asks Davis.

"That's all, gentlemen," says Ward.

CHAPTER SEVENTY-EIGHT

Avi is back at one of his Cap Ferrat hotel homes sunning himself when he gets a text that he has a message on his secure server. He leaves the pool and goes back to his suite. He showers, dresses, and rides his Vespa down to a parking garage at the shopping district. He parks and takes a cab to the freight terminal.

Once in his office, he reads the message. It seems he has not been terminated from employment. Quite the contrary: the CIA wants him to kill Viktor. But this is a YOYO (you're on your own) operation, meaning there is no CIA back-up. This is odd for the CIA who usually covers every detail in a hit. The report contains a detailed layout of Viktor's estate in Tangier. Photos show a fortified estate protected by armed guards. It seems Avi has become valuable again to the CIA.

Avi initially wonders why the CIA did not bring in a fresh hitter for this job, but then he realizes if he gets killed killing Viktor, the CIA will have literally killed two birds with one stone. This is likely his last job for the company one way or the other. Avi smiles. He likes the idea of the challenge. He decides to pick up a little extra traveling money from Uncle Sam for all his trouble.

"Boss, we have traffic back from 57," says the deputy director to Ward. "He wants more money for this job."

"What an arrogant bastard!" says Ward, "How much does he want?"

"One million."

"A fucking million dollars for a hit, damn! What kind of society do we live in now where assassins get paid a million dollars to kill a bad guy? Offer him $500,000—250 up front and 250 after completion. If all goes well, he won't be around to collect it. And tell him we strongly suggest he accept this proposal."

"I'm not sure how easily he scares, sir, considering how he handled the agent in New York City."

"I will pretend I didn't hear that," says Ward.

Avi books a flight for Harry Hareem one-way business class to Tangier via Madrid. He thinks about a return flight, but he loves Morocco and may stay a while after the job is over.

Avi moves a few things around on his calendar, which is relatively clear with Viktor laying low, and makes his way to the Nice airport. He brings a checked bag with a few weapons in pieces so as to not be recognizable if his bag is x-rayed, but since he's flying to Morocco, it's not likely. Avi boards the plane and is disappointed business class is really just a little bit better than coach, but the flights are pretty short from Nice.

Avi has memorized Viktor's dossier and brings nothing to alert anyone to the fact he is here to kill, except the weapons. Avi typically plans out every employment action with precision and timing, but this time he has not yet decided how he's going to terminate Viktor, given the army Viktor has at his compound and the very high likelihood the CIA will drop in a team to finish him after he finishes Viktor. He knows he can improvise using something as simple as a teaspoon to terminate Viktor if needed.

Avi lands and takes a cab to downtown Tangier to meet with his contact. They discuss Avi's needs. He hands his contact an envelope. The contact holds it in his hand, lifting it a couple of times like he's weighing it in his mind. Then he shakes Avi's hand and leaves. Avi gets into the car his contact came in, with a secured cleared driver who will be at his disposal for the entirety of his stay.

Avi has a room at La Mansion and dinner reservations at Al Habib, a trendy Arabic-Asian fusion restaurant which is booked months in advance, but always has a table for special friends. He decides it may be best to have a dinner date, so he calls a friend who arranges for a beautiful guest to join Avi for dinner. Avi loves this restaurant and does not want to pass up the chance to dine here but being alone may draw unwanted attention. Harry Hareem has a very good reputation at this restaurant and the owner will make sure he gets a quiet, discreet table. While Morocco is a Muslim country, the wine list at Al Habib is impeccable.

CHAPTER SEVENTY-NINE

Avi goes to La Mansion to settle in for his Moroccan experience. He is met at the front door by the hotel manager.

"Mr. Hareem, what a pleasure to have you back, sir."

"The pleasure is mine, Mr. Fattah," Avi says to the manager in Arabic.

The manager is overjoyed he remembered his name.

"I have your suite ready for you, and I have personally inspected your pool to make sure your stay is as you would like it." He hands Avi the key to his room. "How long will you be with us, Mr. Hareem?"

"I am not sure at this point, so let's just leave it open. I hope to have some leisure time while I am here and would enjoy a longer stay if I can manage."

"Very well, sir, and thank you for staying with us. If I can do anything to make your stay more pleasant, please do not hesitate to reach out to me personally." He hands Avi his card with his cell number.

"I will, Mr. Fattah."

Avi takes his leave from the hotel manager and walks to

his suite with the bellman carrying his travel bag behind him. A large fruit basket is prominently displayed on a round table as Avi and the bellman enter the suite. It has a note from the hotel manager welcoming Harry Hareem. A nice touch. This suite probably does not get rented very often and may be the most expensive hotel room in Tangier.

"Sir, would you like a butler to unpack your bags for you?"

"No, thank you. I will take care of it," Avi says to the bellman as he places 450 dirhams into his hand. The bellman reacts by half bowing gratefully multiple times as he backs his way out the door. Avi has just bought undying loyalty from this bellman who typically makes about $1.50 an hour. From his childhood, Avi realizes just how little courtesy and regard it takes to receive great appreciation. His actions show the complexity of his character. While he is here to kill one man, he is showing compassion for another.

Avi has a late lunch by a private pool at La Mansion and makes a call to Viktor. He finds Viktor's cell number is disconnected, so he calls Viktor's office in the Caymans. A pleasant-sounding voice answers the line, revealing nothing about the business.

"Good morning, may I help you?"

"Viktor, please."

"I'm sorry, sir. Viktor is not in today. May I help you?"

"I'll leave him a message. Tell him I'm calling about the girl in New York. He can call me back."

"Sir, may I get your name and number?"

"Viktor has both."

"Both, sir?"

"Both my name and my number. Goodbye."

Viktor gets a call from Tom, his second in command at Diversified.

"Viktor, a couple of issues have come up today. We got a request for complete liquidation from the Chinese."

"I figured as much. Go ahead and fulfill it."

"Liquidate the entire amount?"

"Yes, but take your time. You have ninety days. And the other thing? You said there were a couple of issues," says Viktor.

"We got this kind of encrypted message from a guy who said to tell you he was calling about the girl in New York. He said you had his name and number. He didn't say anything else and when pressed, he hung up."

"I'll take care of that. No problem, thanks."

Avi is about to have another glass of champagne by the pool when his phone rings. He connects the line but says nothing.

"Hello, are you there? This is Viktor."

"Viktor," Avi says.

"I thought you were dead. I heard a terrorist was killed in Central Park after the . . . you know, what went on in New York."

"Yes, I know, it just goes to show you about the news, Viktor. You can't count on it to be very reliable. Are you in the Caymans? I'd like to sit down with you about all of this."

"No, I'm away from the Caymans. With everything that went down, I didn't want to get trapped on an island."

"Sounds like a good plan. Now, about the girl—when I left, she was still hanging on, but it doesn't look good for her."

"How do you know?" asks Viktor. "I haven't been able to get any information on her, but I've been trying to be discreet as well."

"I have sources you don't. Anyway, I have reconsidered your proposal to finish the job on her, but I would like to meet you in person to settle some issues first. Apparently, you aren't in a position to advance funds via a secure wire, so I'll need to get the payment in advance, face to face. So, where are you? I'll come to you."

Viktor hesitates at first and then answers, "I don't mean to be disrespectful, but I paid you to kill her and she is still alive. I'm not sure why I owe you more money."

Avi waits to answer. "I think you understand this business. People have been eliminated in the attempt to close her contract. This will require a new contract. You will pay as is customary in this type of arrangement if you want the additional work done. Now, Viktor, I will ask you again, where are you?"

"I'm in Tangier."

Avi is pleased Viktor did not lie to him. It almost makes him hesitate about killing him.

"Ok, that's not far from my current location. I can probably be there tomorrow. How about tomorrow afternoon at 3:00?"

"Oh, okay. Sure."

"Where are you in Tangier?"

Director Ward goes to his deputy director's office.

"You can pull the Tangier team back but not off, as we now have 57 in place. One thing about this guy, he will get the job done, and as I said, if we are lucky, he will get killed in the process."

"What if he doesn't?" asks the deputy.

"Pull a SEAL team over from Madrid and put them on standby in Tangier until we reach out. Go ahead and brief them on the grounds where Viktor is living and make their primary target 57. No one goes in without my personal approval."

"Got it."

CHAPTER EIGHTY

Avi has a wonderful dinner at Al Habib with Eloise, who is no doubt a model in Tangier with larger ambitions. Her ambitions will have to wait for now, because Avi has work to do for his assignment tomorrow. He gets out of the car at Eloise's apartment. The driver slowly moves the car away, and Eloise unlocks the door and invites Avi inside. He kisses her, looking around to make sure no one is watching so she will not have any fallout from this taboo gesture in this part of the world. He turns and leaves. She smiles disappointedly and goes into her apartment.

Avi walks about three blocks and enters a small pastry shop, which is oddly open at this time of night. While the storefront is small, the building goes far back into the block with a courtyard that has a clothesline, a well, and an outside shower with a fully bricked floor. Avi goes up a set of stairs to where an old woman sits at a table with a bowl of mostly unshelled almonds. She is using a hand tool to shell the almonds. She motions for him to move into the left side room. Avi enters and a man rises and embraces him.

"I have what you requested of me, my friend. I will never forget what you did for my family, and I am forever in your debt."

"No debt between friends, Abdel," Avi says, which makes Abdel feel even more affectionate toward Avi. He shows Avi a weapons cache of AK 47s and a few other armaments. The AK 47 is the weapon of choice in this part of the world. It is fairly easy to obtain because there are many ghost factories in the Middle East with the technology and expertise to assemble them. The Russians have made sure parts continue to flow into these factories through governments they support, generating a cottage industry. The AK 47 is really the biggest weapon of mass destruction. It will fire in almost any condition, hardly ever jams, and can be easily used by a 12-year-old African boy.

Avi picks up the sack full of guns, ammo and some grenades, all Russian made, and pulls the strap of the heavy bag onto his shoulder. He embraces his friend again and leaves the way he came in, nodding to the old woman as he passes by her.

Avi's car is in front of the store waiting for him. He gets in the car, changes into dark clothes and a dark ski hat, and they drive out to Viktor's compound. Avi takes three AKs loaded with full cartridges, two pistols, and three hand grenades and walks to a compound bordering Victor's. He straps the AKs over his shoulder and chest, picks up a backpack containing the pistols and grenades, and climbs the outer wall of the compound. In the dark, the wall appears smooth, but Avi feels the cracks in the mortar which he knows are always there in this type of construction. He scales the wall to the top and drops down to the roofline, out of view from Viktor's compound next door. He waits. He doesn't hear or see anyone. He places one AK on top of the wall. It's about 8 feet away from Viktor's wall. He digs the AK down into the wall with his Ka-bar knife. He also plants one Russian F1 hand grenade. He can see the tip of the cartridge of the AK sticking out, but nothing else. From a distance, it looks like wall décor. He places the other two AKs and two more hand grenades in a similar fashion along the wall, spread out evenly across the wall length. He eyes the distance between the two walls confidently knowing it is safe.

From the rooftop of the compound where Avi has stored his weapons, he can easily see Viktor's compound right next door. Avi notices what appears to be a compost operation in Viktor's front courtyard with old food and plant waste decaying in a plant bed. He sits down behind the wall on the roof and waits. An old man comes to the roof of the house where Avi is sitting and sees Avi. He lights a cigarette and begins to smoke it. He and Avi stare at each other for a few minutes. The old man finishes his cigarette, evidently deciding this is none of his business and goes back downstairs. Avi listens at the stairs for a few minutes but hears nothing from the old man or anyone else. Satisfied the old man will remain silent, Avi goes back to work. He doesn't see or hear any movement from Viktor's team besides the sound of a TV and occasional voices. Definitely mercenaries. Most mercs do not look for trouble on the job, and these guys are no exception. A job for hire is no good if you are dead. Avi, having continued to hear low-level noise, tosses one of his pistols into the compost and sees it land near the middle of the plant bed. He waits to see if anyone hears the thud of the pistol and comes to investigate.

Avi climbs down the exterior border wall which is opposite Viktor's estate. He places another pistol in a planter outside the walls. He then texts his driver and waits in the shadows. As his car approaches, he moves out to the street and gets in the car. Avi goes back to La Mansion with the thought of returning to Eloise's house, but he decides against it. He has a busy day tomorrow.

CHAPTER EIGHTY-ONE

Viktor checks the airport manifest online to try and ascertain when Avi is arriving. He finally gives up because he doesn't know what name Avi is using or his departure city. He decides it would be futile to leave a guy at the airport to see if he could recognize Avi. If Avi wants him dead, he will likely die. He just hopes he's worth more to Avi alive.

Viktor meets with his security team leader. "Today I have a meeting with a man who may be coming here to kill me," he says.

"Then why meet with him? Why don't we just kill him when he gets out of his car at the gate?" asks Garrett, the team leader.

"Because if, in fact, he is not here to kill me, I need him to finish a job for me, so I need him alive if possible."

"Boss, you want me and my team to protect you from a guy who may be coming here to kill you, but you do not want us to kill him because you need his services? How will we know when to kill him? After he kills you? This is nuts, man. You are placing my team in harm's way."

"I understand and will triple your daily rate for today just for the inconvenience."

"Well, I hope my men live to spend the extra money. Okay, if we can't kill this guy, then we'll need to do a careful search, including a complete cavity search, to make sure he doesn't have any bombs, in case he decides to kill you and himself at the same time."

"I also cannot afford to piss this guy off too much. If he's not here to kill me, I need him to finish this other job for me as well."

"Boss, have you lost your mind? Okay, only full military pat down in the outside courtyard—is that acceptable?"

"Yes," says Viktor.

"If he's armed, can we confiscate his weapons, or do you think that will piss him off?" asks Garrett sarcastically.

"No, confiscate any weapons he has on him when he arrives, but be sure to tell him the weapons will be returned to him when he leaves."

"Just so we don't piss him off, right?"

"Right."

"Ok, this shit is going in a book someday. What time is he to arrive?"

"3:00 pm."

"Do you know where he is staying?"

"No."

"Do you have a description?"

"Not a very good one."

"How will we know if it's the right guy when he gets here? Maybe he will send a double to blow us all up."

"It's a possibility, but not likely. He and I have business to attend to."

"If he doesn't want to kill you, that is?"

"Yes."

"Ok, this is a new one for me, man. But, fine, I'll try to protect you, but you cannot under any circumstances be alone with this guy unless we put him in a Silence of the Lambs cage first."

"Actually, I need to discuss business with him confidentially," says Viktor.

"You mean alone?"

"Yes."

"I take it without a cage, so we don't piss him off? Good luck with this, but I've got to tell you, I'm betting he kills you, even though I'll do everything in my power to keep it from happening."

"Thanks, that's very reassuring coming from my security team leader."

"Viktor, with how handcuffed you have us, we should probably just do you a favor and kill you before he gets here! Damn, man!"

CHAPTER EIGHTY-TWO

"Do we have anything on 57 in Morocco?"

"No, sir. We sent him in complete dark-op with no support—YOYO as requested."

"Anything happening at Viktor's compound?"

"Nothing that we can tell. He has not left the grounds to our knowledge, but we do not have a way to see in except when our bird flies over every four hours. The ground team is trying to monitor the gate for activity, but it's difficult, sir. We just don't have enough personnel in-country unless we use the SEALs."

"SEALs! They're seek-and-destroy only," says Ward.

"I know, sir. They're about three miles away from Viktor's, sequestered so as to not draw any unwarranted attention. We have some sound, sir, but it's across the street from the compound, and it's downstairs so the reception is not great."

"I guess all we can do is wait this one out and call in the SEALs if we hear the shit hitting the fan."

"Looks that way, sir."

"See if we can add another satellite."

"It's possible, but we have one already tasked to this activity. It may require additional overreach to retask another one, sir."

"Let's stay with the one then. Probably a good call for now."

Frank visits Rachael in the hospital. It's not much of a visit because she's still unconscious. Frank meets with her doctor.

"Frank, she has been through a huge amount of trauma and although the surgeries have repaired her internal issues, she is still not out of the woods. Once she wakes up, she'll need a considerable amount of time to recover from the surgery, not to mention all the trauma from the gunshot wounds. It's just too early to tell what we are actually dealing with. It's better than we had hoped, but our expectations were pretty low. I'm sorry I can't give you better news at this time. It's really a day-by-day thing now, but at least it's not hour-by-hour anymore, Frank."

"Thanks, Doc. I'll keep checking on her."

"Frank, I'm assuming you are her only family? She hasn't had anyone else visit."

"Doc, for our purposes, that's right. I'm family and if anyone comes around saying they are family, I need to know about it. I am hoping to keep two guys at her door for at least a few more days, but I am still concerned an outside force could ruin all the work you have done getting her this far."

"I understand. We will keep you apprised of any changes or anything suspicious."

"Thanks, Doc. I appreciate that."

CHAPTER EIGHTY-THREE

It's 2:00 pm Morocco time, and Avi is preparing to visit Viktor. Avi is dressed in loose, dark pants, a white Moroccan shirt, tennis shoes, a hat, sunglasses, and a white jacket. The sunglasses have an infrared feature that allows him to detect body heat through walls. To the untrained observer, they look like bifocals. He puts a Sig Sauer 9 mm in his outside jacket pocket, a stiletto in his inside jacket pocket, and a .25 pistol in a leg holster. He brings a pack of vapor cigarettes with three blasting caps and two poison darts. Darts and blasting caps are oldies but goodies, as most people do not even look for them anymore. Avi puts each cigarette in its own little box in the pack so they will need to confiscate the entire pack or check each box. He marks each box with a small check if it's lethal then puts the pack in his front shirt pocket. He knows they will likely search him, and they will need to find something to feel like they have been thorough.

Avi gets in the car to ride to Viktor's compound. It's a twenty-minute drive, and he asks the driver to stop about six blocks from Viktor's. He texts his driver to make sure his phone is working. If Avi gets in a jam, he'll text his driver to come to the side wall so he can jump from the roof to the car. They are in sync, and the driver proceeds toward Viktor's compound. They arrive 10 minutes early.

The driver pulls up to the outside gate of Viktor's compound and is stopped by two armed mercenaries. The compound has two gates, and they are allowed to enter the outer gate, which then shuts behind them. Their car is now sitting in an alley inside the outer wall, but not on the house grounds proper. The inner house gate is not opened to allow entry into the inside of the compound until an all-clear signal is received. This keeps any potential disturbance in the car alley, such as if someone rushed through the outer gate, they would find themselves trapped in the car alley—a sitting duck from the wall above with no escape.

Avi steps out of the car in the car alley and is, in fact, a sitting duck. Two armed men search him, while two more patrol the roof. Avi counts five mercs—one on the gate, two searching him, and two on the roof. One man searches Avi thoroughly, while the other keeps an M16 pointed at him the entire time. The searcher finds the sig, the 25, and the stiletto. Avi takes his glasses off and holds them in one hand while they search him. The armed man speaks to someone on a microphone attached to his shoulder, and another man answers. That makes six mercs by Avi's count since neither of the roof guards spoke into their mics. A six-man team to cover one guy in a compound sounds like the right number to Avi. He will keep his eyes and ears open, but six seems right. That's not including the household staff, but they are not likely to get involved. They work for the owner but will run or cower if given the option. At least, that has been Avi's experience. The merc looks at his vapor cigarette pack.

"What's this?" asks the merc.

"I'm trying to quit," Avi says, holding his hands out like he is waiting for the communion.

"The guy has vape cigarettes," he squawks into his radio.

"Keep them. He can get them back on the way out," says the voice.

Avi pays close attention to the voice because the guy on the other end of the mic is the leader.

"How about just one, man? It's a vape," says Avi to the head merc who is checking him out.

The merc puts the entire pack in a basket with the other items they have just confiscated.

"You get all this back when you leave," he tells Avi.

Avi holds his hands together in a Namaste pose to show the merc he means no harm. The merc ignores Avi and calls in the all clear. The outer gate is opened and Avi's driver moves the car out of the compound. Once this gate is closed, the inner compound gate opens, and Avi is allowed into the compound courtyard. He sees the compost garden right in the middle of the stone courtyard, and he walks to the door of the house escorted by the two guards who did the frisk-and-cover routine on him in the alley. The gate is closed by a guard who stays outside the main gate. Back down to five mercs in play. Avi is escorted up a set of stairs to a room with two window walls and a balcony. Avi checks the staircase on the way up to make sure there is not a separate set of stairs to the roof. The balcony is a little problem for his plan. He could not see it from the other side last night. He enters the room, and Viktor greets him warmly, using both of his hands to shake Avi's.

"I am pleased to see you, my friend," says Viktor. "I didn't think you made it out of New York after seeing the news reports and not hearing from you."

"Viktor, your guards took my cigarettes. Do you have a pack?"

Viktor nods to one of the armed guards in the room, who now total three since one was already there when they arrived. Avi figures he is the boss. One of the cover guards goes back down to retrieve the vapor cigarettes from the basket, leaving the boss and the frisk man as immediate threats—both armed with M16s pointed at Avi.

"Please come and sit down. You are my first guest here."

A maid brings in a fresh bowl of dates and places them on the coffee table in front of Avi. He is seated on the couch, and Viktor is seated in one of the armchairs. The mercs are positioned to triangulate Avi if he moves a muscle the wrong way. Avi holds the vapes but does not pull one out. He simply listens to Viktor and doesn't let on that the mercs are annoying him and will probably need to die for this behavior. He is attentive as Viktor goes on about the house and Morocco.

"Viktor, we probably need to discuss the issues at hand," Avi finally interrupts.

"Oh, of course. Would you like to do this now?"

"Yes. Alone."

Viktor nods to the boss and two of the guards leave, but the boss stays.

"Viktor, I get it. I'm okay if he stays, but if he doesn't stop pointing that gun at me, I am going to kill him."

Viktor nods to Garrett, who moves to the door to assume a less aggressive position.

"Is that ok?" asks Viktor.

Avi nods yes.

"So, what about the girl?"

"It's going to cost an additional $2 million."

Viktor gets quiet.

Avi continues, "She has guards on her and is still in the hospital, so it will not be easy."

"Okay then. Two million. I am not in a position to negotiate with you, am I?"

Avi says nothing.

Viktor continues "I can get it to you once you finish the job. I don't have much cash here at the compound."

Avi crosses his legs and fiddles with his vape pack, trying to remember which are vapes and which are darts and exploding caps. He sees his check marks on the packs now.

"I'll need some form of payment today—at least half."

Viktor says, "You know I'm good for it with all that we have been through."

"I can't change my policy just because we are friends now, Viktor."

Viktor gets up from his chair as does Avi, and Garrett comes closer with his gun raised. Avi stares at Garrett while he taps the package of vapes in his hand against the other wrist. He takes one out and puts it in his mouth and inhales, and a small puff of water vapor comes out. Garrett pulls back a little and moves his gun down to a forty-five-degree angle. Viktor goes to the desk, reaches into a drawer, pulls out a drawstring bag, and puts it on the desk. Avi opens the bag. Six perfectly cut, clear white diamonds fall into his hand, each about 4 carats—probably a million or so dollars wholesale. Avi holds the diamonds up and walks closer to Garrett, seeming to need the light to view the stones. He blows out hard on the vape, and a dart charges into Garrett's neck. Garrett reaches for the dart as he falls, and Avi grabs his pistol and shoots Viktor in the neck as Viktor reaches for a pistol in his desk drawer. Viktor is down but not dead. Avi takes the machine gun from around Garrett's neck and double taps Garrett's head as mercs rush the stairs to enter the fight. Avi then shoots a double tap into Viktor and moves to the door to hold off the mercs. Bullets fly into the room, and Avi yells out in a Texan accent, "I've got your boss. Stop shooting or I will kill him."

The bullets stop. It's a stand-off.

"I don't want to kill him and all of you, but I will. It doesn't have to end this way for you guys; it's just a job. Put down your weapons, and everyone but Viktor walks away from this."

"Send Garrett out."

"Not going to happen, guys—it's not a negotiation; I'm just giving you a chance to live."

Avi looks through the infrared glasses and sees three mercs crouching on the stairs, using the wall as cover. He shoots through the wall and hits one, who goes down. Then he pulls back and holds his fire.

"Guys, I'm going to kill you all, so run while you can."

The mercs pull back from their positions, but Avi can see they are still trying to advance up the stairs. Avi moves to the window while they think about the stand-off. The wall is smooth up and down. He goes over to the balcony, which has a rail. Avi goes out to the balcony and climbs onto the rail and shoots back through the door across to the window. Avi can see with the infrared glasses that two mercs have moved downstairs and are shooting up at the window. He sees bullets hitting the wall. Two inside—not a threat. He now sees three outside, so the outside guard must be in play. That leaves just one on the stairway. Avi scales up to the roof from the balcony with his gun and the vapes. He hears gunfire in the room with Viktor and sees that all four have now entered the room, seeing no return fire.

Avi runs for the far wall and jumps from Viktor's roof onto the other compound's roof. He ducks behind the wall and pulls out an AK and a hand grenade. He crawls to the next AK using the roof wall as cover. There is no return fire yet. He sees all four mercs on Viktor's roof looking for him. He kills all four with the AK using only 14 rounds. He texts his driver and goes to the front wall of the next-door estate, then walks down the stairs into the house and hears a gun go off. He has been shot by the old man from last night. Avi sprays the old man with AK fire as his wife cowers in the corner. He hesitates and leaves her there unharmed. He walks out of the estate to catch his driver who is speeding up. His driver slows down, and Avi gets into the car as two hummers approach Viktor's compound. They pass Avi's car driving in the opposite direction.

Avi has been shot in the right thigh, and he pulls his belt off and ties it around his thigh to stop the bleeding, hoping the old man did not hit an artery. Avi tells the driver in Arabic to take him to the shop where they picked up the weapons last night. His driver does so swiftly. On the way, Avi texts a 911 code to his friend. When they arrive, Avi's friend and his father are there to take him upstairs in the back of the house, and a veterinarian friend is on the way to take care of his wound. The veterinarian arrives in less than 10 minutes and begins to work on Avi.

Meanwhile, the hummers are searching the city for any trace of Avi. No one says anything. The SEALs will get nowhere in this part of the world. Still, Avi knows he cannot stay here now the SEALs are looking for him.

"My friend, getting you out of here now will be difficult. The authorities at the borders will be looking for you, especially to Spain."

"That's why I will need to go to Algeria."

"But the border with Algeria is closed—political issues from the last war."

"I know. It's our best bet—with it being closed, they won't check it."

"I understand, my friend, but how do we accomplish this?"

Avi takes out his laptop and pulls up a site for illegal crossings into Algeria from Morocco on the dark web. It seems policing has dropped off dramatically unless one happens to be smuggling petroleum. People do not seem to be a problem currently. Avi uses this site to hire a fake family to meet him at the border to bring him home. It seems the simplest solution is to be part of a separated family because most police turn the other way for this type of crossing.

"We will need a small car, not a truck," Avi says and hands Abdel one of the diamonds he got from Viktor. Abdel looks at the diamond.

"This should be sufficient for the car and a driver, you can keep the rest," says Avi. "Go to Mohammed; he owns Mazanillo Silversmith in the bazaar. He will change it for you and treat you appropriately."

Avi knows Mohammed will not give Abdel the same deal as if Avi were to go, but he will know who it is for.

"You need to stay here for two days if you can, sir, for these stitches to hold," the vet tells Avi.

Avi acknowledges the doctor's recommendation with a nod but opened stitches will not cause as much pain as the SEAL team will if they find him. They have every incentive to kill him. He has finished Viktor, knows a lot, and is now an enemy of the state. When the US is after you, it usually does not turn out too well. The US does not suffer fools gladly if they pop up on their radar screen, and Avi has certainly gotten their attention. When he was their corrupt hitman that was one thing but to make US news and embarrass the bureaucrats who run the world is another story altogether. Even Avi has a slightly uneasy feeling about his predicament. Governments have been toppled for less.

"Abdel, when you get back with the car and the driver, I am going. I am heading for the Algerian border."

"Very well, my friend. I will work as fast as I can."

"I know you will."

CHAPTER EIGHTY-FOUR

Ward is on the satcom with the SEAL team at Viktor's compound.

"Looks like your boy was here," says the team leader. "Everybody in the house who was armed, including Viktor, is dead. He even killed an old man next door."

"Anyone tell you guys anything on the ground?" asks Ward.

"Not a word. It's our war. Your guy must have some help here because he has disappeared . . . hold on . . . wait a minute. The old man had a Colt 45 revolver that was shot once. He must have been in the Wild West to have this old relic. He may have shot your boy, boss; there's no slug for a 45 or a hole for one anywhere in the house . . . Listen, the locals are coming now—we need to bolt. I'm out."

"Now what?" the deputy director asks Ward.

"Now we report to the senator," says Ward.

Avi is sitting in the passenger seat of a four-door sedan with his new driver, who he hopes he can trust. He has a pistol in the bag on his lap just in case there is an issue. The driver has a beard and wears the traditional headdress of what many would call a peasant. It looks like a cloth rolled up and wrapped around the head several times, red and beige in color. He is chain-smoking Marlboros as they drive south. To the right, the sun is covering the desert with an array of colors as it descends on the other side of the world, bringing a new day to some and the end of the day to Avi and his driver. The desert turns to a pale red, then pink, and then darkness. The wind almost immediately picks up as the sun falls rapidly from the sky in the desert. They are traveling south out of Tangier on a two-lane road with no lights anywhere. They have a full tank of gas, and there is supposedly a store about half-way—10 hours away—where they can hopefully stop and take a break. It's a 20-hour trip crossing into Spain and back to make this official, but Avi is not planning to explain anything to the Spanish or Algerian officials about his leaving, especially wounded. It takes about the same time to cross the mountains and desert of Morocco as it does to drive from Spain to Algeria. There are extreme temperatures throughout the entire ride. Avi is really not up to this ride from a medical standpoint. But by using this route, they are less likely to have to deal with any officials but more likely to run into thieves and con men.

They drive into the night for several hours. Avi tries to get some sleep, but he has one eye open just in case he finds himself in a compromising position with this driver. He is vouched for by Abdel, which should be good enough. In this world, you only give your approval for those you know are truly worthy. Many people will kill the person who sends an unreliable person. Avi would not likely kill Abdel because they have a history together, but he would certainly kill this driver if he tried to pull anything. The darkness seems to have taken on different colors, and Avi wonders if he is hallucinating. Then, Avi sees a speck of light up ahead.

Avi's driver speaks in Arabic to Avi, "swaf takhud mn hada," as they see lights sitting in the road ahead.

"Take care of what?" Avi asks his driver.

Avi sees the white object is actually a light coming into focus. He covers his bag with a blanket and places his hands on both of his pistols. They are waved to a stop. Two men approach carrying AK 47s and shine a bright flood light on the car. They can see Avi seated in the front seat by his driver, who is smoking a Marlboro and looking at the men. They discuss the road and the fee for traveling on it at night. His driver is not interested in paying a fee at first, but Avi touches his arm. Avi slips out a carton of Marlboros and dirham equal to about $40. The men seem satisfied with the exchange and motion for two other men to move the truck off the road so Avi and the driver can pass. The whole matter takes about an hour to negotiate in the middle of the night about 75 miles from anywhere. Then, Avi and his driver ascend from the Moroccan foothills into the mountains in pitch black darkness with no guardrails in sight. It is all on this driver to deliver Avi safely to his Algerian family, who hopefully will not try to renegotiate the terms once he is in sight of them and the customs men. Avi will not be in a very forgiving mood if he has to keep paying to get out of Morocco. There is only one more major crossing left before he can move on to Algeria.

CHAPTER EIGHTY-FIVE

Senator Spence, CIA Director Ward, FBI Director Davis, and Homeland Secretary Johnson hold a press conference on Capitol Hill outside where the inauguration of the President is held.

"Yesterday at approximately 4 pm local time, Viktor Ludvidz, a terrorist from Serbia, was killed in Morocco during an effort to take him alive and bring him to justice for his terrorist activity. Ludvidz was the mastermind behind the attack in New York City last week as well as many other crimes. The CIA, FBI, and Homeland Security coordinated the operations through a joint task force using the US military's finest to subdue and ultimately kill this terrorist who is suspected of mass murder beyond the recent New York attack. Various top officials in the Ludvidz organization on the scene were also killed."

"This is a swift blow to terrorists everywhere. The US will act to protect our citizens wherever they are in need," continues Senator Spence. "We have also confiscated approximately $200 million of terrorist funds in this successful operation, dealing a blow to the funding of these organizations. All of these US agencies have proven time and time again they can work together successfully to defuse terrorism."

"As in every operation, several heroes acted with complete valor and no concern for their own welfare to uncover this plot. One is Detective Frank Holland of NYPD, and another is Rachael Lopez, a former Arizona police officer. She is currently recovering from wounds suffered in the New York attack. We all wish her a speedy recovery."

Frank reaches over to the television in Rachael's hospital room and turns it off.

"That is complete bullshit!" Rachael yells.

"Rachel, if you pull those stitches out busting a gut, I'm going to shoot you and put you out of my misery."

Rachael picks up a cup with a straw and tries to drink some water through the straw, only to yell "Ouch, damn it!" She throws the straw out, turns up the water glass, and pours it all right down her neck and onto her robe.

"Jesus, woman! Are you always this much trouble?"

Frank grabs a towel and tries to dry her off.

"I am so much more trouble than this, Frank. I'm going to show you trouble when I get out of here—I'm going to find that son of a bitch who shot me, and I am going to kill him. Where's my gun? Oh right, you didn't give me a gun! I would probably not be in here right now and that bastard would be dead if I had had a gun in the bar. What the hell were you doing while my ass was getting shot up in there?

I'm still pissed at you."

"Hey! I came in the window to save your ass, as you say, so don't give me any grief about you not having a gun."

"Do I need to call the police on you two?" Tony asks as he walks into Rachael's room. "You two are fighting like love birds in here. I could hear you at the nurse's station."

Rachael looks at Frank, who looks back, and then they both look away.

"Good news! Your new boss, Frank, and possibly your boss too, Rachael—if you decide to take the job—is starting a multijurisdictional task force, which may give you two a way to find your perpetrator if you, in fact, don't believe our esteemed federal bureaucrats in Washington were on the level with their assessment of recent events."

"On the level, my ass!" says Rachael. "I have never heard such a crock from anyone. Terrorist! We can't let them get away with that crap!"

"Rachael," says Frank. "You have to learn to pick your battles. If we get on this task force, working together we can bag him. Try not to get so worked up about the process."

Rachael tries to drink water again without the straw, this time with a little better result as Frank holds her head up a little. She smiles briefly but frowns again quickly.

"Rachael, we need you to get well."

"Speak for yourself big guy. How's your arm?"

Frank moves it back and forth to show Rachael it's okay.

"Still, doesn't look like you're quite ready to shoot anyone; you winced a little."

Avi, or rather Dr. Patel, is sitting in an open-air lounge watching an American TV channel at the Havannah resort in Vanuatu. He has his own private physician, Dr. Julia, a 5'8" brunette who arrived from Stockholm yesterday to nurse him back to health as he recuperates from his thigh injury. Ah, the good life again—except for the television broadcast. Senator Spence is holding a press conference with a legion of bureaucrats standing behind him. Avi listens to the end and decides it is time to move to the private pool at his villa. Dr. Julia helps him up as he still needs a crutch to move around, much to his disdain. It took 35 stitches to sew him up, and he has continued to have muscle cramps from the trauma of the gunshot. He regrets not killing the old man when he came to the roof the night before the firefight at Viktor's compound, but what are regrets? Nothing can be done about what did not happen yesterday.

Avi moves on from this line of thinking, deciding to concentrate on Dr. Julia in her bikini lying next to him looking out over the beautiful Coral Sea from the patio of his suite. After 5 minutes of solitude, a restless Avi reaches for his laptop to check for an additional deposit from the Company for doing the job they requested. It's not there. Stiffed out of $250K. He decides to let it go for now and focus on his recovery and Dr. Julia. There will be another day.

THE END

About the Author

Joe was born in Pinehurst, North Carolina, growing up in a 900-square-foot house with two sisters, two grandmothers, one cousin, a Mom and a third-shift textile-worker Dad. He was the first in his family to complete college with a four-year degree. Graduating from the Campbell University, he joined Wachovia Bank, at the time a stodgy old-line conservative financial institution, working as a repo man in an even more rural part of North Carolina than where he was born.

Realizing right away this was no job for an ambitious poor boy who wanted to be rich, he began a monthly routine of begging the manager of Dean Witter Reynolds Securities, Roy Williams – not the basketball coach – to hire him. Without reservation, Dr. Williams immediately and continually said, "Never." After two years of Joe floating around trying to find the right fit in a profession and continuing his monthly phone calls, Dr. Williams finally relented and hired Joe into what was then the Sears Financial

Network, working inside the local Sears store. Thus began Joe's official financial career.

Life moved quickly as Joe's ambitions were realized. Over his years as a global business executive, his experiences ranged from sipping champagne on 200-foot yachts in Monte Carlo to paddling canoes in the jungles of Borneo. Joe was the sixth American to slip behind the Iron Curtain to visit Albania in the early 1990s and see how a dictator operated firsthand. Joe spent time in Venezuela as well as numerous other countries he will not comment on.

These experiences have given the author a wealth of personalities to create his fictional characters.

Joe has served as the Chairman of the Board of Visitors for the University of North Carolina Women's and Children's Hospital in Chapel Hill, North Carolina; The Morehead Planetarium Board; and the IntraHealth International Board, a nonprofit global healthcare facilitator; as well as numerous other boards. He has written several short stories while guest lecturing at various universities about money perspectives and entrepreneurism.

The author and his wife, Markie, support children's homes in Africa and Nepal. The couple also mentors post-orphanage young adults. Joe and Markie and their three children reside in Chapel Hill, North Carolina.

You can connect with Joe on Twitter @jpdaviswrites, on Facebook @jpdaviswrites, or send him an email at jp.davis@jpdavisauthor.com.

57284070R00214

Made in the USA
Columbia, SC
08 May 2019